DOGS

OF

DOGS
OF
WAR

A NOVEL BY

STEVE RUTHENBECK

HARBOR
HOUSE
AUGUSTA

DOGS OF WAR
By Steve Ruthenbeck
A BatWing Press Book/2005
BatWing Press is an imprint of Harbor House

Copyright © 2005 by Steve Ruthenbeck

For information address:

HARBOR HOUSE
111 TENTH STREET
AUGUSTA, GEORGIA 30901

Jacket and book design by Matthew Riddle

Library of Congress Cataloging-in-Publication Data

Ruthenbeck, Steve.
 Dogs of war / by Steve Ruthenbeck.
   p. cm.
 ISBN 1-891799-26-6 (alk. paper)
 1. World War, 1939-1945--Fiction. I. Title.
 PS3618.U7774D64 2005
 813'.6--dc22

                                        2005015128

Printed in the United States of America

10 9 8 7 6 5 4 3 2 1

Thanks to:
Mom and Dad
Les, Lori and Amber
Steve and Wendy Johnson
Curt Gates
James Albrecht

CHAPTER

DESCENT

Yea, they are greedy dogs,
which can never have enough
— Isaiah 56:11

THE *LAZARUS* CRUISED through the night sky like a lumbering whale. A renegade mission gave the C-47 direction and purpose but put it in the wrong place at the wrong time. A hungry shark tore out of the reef-shaped clouds behind it. By the light of the full moon, the Messerschmitt 109 turned its guns upon the American transport.

The Luftwaffe pilot smiled behind his oxygen mask. His crosshairs intersected on the *Lazarus* with inevitable purpose. It was an easy kill—almost preordained. The Nazi fighter thrummed as tracers blasted from its wing

7

ports. They stitched a trail through the black sky and walked straight up the C-47's ass.

Jeckel, a handsome man in a leather cap and flight jacket, piloted the *Lazarus*. A photo of his wife and baby girl was tucked between the altimeter and air speed indicator. How long since he last saw them? He didn't want to think about it. He watched French countryside pass beneath them like an immense jigsaw puzzle, then turned to Hydler.

"How's our heading?"

Hydler's accountant face studied a map and the instrument panel. "Five by."

"Give our passengers the news then. Green light in thirty."

The *Lazarus* lurched like it was swatted by a giant fist. A barrage of twenty- and 7.92-millimeter slugs punched through its sheet metal skin. The wind howled through the perforations like a banshee being drawn and quartered.

"Son of a bitch! We're taking hits! Eyes back, Anderson!"

Anderson plowed fields under a Minnesota sunset. He sat in the bouncy seat of a Minneapolis-Moline tractor while his backside turned numb and his spine felt like it was filled with broken glass. The home place—a house, barn, silo, windmill and granary—stuck up from the horizon like an odd rock formation. But that wasn't right. He wasn't home. He jerked his head up and opened his eyes. Reality replaced the dream. He was on a plane with thirteen black-faced men. The soldiers were loaded down with parachutes, hand grenades, pistols, ammunition, knives and rifles.

Sudden crashes banged through the cargo hold. Flames flashed. Smoke billowed. The smell of cordite seared lungs and brought tears to eyes. The men were no longer silent and grim. They shouted and rolled on the floor, knocked out of their seats by the turbulence. The red jump light bathed everything in a hellish cast, like something out of a Bosch painting. Blood dripped from the ceiling and walls. A hand lay on the floor, trailing tendons and a wrist still adorned with a watch. Anderson couldn't take his eyes off it. It looked like some strange breed of spider.

A voice in his headset: *"Son of a bitch! We're taking hits! Eyes back, Anderson!"*

Anderson struggled over the tangled mass of men while the *Lazarus* rocked like a boat shooting violent rapids. He poked his head into the roof bubble and scanned the sky behind them. The moon was a fifty-cent piece on black velvet. Distant clouds glowed with its silver light. A rogue 109 banked and came around on their tail.

"Messerschmitt! Five 'o' clock!"

The Luftwaffe ace reacquired his target with cruel satisfaction. His first pass was perfect. He scored hits on the C-47's fuselage yet managed to avoid shooting anything vital. Only the best could take a plane down piece by piece. He thought of tearing the wings off a fly as he aimed for the *Lazarus*'s starboard engine.

Someone pinned Kenway to the floor of the C-47. He heaved the dead weight off his chest and discovered that it was Spencer. A hole replaced the New York private's face. Kenway pushed the corpse away with stiff-armed revulsion. The red jump light made everyone look like they were on fire. Maybe they were. Wisps of smoke drifted through the confusion. Other men cried out. Barker wasn't the only one who got hit.

"He's coming around again!" Anderson screamed in a paroxysm of fear as the 109 swooped in like a diving hawk,

9

guns blazing. His mouth and face stretched around the words like melting taffy. "He's coming a—"

A line of bullets punched through the ceiling. One of them took Anderson in the chest and stopped him in mid-sentence. The force of the twenty-millimeter slug threw him across the fuselage where he slammed against the wall with a bone-crunching impact. He tumbled to the floor, his chest as insubstantial as a beaded curtain. His wide eyes stared into eternity with idiotic surprise—What? You mean I'm dead?

"Talk to me, Anderson!" Jeckel shouted. The picture of his wife and daughter vibrated with the rest of the plane. The motion made them look like they nodded their approval of the situation with horrible vigor. "Anderson?" Hissing static filled Jeckel's headset. He turned to Hydler. "Anderson's gone! What do you got?"

Hydler pressed his face against the side window. "Four 'o' clock!"

Jeckel stomped a boot full of left rudder and shoved the control stick forward. The *Lazarus* slashed into a banking dive. Its airspeed ticked toward two hundred miles per hour. Moonlit French soil rolled up in the windshield. Men and pieces of men slid forward and slammed into the bottleneck between the cockpit and the cargo hold.

The Messerschmitt pilot grinned as he zoomed over the diving C-47. They were making a decent game of it at last. He gunned the throttle, and the fighter's engine roared with fuel-injected power. The 109 rolled onto its side and looped around in a boomerang circle. The staccato sound of its machineguns cracked open the night.

Bullets tore through the *Lazarus*'s cockpit. Windshield panes shattered. Jeckel threw an arm up to protect his eyes from flying glass. A loud metal *thunk* sounded off to starboard, followed by a bright flash of light. The plane's number two propeller came to a jerky stop. Flames licked out of the engine's sheet metal seams. Jeckel's eyes widened.

"Cut the fuel to number two!"

Hydler reached for the switch—too late. The engine blew with a hollow crump that shook the entire plane. A steel shard knifed through the window and struck Hydler in the temple. He slumped against Jeckel's shoulder like a girl on a movie date. Jeckel shrugged the dead man away and struggled to keep the *Lazarus* aloft.

The Major lurched to his feet in the C-47's cargo bay. He picked his way through the mess like a man crossing a rope bridge over a canyon. His flinty eyes narrowed in genuine offense that things had the nerve to go awry. One of his parachute straps hooked on Huxley's chin. Huxley's mouth fell open, and blood poured out.

"Goddamn it all!" the Major cursed.

Huxley had been a fine shot, almost as good as Berg, who huddled in the corner and looked white-faced with fear despite his greasepaint features.

"Buck up, son," the Major said. "It's only war."

The Major poked his head into the cockpit. Jeckel struggled with the pitching controls while the wind howled through the broken window. Hydler bounced on his seat like he had a bullfrog up his ass, nothing more than a bag of meat.

"Take us to drop altitude and speed!" the Major ordered.

Jeckel turned to him with a disbelieving expression "You've got to be kidding!"

A snarl creased the Major's face. "Do I look like I'm kidding?"

11

STEVE RUTHENBECK

"We'll be a sitting duck!"

"Don't worry about it. We've got parachutes."

"But *I* don't! That's why we're going for the clouds!"

"Drop us first. Then you can head for the clouds or Timbuktu for all I care."

"The hell with that!"

The Major pulled his pistol, stuck the barrel in Jeckel's ear and thumbed back the hammer. "Take us to drop altitude and speed … now."

"You're crazy!"

"No, I'm doing the job that I signed on for. Your job is to deliver us to the target—a job that will be well rewarded if you survive to collect. That depends on how good you fly after we jump. But let's not get ahead of ourselves. The question of whether or not you live can also be answered right here, right now. Catch my drift, Fly Boy?"

Jeckel looked deep into the Major's eyes. They glowed by the cockpit lights, or maybe they burned from within. Either way, Jeckel saw the truth they contained. He glanced at his wife and child. They urged him to comply by way of earnest nodding.

"Throttling back to one hundred-ten miles per hour at seven hundred feet, Sir!"

"Good choice," the Major nodded. He returned to the cargo hold and switched the jump light from red to green, making the men look like rotten corpses floating under swampy water.

"We're going!" the Major shouted. "Tether up!"

The C-47's behavior puzzled the Messerschmitt pilot. Why did it cease its evasive maneuvers, slow down and level into straight flight? Then the Luftwaffe ace saw the tiny shapes emerge from the transport's side. They blossomed into cottonwood seed puffs—paratroops. The 109 leapt forward, homing in on the *Lazarus*'s smoke trail the way a barracuda follows a track of blood through the deep blue sea.

Kenway stood bow-legged in his equipment. His Thompson submachine gun dangled from his chest, barrel-down. A torrent of cold air rushed in as the Major opened the C-47's jump door. Kenway double-checked the clamp holding his static line to the ceiling rod. It had to be secure; it popped his chute after he jumped.

"Paratroops over the side!" the Major shouted and leapt into the night. The men followed suit, shuttling out the door in assembly-line fashion while bellowing at the top of their lungs. Messerschmitt bullets chewed through the cargo bay, throwing sparks and slivers of aluminum. The soldiers barreled through the maelstrom.

Kenway was right beside the door now, one away from jumping. A frigid wind whistled past his ears and numbed his cheeks. He caught glimpses of the moonlit earth and sky. The man ahead of him exited the plane. It was Lyell—the radioman. 7.92-millimeter slugs riddled his body in midair, disintegrating him.

The *Lazarus* dipped as Kenway jumped. He jammed in the doorframe, twisted around and tumbled into the void.

No chute popped.

Jeckel screamed as a line of bullets punched through the cockpit's ceiling. They shattered the C-47's instrument panel and his shoulder. Blood fountained from the wound. The floundering plane tried to rip the control stick from his hands.

The Messerschmitt came around to put the *Lazarus* out of its misery.

Kenway bounced at the end of his static line. The tether strap fouled around his chest and failed to deploy his chute. Now it tightened with excruciating pressure as the wind slammed him against the C-47's hull.

Earth and sky switched places with each jarring impact. His muscles and bones groaned with the abuse. Screaming, he kicked out and managed to brace his foot against the rear stabilizer, which stopped the flipping.

He rode on his back, head toward the nose of the plane. The static line slipped up his chest. Soon it would wrap around his neck and strangle him. Meanwhile, the Messer-schmitt 109 transcribed a tight circle and came in behind them for another strafing run.

Jeckel's shoulder felt like someone drove a red-hot rail-road spike into it. The C-47's response was sluggish. The remaining engine sputtered. The altimeter dropped to six hundred feet, and airspeed fell to ninety miles per hour.

Soon the *Lazarus* would stall and simply drop out of the sky. What was he thinking when he agreed to this mission, if it could be called anything so respectable? It wasn't a mission. It was a personal venture that sounded good at the time but was now clearly a grave mistake.

"What do you think, sweetheart and baby doll?" Jeckel cackled as he looked at the photo of his wife and child. "Was it worth it?" The side-to-side motion of the *Lazarus* made them both shake their heads.

The Messerschmitt arrowed toward Kenway like a spear thrown by God. The static line crept toward his throat, and he couldn't very well free himself if the *Lazarus* was blown out of the sky. He cocked his Thompson and drew a bead on the 109.

The Messerschmitt pilot waited for just the right moment—the one that comes naturally, seemingly without thought—the one that kills. It has a peculiar weight, like the galleries of heaven and hell sit on the edge of their seats to receive new entrants into their domains. It's the most pure feeling anyone will ever know, and the Luftwaffe ace knew it well. The twenty-three decals on the side of his plane represented his score in that department. Now he would add one more to the tally. The cross that kills overlaid his prey. His thumb pressed the control stick's red button, as natural as breathing.

Kenway opened fire. Flames jetted from the Thompson's muzzle. The *Lazarus*'s remaining engine blew and sprayed Kenway with hot oil as the Messerschmitt's cannons chewed the C-47 into so much metal confetti.

The Messerschmitt flyer gasped in disbelief as he saw the hung-up paratrooper firing at him. Sparks leapt off his propeller. Holes punctured his engine cowling. Steam engulfed the cockpit as coolant sprayed from ruptured hoses and splashed against hot engine walls. The control stick jiggled in his hand, and he pulled back with the unconscious instinct of self-preservation. With each passing second, the stick's vibration grew worse. A peculiar chopping sound emanated from the fighter's prop. Nine .45-caliber slugs struck the propeller, knocking it out of balance. The three blades began to wobble. Bolts loosened. Gaps appeared in seams. Pistons and valves strained as friction built up and precision parts twisted out of tolerance. The propeller shaft tore from its mounts and flew off into space like a huge Japanese throwing star. Deprived of its power source, the Messerschmitt stalled out of its climb and slipped back to earth. The control stick became a lifeless thing in the pilot's hand. He discarded it as the 109's motion de-evolved into a flat spin. Frantic, his fingers worked the cockpit latch. He had to bail out. His altitude, what was his altitude? He couldn't make out the instrument panel due to the steam. What was that peculiar weight in the air, like the galleries of heaven and hell sat on the edge of their seats to receive new entrants? The cockpit latch released. The Luftwaffe pilot looked out to see the earth surge up to meet him. He never even had time to curse before the Messerschmitt buried itself in a smoking crater.

Jeckel hauled back on the *Lazarus*'s control stick to no avail. A primitive sound of futile negation brayed from his twisted mouth. Flames reached into the cockpit, burning his hair and blistering his skin. Blood from his shoulder wound soaked his jacket into a red-sodden sponge. The earth grew larger and larger in the shattered windshield.

Kenway struggled to reach his knife. The wind of increasing acceleration screamed past his ears. He knew what that meant: the C-47 only topped two hundred-thirty miles per hour when it went straight down. The static line sank into the flesh of his neck and cut off his air. The slipstream turbulence increased. He lost his foothold on the rear stabilizer and flapped at the end of his umbilical. His helmeted head bashed against the plane's aluminum skin with a hollow bong again and again. He started to black out.

The C-47 plunged toward the ground like a V-2 rocket. Smoke left a trail to mark its fall from above to its final resting place below. Chunks of the plane broke off yet continued to follow it down. There is no escaping the downward spiral.

G-forces molded Jeckel's face into a death grin. Tears ran back into the burned hair of his temples. At first the approaching Earth was just a mottled texture of shadows. Then trees became apparent ... fields ... bushes ... rocks. Jeckel looked at his wife and baby. When the nose of the C-47 hit the ground—in that split second before he slammed headfirst into the instrument panel—his lips pursed to give them one last kiss goodbye—right before his brain exploded across their images.

Kenway's parachute flapped above his head like a sheet on a clothesline. He watched the C-47 crash and explode into a huge fireball. The flames rose into the sky and pointed toward an approaching storm. Towering thunderheads resembled a cyclopean staircase going down, down, down. As Kenway descended into the stygian blackness, he spotted the town of Le Coeur in the hollow of a shadowed valley.

CHAPTER

GRAVE

KENWAY HIT THE DIRT and rolled to avoid snapping his ankles. The wind caught his parachute and dragged him across the ground. Sharp rocks bit into his chest, and he ate a mouthful of grass as bitter as turning the other cheek. Once he got his feet under him and stopped his forward progress, he undid the chute's straps and let the entire rig sail away. He didn't bother to chase after it and bury it. Enough parachutes hung around France to build a city of circus tents. What was one more? He examined his surroundings and discovered he was in the middle of a hedgerow—the godforsaken foul things.

✠ ✠ ✠

THE ALLIES EXPECTED to make rapid progress when they landed in Normandy on June 6, 1944. The British planned to take Caen and push twenty miles inland on the first day. The Americans figured to cut across the Cotentin Peninsula, turn north and take the port of Cherbourg within a week. Other U.S. forces were to push sixteen miles south and establish an east-west line running through Saint-Lo and Caumont. Things didn't work out that way. Caen was still in German hands by the middle of June. The GIs managed to take Caumont, but they failed to secure Saint-Lo and they were nowhere near Cherbourg.

Terrain delayed the invasion. The land was a patchwork quilt of small fields—five hundred per mile—surrounded by almost impenetrable hedges. The hedgerows were originally intended to mark property lines and protect crops from strong sea winds. They were dense walls of trees, hawthorn and brambles that grew out of dirt mounds several feet thick, with a drainage ditch on each side. They turned each field into a fort and created an obstacle course over one thousand miles square. The Germans dug into the base of the hedgerows where vegetation covered them and made them all but impervious to rifle and artillery fire. In fact, the thickets were so dense that Allied soldiers often found themselves face-to-face with grinning Nazis right before getting mowed down.

The sunken wagon trails between hedgerows were also deathtraps for tanks. The narrow passages made them easy targets for German rocket launchers. Plus, a tank that went off the road and attempted to smash through a thicket was even more vulnerable. As it climbed the mound at the base of the hedgerow, its underbelly was exposed to antitank weapons while its guns pointed at nothing but sky.

To make matters worse, a cold rain fell for much of June and July. The daily precipitation turned the earth into a quagmire. The troops had to crawl and slog through ankle-deep mud as they fought from field to field. Dead bodies quickly rotted in the damp environment, and the smell of corrupted flesh permeated everything. One often came across the grim sight of a hastily erected graveyard filled with crude wooden crosses, boltless rifles and bullet-pocked helmets for markers.

Fighting in such a place was mentally and physically draining. Kenway became so dulled by fatigue that killing produced about as much emotional sensation as losing a button. Whether men were shot in the face, had their guts unzipped by a knife or were crushed under tank treads, it really didn't matter. The hedgerows contained no morals, and if civilization still existed beyond their borders, no one expected to see it again.

At one point, men from Kenway's unit captured a German soldier. In their fury at seeing so many of their friends slaughtered, they beat the man senseless, put bullets in his knees and balls and then stabbed him to death with bayonets. It never occurred to Kenway to stop them. It was war; what could he do? Three days later the reality of the event hit him, and he couldn't stop shaking. The thorns of the hedgerows ripped away more than a man's clothes and skin; they ripped away his humanity.

An eternity later, Kenway stumbled through a screen of brambles and found himself standing on the brink of an open plain. The sun pried through the clouds and threw shafts of light across golden wheat fields. Tears welled up in Kenway's eyes. It was so long since he saw anything other than endless walls and death that he nearly screamed at the nonsense thought that wobbled through his exhausted mind: My God, with no walls to keep it out, this enormous world will devour us all!

✠   ✠   ✠

KENWAY CHECKED HIS WATCH. Its luminous dial pointed out 2315 hours. Le Coeur was at least three miles away, and

20

the rally point was the bridge at midnight. Kenway ran for a break in the hedgerow walls and discovered a cart path. He followed it to the summit of a steep slope that looked down into a valley.

The geological bowl was perhaps ten miles in diameter. The southern and western slopes were grasslands, while trees dotted the northern side. The Seine River meandered through a break in the east wall and bordered the southern edge of Le Coeur. The town itself was nothing more than a small hamlet, maybe a little over a mile square. Cottages nestled against each other with pack mentality while serpentine streets twisted among them. A church steeple was the highest structure in the village and jutted up from the southwest quadrant. A bridge exited the east side of the town, crossed the river and lead to a road, which traveled between groves and hayfields on its way out of the valley.

Thunder rumbled, and Kenway looked back at the storm building on the horizon. The mass of clouds now resembled an army on the verge of marching forth and destroying all that lay in its path.

They were in for some wet work.

The moon peeked through the gnarled branches like a man spying on a woman through a keyhole. Kenway hurried down a path between the trees. Dry leaves rustled in the wind, and night birds twittered. The grove bordering Le Coeur was thick but nothing like the woods of Maine. There, the foliage grew so dense you could stumble off a cliff and not even realize it until you were lying in a broken heap at the bottom.

Kenway spent a lot of time hunting in those woods as a boy. His mother couldn't afford store-bought meat after his father died. The job of provider fell to Kenway. While his brothers, sister and mother were as close as peas in a pod, he was the odd piece of the puzzle that didn't fit. Whether that was their fault or his own, he didn't know. He just knew he felt connected to them when he brought home food. They counted on him for that, and that made him important. Then his mother married a dentist. That ended their need for wild game and their need for Kenway. He dried up and drifted away like a leaf on the fall wind. For a time, he thought he found his place with a girl named Jennifer. That ended with him being even more lost, so he joined the military. He figured the army was a family and being a soldier was just hunting on a grander scale.

Something howled in the distance, a wolf maybe. The animal's mournful baying drifted on the wind and made the hairs on the back of Kenway's neck stand up. The atmosphere of the moment was as gothic as any Universal horror movie. All the icons were there: the dark forest, the full moon, the coming storm and the solitary traveler in the woods. The thin tendrils of a ground mist wormed out from among the tree trunks to give the scene that added spooky touch. Kenway unconsciously tightened his grip on the Thompson and thought of grim fairy tales with nasty villains.

What big teeth you have ...

Kenway remembered seeing wolves on one of his childhood hunting trips. He spotted three of them as they drank from a stream. He just happened to top a rise about fifty yards away and downwind. Even from that distance the animals appeared powerful and ghostly. Their fur was a rough gray. They moved with a fluid grace that exhibited elements of purity, strength and perhaps divine knowledge. Even though he thought he was invisible to them, one of them, a large male by the looks of it, snapped its head in his direction, and Kenway knew he was spotted. The other two wolves disappeared into the trees as if by telepathic command. The gray stayed a moment longer, just looking, perhaps to prove his superiority. His blue eyes meet Kenway's with unshakable faith in his purpose. The he, too, melted into the dense foliage. Kenway wished he could go with them in that moment. He thought it must be wonderful to be a part of the pack, to always know your place and destination. Belonging was all he wanted.

As the wolf cry faded, Kenway realized the sound of the night birds had also ceased. The air took on a sour psychic weight, and a prickling sensation made the base of his spine itch. Instinct told him he wasn't alone.

Someone watched him.

Kenway's eyes tried to pierce the gloom. A multitude of shadows filled the general murk and were dark, deep and anything by lovely. He spotted a hundred different threatening shapes. Any branch could have been a gun barrel. Was that a hump of soil, a fallen log or a creeping soldier? He squinted at a head peeking around a tree and realized it was nothing more than a leafy branch. A twig snapped off to his left. Kenway whirled around and saw nothing but ominous dark places. Sweat trickled down his cheek. Maybe the presence was an animal—a predator. That would explain the silence of the forest creatures. Or maybe it was one of the men from his squad. A Frenchman out for a midnight stroll? How about a German soldier with a rifle?

Move!

Still he stood frozen. The sensation was like that last time he went to see Jennifer. He thought it might be love. She felt like home. He supposed when you felt that way about someone you should tell them, so he picked a bouquet of tulips and went on his way. He got to her house and knocked on the door. No answer. He was about to leave when he heard voices around back. Maybe Jennifer was helping her mother in the garden. The thought of giving a girl flowers in a garden made Kenway smile like a fool. Yes, it was definitely love. He went around the house and the voices grew louder. It was like no kind of conversation he ever heard, however. He looked over a white-picket fence and saw his love down on all fours while another man thrusted behind her. He just stood there, unable to move, only able to drop the tulips into the dirt at his feet.

Another branch cracked—this time to his right.

You're bracketed!

The realization finally forced motion. Kenway exploded into a mad dash. His boots thudded against soft ground. His arms pistoned at his sides while his equipment bounced in its harness. Intuition told him to get off the path and into the trees so that a rifleman couldn't draw a bead on him. He cut a hard left, dodging tree trunks and leaping mossy rocks. Were those footsteps behind him? He ran harder, ducking under branches when he could, letting them slap his face when he couldn't. His heart thudded in his chest. His breath flapped his lips. Sweat ran down his face. A broken limb tripped him up. He hit the ground—*they're right on me!*—rolled to his knees and aimed his Thompson back along his trail. Shadows. Trees. And nothing more.

Kenway swallowed his fear. The gulp was overly loud in the stillness. He caught movement out of the corner of his eye and whipped the barrel of his Thompson around to cut his pursuers in half. Nothing moved but the branches. They groaned with forlorn creaks as they swayed in the wind. Clouds cast creeping shadows beneath them.

Then the sharp edge of a knife pressed against Kenway's throat.

CHAPTER

LIVING IN THE PAST

KENWAY'S BLOOD RAN as cold as the steel against his jugular. How would it feel to have one's throat slashed? Which would be worse—the pain of the cut or the sensation of being soaked by one's own blood?

Kenway figured he was about to find out ... at least until soft lips touched his ear and a familiar voice whispered hard words:

"Surprise, you're dead."

Kenway's angry eyes narrowed. "Get that knife off me, Mac."

"Or what? Anyone stupid enough to let someone else get within cutting distance deserves to die. It's called survival of the fittest."

"Maybe you shouldn't have gotten so close then." Quick as a snake, Kenway spun around and twisted the knife hand away from his throat.

25

Mac stood six foot two and looked like a shaved gorilla. The bulges of his gear were lost amid the bulges of his muscles. His fatigues strained to contain his physique the same way his skin strained to contain the bastard seething inside of him.

Mac's eyes glinted with diamond-hard light and his teeth gleamed like a shark's in the middle of his murky features as he rubbed his wrist. "You're lucky that I don't bleed for that, asshole. Mr. Messerschmitt already cut some shares; what's to stop me from cutting one more?"

Kenway hefted his Thompson. "This'll stop you just fine."

A vicious grin creased Mac's face. He twirled the knife through his fingers and stabbed it back into its sheath. "Perhaps some other time then."

"You'll need help. Where are the others?"

"Hell if I know. I got lost during the jump. That's why we have a rally point."

"Then let's get to it. You could have given me the sign/ countersign instead of chasing me over hill and dale. That's pissing away valuable time."

"Chasing you? You came bumbling into me. I wasn't going to call out and give away my position. For all I knew, you could have been Hitler himself."

"You weren't chasing me?"

"Hell no."

Kenway faced the trees, sinking into a wary posture. "Then someone else is out here."

Thunder rumbled. The gathering storm swallowed most of the moon's light, and now the grove was lit only by lightning flashes. Every direction contained potential danger. They could have been surrounded by a regiment and not even known it.

Mac shrugged his Thompson off his shoulder. "How many?"

"I don't know."

"Maybe it's one of us?"

"Maybe …"

The minutes ticked by and nothing happened. They stared into the murk until their eyes burned and their Thompsons trembled at their shoulders. Dead leaves rustled. An owl hooted. A frog croaked near an unseen water source.

Eventually, the night birds restarted their chorus with hesitant chirps and sporadic tweets. The hunted feeling Kenway experienced earlier dissipated with the broken silence.

Mac sensed the current lack of danger. "Fuck it. If someone's out here, we'd be dead already. You sure you didn't just get spooked from being out alone after dark?"

Kenway thought of a two-word answer but didn't bother speaking the reply. He turned his back on Mac and headed for the bridge, wondering about the uneasy feeling worming through his guts. It told him they were in for some bad business.

Mac followed with a cruel smirk.

✠   ✠   ✠

MAC DROPPED OUT of school at age fourteen. He tried working in a factory but couldn't stand the monotony. For a time, he worked as a carpenter, a bulldozer operator and a mechanic. He even worked for a veterinarian and helped castrate hogs—badly.

None of the jobs lit a fire under his ass. He finally joined the army on a whim. It proved to be the right decision. Learning to fight, learning to kill—it was a playground. Only one problem existed: every playground has a bully.

Fort Wilder—named after a Civil War General who killed wounded soldiers with his saber—was located ninety miles from civilization in the middle of the Missouri Ozarks. The location was a sprawling complex of barracks, administration buildings, obstacle courses and firing ranges that rose out of the swamplands like pre-fabricated pyramids. Rectangular formations of soldiers constantly jogged around its perimeter, hefting rifles over their heads and shouting cadence like they had a pair.

Kill 'em all with no regret! Kill 'em all with bayonet! Killing people is what we do! Fuck with us, we'll kill you too!

Mac was one of the sixty men who formed Second Platoon. If Second Platoon needed a bully, Mac felt he was the best choice for the position. Unfortunately, the Sergeant was already tenured.

The Sergeant was just a runt of a man at five foot five (with his hair spiked up an inch) and weighing no more than one hundred twenty pounds soaking wet. His narrow chest was constantly puffed out like a cocky rooster, and he had a mouth on him that would not quit—ever.

Look up "Napoleon Complex" in a dictionary and you'll find a picture of the Sergeant. Mac hated the man with a passion.

The Sergeant strolled through the barracks each and every morning while Second Platoon stood at attention. His boots made equine clops on the floor. Starch turned his shirt as crisp as glare ice. He carried a walking stick under one arm and wore a bush hat on his head. His beady eyes didn't miss any mistake: an unpolished boot, an unshaven face, or a footlocker improperly stowed.

"Kiminski!" the Sergeant bellowed into the face of a nerdy looking private with a wrinkled bedspread. "Your bunk looks like it belongs in a house of moral turpitude! Did you have a whore here last night?"

"No, sir!" Kiminski shouted at the top of his lungs. If you didn't shout at the top of your lungs, you got the butt end of the Sergeant's walking stick in your gut.

"That makes sense. A cheese dick like you wouldn't know what to do with a whore even if she had an electric arrow pointed at her kooze. Let me give you some advice for posterity, Kiminski. You remember what your peanut-puffing sister did to every Tom Harry Dick back in whatever piss hole you hail from? That's what you do with a whore! Now drop and give me fifty!"

"Yes, sir!"

The Sergeant turned his attention to a freckle-faced redhead. "And what do we have here?" He hunkered down to get a closer look at Freckles' feet. "This toenail is not properly clipped! By God and sonny Jesus, why is this toenail not properly clipped?"

"It broke off, sir!" Freckles shouted. His voice cracked like a nervous teenager. Come to think of it, he was a nervous teenager.

The Sergeant straightened up to his full height of shrimp. His face looked like it was dipped in cement. "And how, pray tell, did it just happen to break off?"

"In my boots during PT, sir!"

"Bullshit!" the Sergeant scoffed. "I think you tore it off while daydreaming about your fuck buddy sheep baaing back home at the county fair!"

Freckles gulped.

"Do I make your nervous?" the Sergeant screamed. "Does the army make you uneasy? Does it give you ulcers? Do you pick your toenails to alleviate the stress? Hell, I bet you even play with yourself, don't you?"

"No, sir!"

"You do not rip your toenails short, maggot! That will cause an ingrown toenail. Then your buddy will get too-fucking killed because you're too-fucking hobbled to save him. That's the price for being too-fucking stupid to not pick your too-fucking toenails!"

"No, sir!" Freckles denied the Sergeant's prophecy.

"Yes, sir! You know I'm right! Everyone knows I'm right!" the Sergeant raised his voice and addressed the whole room. "Right?"

"Yes, sir!" bellowed Second Platoon.

"But how can I convince you, Freckles?" An evil smile broke across the Sergeant's features. "I know, grab your toothbrush and get your ass into the latrine, double-time! I want those toilets sparkling when I come in to take my afternoon dump! I want a celestial choir of angels to sing in harmony with my farts amid all that shiny porcelain splendor! Halle-fucking-luyah! Is that understood, private?"

"Yes, sir!"

"Then get moving, you worthless fucking retard!"

Freckles ran to the head, stopped halfway and realized he forgot his toothbrush. He ran back and rummaged through his footlocker.

"Take your time," the Sergeant said. "Heaven forbid that you get the lead out of your ass this one goddamn instance! That might make your mother proud, and we certainly don't want that, now do we? When all the other dried up old cunts at her bridge club brag about their sons and ask how you're doing, we want her to say, he's doing as well as can be expected for a worthless fucking retard!"

Freckles found his toothbrush and ran to the latrine like a whipped dog.

"I'm working with a bunch of mental incompetents here," the Sergeant spoke in a weary voice. "But I will mold you into men of action if it's the last thing that I do!" He passed Mac and his face went red, fuming like a volcano about to explode. Mac tried to think of what he missed. His bed was perfect. His nails were perfect. His footlocker was organized, closed and locked. Shoes polished. Shirt tucked ...

"Jumped up Judas in a chariot-driven sidecar!" the Sergeant pointed at Mac's crotch with a startled finger. "What the fuck is that?"

Mac looked down. Son of a bitch! He forgot to zip his fly.

"Once more, for the cheap seats, what the fuck is that?"

"I forgot to zip up, sir!"

"Horse apples! No man just forgets to zip up! The zipper is the last line of defense for a man's cock, and a man's cock is precious to him, is it not?"

"Yes, sir!" Mac shouted. The Sergeant did have a point there.

"Hence, you exercised a conscious effort to expose yourself to me!"

"No, sir!"

"Are you trying to hit on me, private?" the Sergeant asked in all seriousness.

Mac shook with measured fury. He didn't like where things were going, and if the Sergeant thought about taking them there, then he better have a good doctor friend. Mac wasn't no queer. When he spent that week in jail and he and his cellmate took turns giving each other hand jobs, that didn't mean shit. That was just men scratching an itch. Same for when Freckles blew him during all those midnight meetings in the john.

"No, sir," Mac growled.

"There's nothing I hate worse than a lying faggot, and you look like a lying faggot to me! I come over here

31

and see a man waiting with his fly down. You don't need a flashlight and a roadmap to figure out which way that man swings!"

The Sergeant noticed Mac's growing anger. "Am I offending your delicate sensibilities, private?"

"No, sir," Mac managed through gritted teeth.

"Goddamn lying faggot!" the Sergeant screamed. "But I suppose it's second nature to you. How else does a short-dick-waste-of-sperm get a man in the sack? Do you tell them you're rich? Do you tell them you love moonlit walks and flowers, puppy dogs and water sports? Do you tell them King Kong doesn't have shit on the boa constrictor in your pants and you'll show it to them for a dime?"

"No, sir!"

"Don't give me any lip!" the Sergeant erupted. "But I probably shouldn't have said that, should've I? You probably want to give me all the lip that you can!"

"No, sir!"

The vein in the Sergeant's forehead stuck out. "Okay, shit for brains! You have asked for it! Contrary to what you pukes might think, I don't enjoy ripping your asses to bloody shreds, but you beg for it over and over and over again! You may think you've heard it all, that the all-powerful, all-knowing Sergeant can't possibly spew any more venom from that poetic cakehole of his! Well, you're wrong, assholes! This ripping shall be my masterpiece! The words and phrases that are about to come out of my mouth shall be a revelation to you all! Your perceptions will forever be altered! Should any of you ever butt-fuck your own grandmother, you will think, well, that was certainly prim and proper compared to the ass-chewing the Sergeant handed to Private Mac Grady on June 18, 1940 at zero five hundred thirty-eight hours!" He met Mac's eyes. "Are you ready for this, you lying piece of dog shit cocksucker?"

Mac's fist lashed out and broke the Sergeant's jaw.

Mac spent the next six months in the stockade. Whenever he sat with a fellow inmate's head bobbing in his lap (and he wasn't a fag; there just wasn't anything better to do), he thought of the crunch his knuckles made against the Sergeant's teeth and smiled—the same smile he had on his face as he and Kenway headed for the bridge.

CHAPTER

DYING FOR THE FUTURE

CLOUDS OVERRAN THE LAST remnants of clear sky and blotted out the moon. The celestial orb made the thunderheads glow with a silver light as they swirled across their occupied territory and grew gravid with precipitation. Eventually, lightning bolts tore open their bellies. Rain burst from the wounds and drenched Le Coeur.

Le Coeur was one of France's oldest cities. Julius Caesar camped there during Rome's conquest of Gaulle; Siebert's armies devastated it in 574; King Thierry of Bourgogne followed in 600; and the Normans plundered it again in 858. It experienced religious unrest when Saint Altin converted it to Christianity in the Fifth Century and a bitter battle waged between the converts and the indigenous Druids. It created a political stir during the Middle Ages when it became the seat of a dissenting bishop who called the ruling family, "A nest of vipers swallowing the soul of France." Fire destroyed the town in 1723, and the great architect Jules Hardouin Mansanart drafted the plans for its reconstruction. In 1870, it held off the Germans, who visited it again in 1916 and returned in 1941.

Le Coeur retained a population of roughly two thousand souls who made their livelihood in the areas of fabrics, metal, leather, crops and prostitution. Despite the hardiness bred into the Le Coeur folk by fourteen hundred years of strife, they only lasted a single night against what invaded their hamlet one hot August evening.

Then the survivors ran for the hills.

Eight of the soldiers survived the flight of the *Lazarus*: Kenway, Mac, Jacobson, Cain, Chaplain, Berg, Ritter and the Major. They lay beneath a copse of trees like a row of cigars in a box. The rain soaked them to the skin while they scoped out the sentry on Le Coeur's bridge. The Major turned to Chaplain and made a throat-slashing gesture.

Chaplain nodded, set his gear aside and removed his boots. Then he crawled back into the grove and crept parallel to the Seine—a thin, lithe apparition with malevolent features and somehow arachnid-like limbs.

Once he was beyond the sentry's range of sight, he submerged himself in the river. He ignored the pain of the freezing water and waded toward the bridge—a brick structure sixty feet long with four ventral archways.

He swam past the church and would have uttered a lamentation had his mouth been above water. Instead, he focused his hate on the sentry, who stood with disciplined posture and ignored the elements; the man didn't even turn his collar up to the rain.

Chaplain reached the bridge, drew his knife and slithered from the water. Lightning cut his troll-like shadow across the riverbank as his senses tuned to the man above.

Who's that trip-tramping on my bridge?

He remembered reading *Three Billy Goats Gruff* to Ruth and resisted the urge to slash the blade across his skin. Physical pain was preferable to internal anguish, but he didn't need to resort to such methods now. He had an enemy to cut. That was better. He could imagine faces on the enemy.

This is Farrow and Phil LeSteen.

Chaplain peeked at the sentry's back through the bridge's guardrails. The man wore a tattered shirt and trousers rather than Wehrmacht fatigues. His scraggly hair waved in the wind, and he leaned on ... crutches? Chaplain frowned; then his forehead smoothed. His was not to reason why; his was but to make the man die. He clenched the knife between his teeth and slipped over the guardrail. His eyes glittered like an animal's as his feet padded across the cobble surface. He clamped a hand over the sentry's mouth and aimed to shove the knife through the base of his skull. Chaplain knew something was wrong as soon as he touched the man. The guard's skin was snow cold, and his flesh was as stiff as a frozen fish. The "crutches" were nothing of the sort. They were just scraps of wood used to prop the sentry up. The corpse toppled off its mounts and hit the ground.

Lightning flashed. Chaplain caught staccato glimpses of the body. Green skin. Bird-pecked eyes. A ragged word carved into the man's chest: *Hölle.*

Spinning déjà vu sucked Chaplain down like a bitter-water whirlpool. He smelled the phantom stench of burned flesh, fell to his knees and vomited.

Where is a pig who is on fire from?

Chaplain slashed the knife across his arm with bitter relish.

"Christ," he whispered as he cut. "Christ, oh Christ, oh Christ."

"Situation report?" the Major demanded.

Chaplain flopped between Kenway and Berg. "The guy was already dead, one of the townspeople from the looks of him. Someone carved *Hölle* into his chest."

"What's *Hölle?*" Berg asked, his Ichabod-Crane face looking puzzled.

"Psychological bullshit," the Major answered. "That's it. That's all. The Germans only have four men here. They're using fear to control the population. We head for the church. We'll use it as a staging area. Then we hit them."

The group rose from their hiding place, crept to the bridge and flitted across it in a single-file line. They paused beside the mutilated corpse. Distaste pinched Ritter's severe, woodcut face. "Sick Nazi bastards," he cursed. He was one to judge, after all. He was as good as they came—the three French women he raped since arriving in country and the bag of German ears he kept for luck non-withstanding.

The corpse stared at the grim soldiers with black eye sockets and a plaintive expression on its rotten face.

I can't see! I'm blind!

"Prop him back up," the Major ordered.

Ritter turned with a questioning expression. "I don't think—"

"You're not here to think, private. You're here to do as your told. The Germans set him up as a scarecrow. They might happen by and notice he fell. Maybe they'll figure the wind did it ... or maybe they'll figure that a bunch of mean motherfuckers just entered town to take what they got, so prop him back up."

"Yes, sir."

Once reset, the corpse resembled a demonic concierge. *Welcome, gentlemen. We've been expecting you.*

The word *Hölle*—German for hell—was its badge.

No lights glowed in the narrow streets. The Allied invasion knocked out Le Coeur's electricity. The town's buildings looked medieval compared to American structures. Most were brick and mortar rather than wood. They had high-banked roofs with clay tiles and skylights. The cottages formed a geometrical mountain range of saw-tooth peaks and tombstone walls. Plank fences ran between many of the homes and were adorned with soggy posters that read, *Viva le France!* The place smelled of stone and rotten age. Its odor was compounded by the rain, which flowed around strange bits of street trash: an ax, a broken pitchfork, and a large pile of rags.

Cain wiped nervous sweat from his gaunt face. He stopped a moment to rub the black greasepaint off his fingers and then noticed a hand sticking out of the rag pile at his feet, palm up, like a beggar. He did a double take, and a crack of lightning revealed a bloody skull peeking out from between the soggy folds of cloth.

"Major," Cain hissed. "You better have a look at this!"

The Major came forward and crouched next to the human remains. He chewed on his lower lip in contemplation. Lightning revealed another pile of *rags* a short distance away … then two more … three … four … the street was littered with them.

"Jesus Christ," Cain whispered. His voice wavered at the sight while the rest of the men hugged their rifles closer to their chests for comfort.

"Keep moving," the Major growled. "Stay together."

The church was a paradox of elegant lines and arches matched with rough stone walls, which gave the artistry a backbone. Twin spires and a steeple jutted above its roof. A gaggle of gargoyles held a conference around its bell. They watched Chaplain lead the other soldiers through the church's oak doors. The troops moved into the building as a single creature—one went ahead, checked things out and another advanced beyond him. Lightning flashed through the stained-glass windows. Their brightly colored art depicted acts of martyrdom—crucifixions, beheadings, burnings and lions. The diffuse light wasn't enough to pierce the darkness, however. The men used their flashlights.

The beams of illumination revealed more dead bodies.

Two corpses lay in the center aisle, their limbs thrown out at unnatural angles. Three more flopped over the backs of pews. The legs of one stuck into the air in a V-shape. The corpse's pants legs slipped back and revealed hairy shins and white flesh.

The Major swept his flashlight over the rest of the church. Four rows of pews filled the main worship area. In the rear, steps led to a balcony where organ pipes reflected the Major's flashlight. He pointed at Kenway and Jacobson. They nodded and moved up the staircase to check out the gallery.

The Major swung his light to the front of the church, illuminating a pulpit and a door. An altar stood next to the pastor's perch, and a six-foot crucifix hung over the cloth-covered table. Christ's face was full of misery and love. Rags hung from his waist, and nails pierced his palms and feet.

"*Eli, Eli, lama sabachthani*," a voice whispered.

The Major found Chaplain standing beside him. Chaplain stared at the crucifix with hard eyes. His face was as haggard as the corpses they had so far encountered.

"What did you say?" the Major asked.

Chaplain didn't hear. He rubbed the cuts on his forearm with trembling fingers. The fresh scabs broke open and blood began to flow.

The Major noticed the ladder of scars below Chaplain's elbow. Great, the last thing he needed was a Section Eight soldier. They already lost damn near half the squad to the Messerschmitt. He decided not to draw attention to the self-mutilation, however. He only needed Chaplain to last for one lousy night. Then the man could go crazy on his own time. "Private!"

Chaplain blinked out of his revelry. "Sir?"

The Major pointed his flashlight behind the pulpit. "Check that door."

Alertness and composure returned to Chaplain's demeanor—much to the Major's relief. He opened the door and pointed his rifle and flashlight inside. The small room contained nothing more than a desk and a chair—the priest's chambers.

"Clear," Chaplain murmured.

Other whispers of "clear" echoed through the church. The Major shone his light toward the balcony. Kenway looked down and gave him a thumbs up.

Meanwhile, Mac knelt beside one of the corpses lying in the aisle and rolled it over with a grunt of distaste. The dead man had a scream frozen on his face. Most of his throat was ripped away, and his eyes were gone.

Berg took in the sight with great unease. It wasn't right to see murdered bodies in a church. Churches were supposed to be ... what was the word? Sanctities? Sacrileges? No, that wasn't right. He thought harder. Sanctuaries! Churches were supposed to be sanctuaries. If a person could get killed in a church, they could get killed anywhere.

"*Hölle*," he whispered.

"What the hell happened here?" Ritter wondered aloud.

"You know damn well what happened here," the Major said through clenched teeth. "Nazis. This is what they do. They're animals. We'll take thirty. Get your heads on straight. Then we hit the bank. Cain. Tower. Watch."

CHAPTER

BEAST

ERICK STARK THREW his arms wide and let a barrage of hail lash his chest. Cold rain ran down his sharp Aryan face. He wore civilian clothes and a Nazi SS field cap. No silver skull and crossbones gleamed above its brim, however. A nickel-plated wolf skull was pinned there instead, engraved with the words: *Das Wolfsrudel.*

The storm had as little effect on Stark as it did on the fifteen-foot statue dominating Le Coeur's town square. The sculpture depicted Michael the Archangel and the Dragon from Revelations engaged in combat.

Fangs filled the Dragon's mouth. It coiled up in a series of serpent-like humps, on the verge of striking. Michael waited for the attack with a stoic face, spread wings and a raised sword.

An inscription read: *A great war broke out in heaven. Michael and his angels fought with the Dragon and his legions. The Dragon was cast out, that serpent of old, called Satan, who deceives the whole world. He was cast to earth, and the fallen angels of his rebellion were cast out with him.*

Phantom voices rang in Stark's head: *Tekeli-li! Tekeli-li!*

He didn't bother to pursue the memory. *What's done is done.* He breathed deep instead, sucking in the power of the storm. It was nothing compared to how powerful he felt.

It hadn't always been that way, of course. He was of a weak constitution before the war—pale and scrawny, with a sunken chest and a crooked back. Furthermore, he suffered an attack of osteomyelitis in his youth—an inflammation of the bone marrow—and doctors had to operate on his left leg. The surgery was unsuccessful. The limb remained shorter than his right and grew withered in appearance.

Such physical defects caused Stark to be ignored and shunned. He laughed when he saw Claude Rains in *The Invisible Man*. A person didn't need a serum to make them invisible. They just needed a handicap, and everyone's eyes would pass over them as worthless. And in those days it was quite a feat to be worthless in Germany. Worthless was the common standard during the Great German Depression.

✠ ✠ ✠

PRIOR TO HITLER coming to power, nearly six million people—50 percent of the nation's workforce—were unemployed. Inflation ran rampant. At one point, a glass of beer cost one billion marks. People were desperate, broke, and had no way out. Many lived in the streets, and some men were willing to murder those with jobs so they could apply for the open position as soon as it was posted.

Hitler changed that when he became Chancellor. By 1939, unemployment had all but disappeared thanks to some dubious progress and creative record keeping. For example, women were no longer included in the statistics, nor were Jews, even though many lost their jobs at the start of Hitler's reign. Furthermore, conscription removed 1.4 million men from the unemployed classification.

Factories were then built to supply the military, which created jobs out of thin air. The Nazis also introduced the National Labor Service. It took unemployed people off the streets and made them dig irrigation ditches, build autobahns, and plant new forests. The men wore military-style uniforms and stayed in barracks at the work sites. They were paid only pocket money, and if they refused to work, they were classified as "work shy" and put into concentration camps.

The German Labor Front was then set up to "protect" workers and increased the number of hours worked per week from sixty to seventy-two.

Even the leisure time of workers was carefully regulated by the Kraft durch Freude. It allocated each worker a finite amount of yearly free time to pursue state-provided activities, which were meticulously recorded. For example, in the Berlin area between 1933 and 1938, approximately twenty thousand theater performances were held and over eleven million people attended them.

Ever the thoughtful organization, the Kraft durch Freude also introduced a program to provide workers with cars. Fredinand Porsche designed the Volkswagen Beetle to be affordable at a cost of 990 marks. That was thirty-five weeks of wages for the average worker. To pay for one, workers went on a purchase plan where they paid five marks a week into an account. Few ever received a vehicle, however. The money was funneled into the rapidly expanding weapon factories.

Nevertheless, compared to the failures of the Weimar Government and the financial misery of previous years, many felt the Nazi Government at least made an effort to improve their lot—despite the obvious problems with the programs.

In such an environment, an invalid had to take whatever job he could get, and sewing buttons on coats was all Stark could manage. He worked twelve-hour days, six days a week, and received a pauper's wage. All of his co-workers were women. Most afforded him the attention and respect due a crippled male seamstress—which is to say, none at all.

Sometimes, he suspected they laughed at him behind his back for being such a pitiful excuse for a man. Other times, he was sure they laughed at him. Too often, he heard whispers aimed in his direction and the subsequent suppressed snickers.

Only Elsa acknowledged his existence. She was a pretty blond girl from Dresden, simple and good-natured. Each morning she would say, "Guten Morgen, Erick," and in the evening she would say, "Auf Wiedersehen, Erick." Sometimes she even shared a bit of cake with him from her lunch.

Since no girl ever paid him so much attention, Stark fell in love with her, but he put no stock in the feeling—none at all. He had no illusions she would ever love him. At best, he was just a pet to her, something to pass the day by talking to—not with—and something to occasionally slip a treat, like a pathetic puppy.

Besides, Elsa belonged to someone named Emil. She spoke about him often. He cut down trees for one of the mills on the outskirts of Berlin and fought in the trenches of World War I. Elsa was also sure to mention that Emil was very strong and very handsome.

Elsa didn't do this to wound Stark's pride—of course not. It was just a matter of her simplicity and the fact that you don't have to watch what you say around a pet.

Some nights when Stark couldn't sleep, he would lie in bed and compose verses about Elsa. He would speak them aloud and imagine she heard them and praised him for his poetry. Perhaps she would even give him a kiss on the cheek.

Your lips are like rose petals, soft and true, glistening with morning dew ...

Then Stark would touch his fluttering heart and feel his scrawny chest and think of his weak lungs, back, and wrinkled leg and grind his teeth until he finally slept.

He often dreamed he looked down on a map of the world. As he watched, the country of Germany grew black. Strangely familiar yellow eyes appeared in its heart. The borders of Germany then spread under the beastly gaze.

Black tendrils inched into Poland, Austria and Czechoslovakia. They probed into France and absorbed it, spilling ever onward, over mountain and over sea, until the gleaming yellow eyes owned the whole world—from the United States to China, from the North Pole to the South.

Faces struggled under the surface of the map, like people with black rubber sheets pulled across their features. Stark recognized some of them. One of them belonged to Elsa. Another belonged to his boss, Mr. Leberwitz, the bastard.

Mr. Leberwitz was in his eighties and walked with a hunched posture while leaning on a cane. A thick gray moustache hung beneath his bulbous nose. The light shone bright and severe off his bald scalp. He hobbled between the tables and inspected everyone's work eight times a day. If he felt you weren't working fast enough—*whack!*—he smacked you over the head with his cane. Daily, Stark went home with a bruised skull. No matter how fast he sewed, it was never fast enough.

Stark suspected Mr. Leberwitz enjoyed having a man around who was weak enough for even him to bully. A man can get enjoyment from putting down a woman, but he can get fulfillment from putting down a man. Mr. Leberwitz was also a master of verbal whacks.

"What's the matter, Stark? Can't you keep up with a bunch of women?"

"Is your sense of time crippled as well, Stark?"

And Mr. Leberwitz's favorite, delivered with perfect timing after a particularly viscous cane strike: "You only reap what you *sew*, Stark."

Then the old man would shuffle off, a raspy chuckle bubbling up his throat, leaving Stark red-faced with shame. For a time, Elsa would never speak to him after such encounters, like she was ashamed of him, as well.

This was because Mr. Leberwitz was a Jew.

Most Jews in Nazi Germany suffered greatly. Hitler made plain his hatred for them in his book, *Mein Kampf*, where references to the "filthy Jew" litter the pages. He considered them animals that polluted mankind's purity through malicious inbreeding. He even blamed them for all of Germany's problems. Most German citizens thought that was utter nonsense—until the Depression hit.

Hitler's labeling of a scapegoat became a lot more popular when the people were unemployed and helpless. Everyone wants someone to blame and hate for their misfortune.

The Nuremberg Laws classified Jews as subhuman in January 1933. Policing Nazis stopped Germans from shopping in Jewish stores. By 1934, all the Jewish shops were marked with the yellow Star of David—a Passover of a different sort. Jews had to sit in special seats on buses and trains. German school children were taught anti-Semitic lessons. Jewish youths were openly ridiculed by the teachers, and bullying of Jews on the playground went unpunished.

In 1935, the Jews lost their right to be German citizens, and marriage between Jews and non-Jews was strictly forbidden. Violence reached its pre-war peak in November 1938 with Krystalnacht—Night of the Broken Glass—when the third secretary of the German Embassy in Paris was shot dead by a seventeen-year-old German-Jewish refugee. In retaliation, Hitler ordered a seven-day campaign of terror against the Jews in Germany. Ten thousand Jewish shops were destroyed and many homes and synagogues were burned.

As an added insult, Hitler ordered the Jews to sweep up the mess and made them scrub the streets clean. Some were even forced to do the job with their tongues.

But a thing exists that can overcome racism, prejudice, and violence: money. And Leberwitz had plenty of it. He paid off Nazi officials, and they allowed him to operate his business without oppression. His windows were never broken. His products were never boycotted. And if he happened to hit his workers—his German workers—over the head with a cane every once in awhile, well, what goes on under a man's roof is his own business—thank you very bribe.

So that was Stark's life: being a cripple, performing menial labor, pining for a girl he could never have, and being abused by his boss. He didn't have what it took to change any of it either. Beaten dogs stay beaten … unless they turn mean. Stark shifted from one to the other the night of January 30, 1939.

People crowded the Berlin streets that night. Great bonfires filled the air with smoke and cast the light of flames over all who took part. Columns of soldiers goose-stepped down the boulevards in perfect formation. The cheeks of their blank faces jostled with each jarring slap of their boots. They carried banners and torches. Ranks of uniform-clad children marched behind them, banging drums and blowing trumpets and flutes.

Overhead, spotlights stabbed the night sky, and fireworks burst among their beams. People packed the sidewalks, cheering and screaming—a throng that willingly gave up the humanity of the individual for the beast of the mob. All the militarism of their German blood surged to their heads. They raised hands in slavish salutes and clutched their hearts as their faces contorted with excited hysteria. Their eyes burned with fanaticism, glued on the new god who stood on a great stage. Huge red banners hung behind him. A giant eagle spread its wings above him and clutched a swastika.

The god held sway over all with a demonic magnetism contained in a prissy frame. Wire microphones stood in front of his pasty face, which was topped with slick black hair. A Charlie Chaplain moustache covered his upper lip. He wore a brown *Sturmabteilung* uniform with a red armband. He continually jacked the arm out over the crowd at a forty-five degree angle. They cheered louder—old men, old women, young men, young women, children—everyone who had a voice cried out.

The noise surged and subsided like a series of tidal waves as the collective group drew and expelled breath together. The god lowered his head in all humbleness, waiting patiently for silence.

Stark stood alone against a wall with a broken brick between his feet. He watched Elsa and a man he presumed to be Emil. Emil did, in fact, appear to be very strong and very handsome. He was tall and confident, with a square face and thick blond hair. He stood behind Elsa with his hands around her waist. She leaned into him. They appeared to be very happy. Stark clenched his fists, outside of it all, as usual.

The god's voice boomed out over everything, coming from many crackling speakers and rising into the night. His speech was a curious paradox of rambling with singular purpose. The people quieted and listened with rapt attention.

"We used to stand on the outside looking in, laughed at and ridiculed. Faith was a maiden with other suitors. Yet, the tide shifted because we had the will to persevere! Six years ago today, tens of thousands of National Socialist fighters passed through the Brandenberger Tor to express feelings of overflowing joy and confess loyalty to me, the new Chancellor of the Reich! The anxious eyes of oppressors watched with disbelief as some thirteen million German voters then stood beside me!"

Applause and spirited shouts filled the air. Stark watched a father help his toddler clap. He watched a woman cry with the emotion of it all. But mostly he watched Elsa and Emil. He watched and cursed whatever twist of fate caused him to be born like the crooked man from the nursery rhyme.

There was a crooked man, who walked a crooked mile ...

"Many rallied against us, united in their hatred for National Socialism, hatred born of guilty consciences and worse intentions. The priests of the Center Party, the communist atheists, the socialists out to abolish private property, the capitalists who worship the stock exchange, the democratic apostles who force the Versailles Treaty upon us, they all aimed to destroy the Reich and made common cause with Jewry!"

The mood of the people changed. Their features became cross, and strident cries of anger rang out with flaming animosity. Stark perked up at the sound. It was a mood he could identify with—bitterness, hate and rage.

"Jewish agitators convince other nations to hate Germany. Yet, such nations will soon realize Germany does not want war. All the assertions of our intended attacks on other countries are lies, lies born of morbid hysteria and a mania for self-preservation on the part of the Jewish world enemy! For the Jew gains by war. He prospers financially, and his thirst for revenge and entertainment is satisfied by watching others die. His lies are the grossest defamation that can be brought against our peace-loving nation!"

Something swayed inside of Stark as he listened to Hitler's speech. The dictator had made no great impression on him previously. Stark was too cynical to be drawn to causes. Life taught him that passion made no difference if the situation dictated defeat. Yet, the mood of the night swept Stark up. The energy of the people was impossible to ignore, and it felt as if Hitler spoke to him directly.

Stark knew what it was like to be oppressed by circumstance—*his twisted back and withered leg ached*—and conspirators—*his head throbbed from Leberwitz's blows, and his heart ached from all the laughter and jokes at his expense*—to be denied the fruits of happiness—*he looked at Elsa and Emil and snarled.*

Something inside of Stark seethed against everything, thwarted by the unfairness of it all. Hadn't he paid his dues? Didn't he deserve even a modicum of satisfaction?

"When the German nation was deprived of its savings, which it had accumulated through years of honest work, by inflation instigated and carried out by the Jews ..."

When I was born crippled ...

"After we witnessed almost one million milk cows be driven from our lands in accordance to the cruel paragraphs of the Versailles Treaty, and more than eight hundred thousand German children died of hunger and undernourishment at the close of the war ..."

And all self worth was stolen ...

"Over one million German prisoners of war were retained in confinement for no apparent reason for a whole year. Over one-and-a-half million Germans were whipped out of our frontier territories with nothing more than the clothes on their back. We endured having millions of our countrymen taken from us without their consent and without their being afforded the slightest possibility of existence ..."

And all my efforts meant nothing ...

"I could supplement these examples with dozens of the most cruel kind. Suffice it to say, Germany was left beaten and robbed on the side of the road, but no Good Samaritan came along to save us. All shunned our pain. We were left to die!"

Alone. Nothing to nobody.

"But we will not be denied! We will snatch destiny from the heavens! We will embrace the strength in our hearts and pluck what we want from the tree of life!"

Stark reached down with trembling hands and picked up the brick at his feet.

Auf Wiedersehen, Erick ...

"I have often been a prophet in the course of my life and usually ridiculed for it. When I said that I would one day take over the leadership of the State, and with it, the entire nation, many laughed ... but they aren't laughing anymore. Tonight, I will once more be a prophet: if the Jews again insist on plunging the nations of the world into war, then the result with not be the Bolshevization of the Earth, and thus the victory of Jewry. Rather, it will be the annihilation of the Jewish race in Europe and the beginning of Germany's ascension to a position of glorious power!"

Stark fondled the brick and watched Elsa and Emil.

Guten Morgen, Stark.

"Tonight, let us look to the future and not forget our children in the process. We shall see them educated. In fact, we have already begun. We will teach them to take what they need and seize what they want with an iron fist. Right now, tonight, let us put all our hopes, dreams and strength into a box, and fight for it, so that we may pass it on to a dynasty of Aryan generations who will lead the world to perfection!"

Stark stood numb among the cheering. It took him several minutes to realize his voice was one of the many that made up the cacophony. Even though he didn't realize exactly why he cheered, something inside of him knew, and that was enough.

Yellow eyes. Enveloping blackness.

Stark suddenly realized why the yellow eyes of his dream were recognizable. They were misshapen, but clearly his own.

The Earth seemed to move under his feet, and Stark let himself be carried along by the invisible wave. All inner turmoil quieted. Limits disappeared; boundaries ceased to exist. He didn't have to struggle anymore. The answer was right there and so apparent: *if you can't make it, break it.*

Eventually, the rally dispersed. Hitler withdrew from the stage. The last of the army marched through the streets. The crowd broke into small groups, which broke into couples, which broke into solitary figures as everyone returned to their homes.

One solitary figure followed a couple with a brick in his hand.

Excerpt from a pamphlet entitled: *Das Schicksal Deutschland:*

"Germany had been brought low. It has been knocked down and trodden upon. It is the nation that no one sees, the nation that is ignored, the nation that does not matter. But it shall rise again, transformed like the Phoenix from the ashes. It shall rise to glorious heights and reap the fruits of desire, from stepping-stone to foundation to tallest spire. This destiny it will pluck from history's heart with its own hands, and it shall bash in the heads of its enemies with the rock of strength!"

Excerpt from *Mein Kampf*:

"The Jewish youth lies in wait for hours on end ... spying on the unsuspicious German girl he plans to seduce ... He wants to contaminate her blood and remove her from the bosom of her own people."

Excerpt from a pamphlet entitled *Erster Paraphilie*:

"The Aryans were once a race of perfect giants. The Jews were foul dwarfs who hated their beauty and wisdom. They knew that the only way they could defeat the Aryans was to dilute their purity. They kidnapped Aryan women and impregnated them, tainting the Aryan blood with the Jewish spoor and weakening the once great race with imperfections until it was cast down."

A drawing inside the pamphlet: A vile pig man with a hooknose and fat lips forced himself on a beautiful blond woman. A mustachioed pig female with a hooknose and fat lips helped hold the beautiful blond woman down.

Stark wondered if her bastard child ended up a cripple.

Newspaper headline, September 1, 1939:

BLITZKRIEG!
The Wehrmacht Army struck Poland today. Heroic
soldiers of the Fatherland penetrated deep into its
borders and overwhelmed Polish forces with su-
perior equipment and tactics. Stukas, Panzers and
stormtroopers marched forth ...

Stark sewed buttons without looking. The needle pricked his finger again and again, drawing blood. He didn't notice as it dripped on the table. He watched Leberwitz. The old man looked more sleazy and greasy than ever. He hobbled between the workers, a vile pig in a shiny suit with a hook-nose and fat lips, ogling the women.

No Elsa to ogle, though.

Elsa was... gone.

She can't have her cake and eat it, too.

If an Emil falls in the forest and no one is around to hear him, does he scream?

Leberwitz caught him watching.

"What are you looking at, Stark?"

"A pig."

Leberwitz's eyes grew to the size of saucers. He hobbled toward Stark as fast as his cane could carry him. He looked like a vulture that came to tear the best from them all—no eagle carrying an olive branch twisted into a swastika.

"What did you say?" Leberwitz demanded.

"I called you a pig."

"You, dog!" Leberwitz roared and raised his cane. It was the cane whack to end all cane whacks. He brought the walking stick down on Stark's head. Stark ignored the blow and pushed himself to his crooked feet, launching himself at Leberwitz.

Blitzkrieg!

There was a crooked man who couldn't straighten out, so he broke the world.

Stark and Leberwitz hit the floor between tables. Women shrieked and parted from their flailing limbs. Stark found the cane in his hand. He wrestled it away from Leberwitz and struck him with it. Leberwitz let him go. Stark got to his feet and hit the old man again and again and again, screaming at the top of his lungs.

"Abandoner!" *Whack!*

"Shunner!" *Whack!*

"Hater!" *Whack!*

"Rejecter!" *Whack!*

"Frustrater!" *Whack!*

"Disappointer!" *Whack!*

"Abuser!" *Whack!*

"Crippler!" *Whack!*

Leberwitz cried and pleaded under the assault. Drops of red splattered Stark's face. Leberwitz's bloody features twisted into those of Elsa and Emil. The way they looked that night, so surprised, so shocked that the pet had teeth *and* desire.

Finally, Stark's own face appeared in Leberwitz's battered countenance. It looked up at him with yellow eyes and begged for the coup de grace. He paused a moment, but only a moment, and then brought the cane down a final time.

Stark dropped the bloody walking stick. His lungs heaved. Spots danced before his vision. His heart pounded in his chest with enough force that he thought it might explode. Something in his back was strained, and agony burned up and down his spine. He embraced the pain and held on to consciousness with grim intensity.

Stark saw the women staring at him. They couldn't take their eyes off him.

He wasn't invisible anymore.

Stark arrived at the enlistment barracks before dawn of the next day. It was a cold and sterile brick building. He stood in a line of men that shuffled eagerly forward, almost jostling to get through the door. When Stark's turn came, he gave his name and personal information to an elderly female typist with a hairy mole on her upper lip. She recorded the information with machinegun bursts of typewriter keys.

Stark was ushered into a large room for a physical. Anonymous men stood around him like factory products fresh from the assembly line, waiting to be shipped out. Countless eyes judged him as unworthy to join the ranks. He stared back in defiance until a blond nurse led him behind a curtain and told him to disrobe, the doctor would join him shortly. Stark did and waited for the inevitable verdict.

But he had to try. Nothing else existed.

The doctor was a tall, thin man who wore wire-rim glasses that shielded squinty eyes. Messy hair topped his oblong face. A sparse moustache grew on his upper lip like a patch of grass dying on an arid mountainside. Stark thought the man looked like he was made from a flagpole and broomsticks. A nametag identified him as Dr. Rascher.

Rascher didn't bother to put a stethoscope to Stark's chest or even go so far as to shine a light in his ear. He simply looked Stark over from head to toe and dismissed him with a wave of his surgical hand.

"Unfit for service," he declared.

But Stark didn't leave. He stood naked and puny on the cold floor, shivering from more than the cold, shivering with the effort to rage against dismissal. He informed the doctor of his will. He would do anything for Germany, anything for the Fuehrer.

Rascher looked at Stark with interest for the first time. "Anything?" he asked, eyebrows raised.

"Anything," Stark affirmed.

Rascher considered the answer, staring at Stark but not seeing him. Finally, he reached into his pocket and pulled out a black marker. He drew an X on Stark's forehead. "Go to the checkout table. They'll take care of you." With that, Rascher left.

Stark dressed and limped to the far side of the room, rubbing at the mark on his forehead. It caused the other men to stare at him even more. He ignored them. His eyes were drawn to the black uniform of the SS trooper standing among all the white smocks of the medical personnel. The man was everything Stark wished he could be—handsome, strong, and important. To Stark's surprise, the SS trooper approached him.

"You're marked. Follow me."

The man led Stark to a bench outside. "Wait here."

Stark shivered in the chill morning mist for two hours, wondering what it was all about. Three other men with X's on their foreheads joined him. One was an old man. Another looked like a scrawny weasel and had a tick in his cheek; occasionally, his limbs let out a flurry of twitches, as well. A fourth man looked normal but turned out to be a deaf mute. None of them were ideal physical specimens. None of them were good enough for the army, but they were good enough for ... something.

Truck headlights materialized out of the mist like dragon eyes. The sound of its engine was offensive in the morning stillness. A bull of a man in another SS uniform exited the cab. He stomped to the back of the truck and pulled the canvas flap open.

"Get in."

The ride lasted for hours. Stark's back screamed with discomfort. He smelled sweat, despair, and the odor of someone's weak bladder. It turned out to be the old man; Gunther was his name. The man with the tick was Verning, and the deaf mute was Hagen. Exhaust leaked into the cargo bed, and Stark felt like simultaneously passing out and throwing up. His head nodded forward for a time, and he slept a fitful sleep filled with dreams of being eaten alive by shadowy beasts.

Finally the truck stopped. The driver pulled the flap open. Setting sunlight flooded in, and Stark and the rest of the men shielded their eyes. They found themselves in the courtyard of a castle. It had three towers and walls in between. Soldiers walked its perimeter with rifles and German shepherds. One of the dogs marked Stark with baleful yellow eyes and seemed to grin. Stark looked back and shuddered. He realized where they were: Wewelsburg—the castle of Henrich Himmler.

✠　✠　✠

BUT THAT WAS a long time ago. Now was now. Stark continued to let the storm try to beat him down. It couldn't. Nothing could anymore. He was beyond it all. He was iron. He was strength. He was no longer the crooked man. He was *Übermensch.*

A bank stood along the east side of the courtyard. The building was a squat two-story structure with large double doors. Stark could see Hagen and Gunther through one of the barred windows. They sat at a table and ate cheese and sausage by firelight. Gunther still had gray hair, but his face was free of wrinkles. His skin was almost as taut as Hagen's even though Hagen was a much younger man. Watching them eat made Stark's mouth water. He was always hungry now.

A naked man materialized out of the shadows like he floated up from the depths of dark waters. He came through a gate in the eight-foot wall surrounding the courtyard and marched toward Stark with purposeful strides. The rain ran down the many striations of his well-defined muscles. His blond hair was matted to his forehead, and his eyes glittered with sharp intensity.

"Verning," Stark greeted him. "Your report?"

"Americans are here."

CHAPTER

W●RRY

A PERSON SHOULDN'T BE up here in weather like this. What if lightning hits the steeple? What if there are bats? What if they bite me and give me some kind of disease? What if I fall? What if a German sniper has me in his sights?

The wind drove a cold rain through the bell tower. Stinging drops beat a calypso rhythm on Cain's helmet and washed clean streaks in his greasepaint. It made him look part-man, part-tiger. A chaotic grid of gable roofs stretched below him. Nothing moved on the twisting streets. The town looked dead, and they saw no signs to the contrary, just the opposite in fact. Cain thought of the carved-up corpse.

Hölle—Hell.

He couldn't shake the feeling the whole damn mission had edged into Bad-Idea territory. First the Messerschmitt and now a village of the dead. What next?

It's not a village of the dead. You saw a couple of corpses. That's all.

Then why did the townspeople leave them there?

They're afraid of the Germans.

Why haven't we seen any signs of life?

It's after midnight. The people are asleep.

Those logical arguments came from the part of Cain's mind that always believed he'd win the sweepstakes or be identified as the long lost nephew of some rich uncle. It was the part that believed in brass rings and their attainability.

If it wasn't for that part, Cain would just say 'fuck it' and desert. It wouldn't even be AWOL. They were operating outside the system. But *What If … What If* it was all true? *What If* they got what they came for, lock, stock and barrel?

Why it would mean everything. *Everything!*

A more reasonable part of Cain spoke up and told him not to be so stupid. If something sounds too good to be true, then it usually is too good to be true; pursuing it will only end in folly.

It was like losing one's life savings in poker by thinking the next hand would win big. And the next hand becomes two, then five, then ten, and each deal of the cards costs you more and more and more until everything is gone.

But … *What If?*

"The hell with it," Cain cut the internal debate off. "Everything'll be fine."

The gargoyle who shared his vantage point was the only one who heard the declaration. It didn't give its opinion on the matter one way or the other. It just crouched on the window ledge and gazed into the streets, waiting for someone to venture out so it could swoop down and carry them back to its roost. Then it would gibber and rend and eat.

What if the gargoyle did come to life? What if it did eat the townspeople? Now I'm alone with it ... and it's probably hungry.

A bolt of lighting blazed Cain and the gargoyle in white light. Cain jumped. The monstrous statue grinned—devilish and hungry. A terrific peal of thunder rattled the entire church. The downpour increased and roared like a passing locomotive.

Cain reined in his jittery nerves and stamped his feet to keep warm, He couldn't tell where the stock of his Thompson ended and his numb fingers began. Snot dripped from his nose. His throat felt raw and dry. He forced his eyes to probe the rain-beaten shadows below.

Even if a brigade of Nazis came down the street with MP-40 machine guns blazing and potato masher grenades flying, he would have a hard time seeing them. Tension turned the muscles of his neck into steel bands. He tried to relax, but it wasn't in his nature to loosen up. He was always on edge. Some part of him always wiggled or twitched or spasmed—his foot, his fingers drumming on his knee or his tongue obsessively licking his lips. Plus, the compulsive worrying ...

What if a grenade puts me in a wheelchair? What if I get run over by a tank? What if my gun jams in the middle of a firefight? What if I get captured?

The fact he knocked his wife up prior to shipping out made things even worse. The baby was supposed to be born six days ago. Cain had yet to receive word on the outcome. Visions of his wife screaming in the delivery room tortured him, her sheets soaked with blood and the doctor between her legs, yelling, *begging*, for a nurse to assist him. And so much more than just that existed to worry about.

What if the baby was fine but Cheryl wasn't? What if Cheryl was fine but the baby wasn't? What if it was a Mon-

goloid? What if it had cerebral palsy? What if it had TB? What it if had polio? What if Cheryl dropped it on its head? What if the baby was blind? Deaf? What if it was born with its heart on the outside of its chest? What if it was twins? Then twice as many things could go wrong ...

Cain wished he and Cheryl hadn't bothered. A child was more than a responsibility; it was a ball and chain around one's neck—so was marriage, actually. And now Cheryl would get a fat ass after giving birth. They all did. Then he'd spend the rest of his life with a disgusting spouse and some snot-nosed brat who drained away his paycheck.

Wasn't that why he came to Le Coeur? Wasn't that what the prize meant to him—freedom? He'd never have to go back, if it really was—*everything.*

How wonderful to be free of responsibility and worry, living only to satisfy the self, taking what you want without consequence—

Something grabbed Cain's foot. He managed to contain a shriek.

The gargoyle's got me!

Jacobson's face peered up through the trap door. "It's time. Let's go."

Cain's thudding heart calmed by minute degrees. He gratefully followed Jacobson down to the main level of the church. The other soldiers sat among the pews, bowing their heads over their weapons like a congregation worshipping at the altar of violence. Mechanical clicks and snaps filled the air. Palms slapped clips into Thompsons. Fingers tightened bootlaces and gear straps. Grenades hooked into vests. Knives and pistols hung along legs. Unconscious snarls curled lips.

Cain recited a boot camp prayer while he locked and loaded his Thompson.

"This is my rifle. There are many like it, but this one is mine. My rifle is my best friend. It is my life. I must master it as I master my life. Without me, my rifle is useless. Without my rifle, I am useless. I must fire my rifle true. I must shoot straighter than my enemy. I must shoot him before he shoots me. My rifle and I know that what counts in war is not the rounds we fire nor the noise of our burst. It is the hits that count. We will hit ... My rifle is human, even as I, because it is my life. Thus I will learn it as a brother. I will learn its weakness, its strength, its parts, its sights and its barrel. I will ever guard it against the ravages of weather and damage. I will keep my rifle clean and ready, even as I am clean and ready. We will become part of each other. Before God I swear this creed. My rifle and myself are the defenders of my country. We are the masters of our enemy. We are the saviors of my life. So be it, until there is no enemy, but peace. Amen."

It occurred to Cain that the prayer was no longer appropriate. They weren't in Le Coeur for peace or country. They were in it for themselves.

CHAPTER

INFLUENCE

THE MAJOR PROWLED up and down the row of black faces and beady eyes. His muddy boots left tracks on the church floor as bristled aggression charged the air. "Now this is what I want to see," he growled, "a bunch of glorious bastards who can't wait to eat their own balls and ask for more! Gentlemen, are you hungry?"

"Yes, sir!"

"Are you mean?"

"Yes, sir!"

Kenway stood on a verge, as still as when he waited for a deer to enter a clearing in the forest. Chaplain stared into a void only he could see. The sight of it drew deep lines in his face. Ritter clutched his Thompson in a white-knuckle grip and rubbed a severed ear in his freehand like an Indian fiddling stone.

"Cruel?"

"Yes, sir!"

"How cruel?"

"*Fucking* cruel, sir!"

Berg's face was a blank slate waiting to be written upon. He couldn't understand but was willing to learn. Jacobson's jaw clenched and unclenched. The muscles of his cheeks pulsed like beating hearts. Cain's entire body thrummed like he was hooked up to an electric generator. Mac tried to hold back a frightening smile.

"Are you ready to kick some Nazi shits off the planet?"

"Yes, sir!"

"Are your ready to make the American dream come true?"

"Yes, sir!"

"Then let's do it, assholes!"

"*Hoo-yah!*"

The Major led the troops out of the church and into the storm. Whether or not they lived through the coming battle was of little concern to him. They were dead men walking either way. In the end, there was just too much at stake to share.

✠ ✠ ✠

ROUGHLY TWENTY-FOUR HOURS before jumping out of the *Lazarus*, the Major was with the U.S. First Army near the town of Ame. He sat in his spacious tent and sipped coffee laced with brandy—or maybe brandy laced with coffee was a better way to put it—while he nibbled on a box of chocolates liberated from a nearby chateau.

A music box, likewise liberated, tinkled with the thin strains of Prokofiev's *Peter and the Wolf.* Important maps and documents lay around the Major's feet. Responsibility required him to study them before the next day's operations, and he would—just as soon as he finished studying a French girly magazine … if he was still sober by then, of course.

A passing tank column drowned out Prokofiev. The Major loved the grumble of their engines and the squeak of their treads. It was the sound of progress—wheels, industry and violence. That's what made the world go round.

An enterprising man could do well in such an environment, and the Major did. Boxes of loot filled his tent. He had jewelry, silver candlesticks, silk tablecloths, cash and even a few exotic items like a golden helmet and the ceremonial dagger of some forgotten cult.

It was quite the collection to be sure, but it wasn't enough to put him on easy street. By the time he paid off all the small fish and gave the Colonel his share, he'd have just enough to get started somewhere else, but not enough to live the way he wanted to live. Wheeling and dealing one's way to fortune was not the way to go, the Major realized. It took too damn long. He needed the *Big One*.

The Big One was the mythical score to end all scores—the one that netted everything in an instant. It was out there somewhere. He just had to find it.

Or maybe it would find him, if he just wished hard enough …

"Major?" asked a voice from outside the tent.

The Major frowned and checked his watch. It was far too late to be bothered. He needed his rest. Running a black market and fighting a war on the side was exhausting. He didn't reply, hoping the owner of the voice would go away. No such luck.

"You in there, Major?"

The Major's frown deepened. For shit's sake, didn't they realize he was off the clock? It's not like he got overtime. He consulted a pair of French tits to see if they agreed with his position; he certainly agreed with theirs.

A chubby private shoved his head through the tent flap. He spotted the Major and a tentative grin split his moon face. "Oh, there you are —"

The Major shot up from his chair. "Just what in the blue fuck do you think you're doing, private? Did I give you permission to enter?"

The smile left Fatty's face. "No, sir!" He tried to stand at attention and snagged his helmet on the tent's entrance. The steel headpiece tumbled to the ground with a dull clunk and rolled toward the Major's feet.

"Then why is your fat head *and* your helmet inside my tent?"

"The Colonel wants to see you!"

"The Colonel can kiss my ass. Now get the hell out!" The Major hooked a toe in the private's helmet and kicked. The headgear flew across the room and hit Fatty in the stomach. He managed a fumbling catch and a fumbling response:

"I don't think—"

"Of course you don't. You're too stupid to even *listen!*"

"He says it's important!"

"What could be that important? It's damn near midnight!"

"An interrogation, sir!"

The Major's indignation ceased and his eyebrows rose. He did have other hobbies besides drinking and naked women. "An interrogation, you say?"

"Yes, sir! An expedition force hit a Nazi convoy a couple miles east of camp. They took a prisoner."

Fatty wondered if the Major's sudden acquiesce was just a trick and an order to dig foxholes and fill them back in again would soon follow. The job would last until he learned to keep his fat head out of an officer's quarters.

The Major spared him the shit detail, however. He grabbed a black leather bag from his footlocker instead. Then he headed out of the tent on light feet, like a man going on a date with a special girl.

"Out of my way, shit for brains."

Fatty stepped aside and let the Major pass. The officer disappeared into the depths of the camp, lost among the equipment, vehicles and milling soldiers—a solitary figure cutting his own swath through the ripe fields. The private was glad to be out of his presence. It was too much like standing in a cage with a hungry tiger.

The Colonel sat behind an oak desk that he insisted traveled everywhere that he did. He was sixty-six years old and still iron. His shirtsleeves strained to cover massive forearms. His jaw muscles clenched on a cigar. Its smoke drifted past his wide nose, past his penetrating eyes and above his gray hair. His crew cut was combed into spikes so sharp they seemed to draw blood from the air.

An old man was tied to a chair in front of the Colonel. Unlike the Colonel, he showed his age. A bald spot gleamed in the center of his white hair and he had a bird-shaped birthmark on one wrinkled cheek. An oversized SS uniform clung to him like a burlap sack on a barbed-wire fence. A shoulder patch showed an eagle holding a swastika—the symbol of the Reichsfuehrer's Personal Staff.

So far all the Major got out of him was his name—Franz.

"Ask him again," the Colonel ordered. His voice sounded like his teeth were made of wood and rasped against a sandpaper tongue.

"Why are you here?" the Major spoke in German. "You're not a soldier."

Franz sweated and his lips trembled. Nevertheless, he refused to answer.

The Major turned to the Colonel with a hopeful expression. The Colonel nodded. The Major opened his bag, reached past a hammer and a straight razor and grabbed a pair of leather gloves. He pulled the gloves on and tightened a hand into a fist. The leather creaked. Franz winced. The Major gave him a reassuring smile. Then his fist jacked through the air.

Franz's nose exploded in a burst of blood. The German cried out. The Major waited for Franz to grow accustomed to the pain. Then he jabbed the man's nose again, pulverizing it, grinding it into mush. This time Franz screamed.

"Why are you here?"

"To fight," Franz wheezed in his native tongue. The harsh light of the Colonel's desk lamp threw his battered face into sickening detail, like a patient on an operating table. The bird birthmark looked like it took panicked flight.

"Bullshit. You're too old to fight. Why are you here?"

"Army depleted. Every man must fight. Old. Young. All."

Maybe. Maybe not. The Major tried a different question—one to which they already knew the answer. "How many men were in your unit?"

"Twenty-five."

"Vehicles?"

"Two tanks. A truck."

"Very good," the Major smiled. He patted Franz's head. The German flinched like a beaten dog. Blood dripped from his nose as thick as mercury.

"Ask him where they were going," the Colonel ordered.

"*Wohin haben Sie gefaehrt?*"

71

Franz didn't answer. He was trying to be a solider again, the Major knew. He gave in once. Now he was ashamed and determined not to weaken again.

The Major paced back and forth, throwing Franz into light and shadow. "Just tell us. Everyone has a breaking point. There's no shame in that. Don't make me take you to yours."

Silence from Franz but for the whistle of breath between his teeth.

The Major bent down and put a hand under the German's chin, gently, like a lover lifting his soul mate's countenance for a kiss. "Where?"

Franz spit in the Major's face. The Major straightened up with a disappointed sigh, removed a glove and reached into his pocket for a handkerchief. He wiped the spittle from his face, never taking his hard eyes off Franz.

"I'm sorry," Franz babbled under the icy gaze. "I'm so sorry!"

The Major replaced the hanky. He pulled the glove back on with deliberate slowness, making sure it fit tight in the fingers. Then his hand lashed out as quick as a striking snake and caught Franz's broken nose between his thumb and forefinger. He twisted. The German shrieked, tears shooting from his eyes.

"*Wohin haben Sie gefaehrt?*"

"Le Coeur," Franz relented. "We were going to Le Coeur."

A map of France stood on a nearby table. A pencil sharper marked a British regiment. Paper clips showed a Polish paratroop infiltration. A beret symbolized German tanks. The whole thing was cluttered with every day objects that represented soldiers fighting for their lives. It was easier to move a fifty-cent coin across a piece of paper than it was to send a hundred men to their deaths. The Major located

Le Coeur after a few seconds of searching. He reported the information to the Colonel.

"It's a small town out of the fighting. Doesn't look very important."

The Colonel sucked on his cigar. Its tip glowed like the devil's eye. His voice was devoid of inflection as he spoke.

"Then why were they going there?"

"*Warum haben Sie da gegangen?*"

Franz slumped forward. The Major grabbed a handful of his thin hair and pulled him upright again. Franz's eyes showed white; he had passed out from the pain. Nonplussed, the Major rummaged through his bag and pulled out a saltshaker.

The Colonel waited as patiently as a trapdoor spider. He knew how the drama would play out—the same as it always did.

The Major rubbed the salt into Franz's ravaged nose. The man woke up and uttered a high-pitched scream. The Major gave him a precise uppercut to the chin. The German's teeth clicked together and a severed piece of tongue fell into his lap.

"Why was your unit going to Le Coeur?" The Major held Franz's mouth shut, forcing him to swallow the blood. "When I let go, you better answer. Understand?"

Franz nodded. His eyes rolled with revulsion and pain.

The Major released his grip. Franz turned to the side and coughed out a gleaming mouthful of blood, again and again, retching in between the hacks.

"Talk, damn it!"

"To reinforce the garrison," Franz managed around gags.

"How big is the garrison?"

"Four ... four men."

73

What the fuck? Why send a small force to an unimportant town with a garrison of only four men? And why would a guy try to resist torture over it?

"What's so important about Le Coeur?"

"A bridge," Franz sputtered.

"Bullshit! There's no major bridge there."

"A rail yard, I mean."

"This is a waste of time," the Colonel declared. "He doesn't know anything important. He's just making stuff up to prolong his life. Shoot him."

Smiling, the Major drew his pistol and pressed it against the German's temple.

"No!" Franz cried out in English. "Don't shoot!"

"Well, well, well," the Major observed, "the Kraut speaks our language. I wonder if he has any other talents, like the ability to stop a bullet."

"Please," Franz begged. Blood poured from his mouth and down his chin. His salted nose looked like raw hamburger covered with powdered sugar. "Don't kill me! I'll tell. I'll tell you everything. If you let me live. If …"

The Major lowered his weapon. "You better make it a damn good story."

And then Franz spilled the details through blubbering lips. His watery eyes shone like new quarters as he spoke, almost as bright at the Major's once the story was done—for Franz's little yarn was about the Big One. The Major's stomach did queasy loop de loops in his gut. Here it was at last, after all this time. It just dropped out of the sky, landed on his face and started wiggling. He willed himself to be calm.

"You'll let me go now?" Franz asked.

The Colonel considered and decided in two seconds. "Kill him."

The report of the Major's pistol was deafening in the enclosed tent. A large hole appeared in Franz's chest, just over his heart. Blood pumped from the wound in weakening spurts. He looked at them with wide, shocked eyes.

"You bastards," Franz whispered, and then he did a peculiar thing: he laughed. It came out as a series of dry huffs—cruel laughter for men to be pitied. Two more words tumbled from his bloody lips just before he expired: *"Das Wolfsrudel."*

"What did he say?" the Colonel asked.

"Hell if I know," the Major shrugged. "He probably called me an asshole. I can live with that. So how do you want to handle this?"

The Colonel leaned into a predatory position and pulled a plan out of thin air. "You leave tomorrow night. I'll arrange a flight. Take a Zombie Squad. Make sure they're expendable. We won't need them after we secure the objective. Is that clear?"

"Crystal."

The Major exited the tent. The night air did nothing to cool his fevered brow. He held a trembling hand up, made a fist, closed his eyes and took a deep breath. Two types of men existed in the world—those who could make opportunity their own and those who let it fumble through their fingers while pissing their pants.

Christ, the Big One. The Major opened his eyes and his hand; its fingers were now steady. He turned back to the Colonel's tent and got the feeling that the selected men weren't the only ones who would be expendable once the Colonel got his hands on the objective. He and the Major were business partners, but business partners were meant to be fucked.

That was fine. The Major could respect that, but he wouldn't give the Colonel a chance to doublecross him. Once he had the prize, he'd keep it for himself.

CHAPTER

PROCESSION

I AM A STRANGER in a strange land.

Kenway followed the rest of the soldiers down a narrow street, the line of them looking like a giant snake slithering into the dark hole of storm. They passed through a creaky gate and slunk between silent houses with black windows.

Kenway looked at the homes and tried to comprehend the fact that real people, not dolls, lived inside of their box shapes—people that ate, drank, laughed, loved, hated, and cried with desperation when all hope fled. In the end, the concept was mind-boggling to the extreme. The realization that the universe is bigger than the space between your skull is a frightening thing, and disconcerting when you can't find a place in all that emptiness. With nowhere to stand, the world is as large as fear and as small as you. It's claustrophobic and barren, a wasteland and a tomb, an unknown expanse without reason and populated by beasts. To consider the reality of it was to tempt madness.

How did a boy get squeezed out of his own family? How did a boy lose a girl named Jennifer? How did a boy end up screaming with a pack of other boys with rifles and bayonets? Then ending up in France? In a war? It wasn't his fight. He just happened to sign his name on a dotted line. And other boys trying to kill him, boys he'd never met? He wasn't good enough to mean anything to anyone in life, but he was good enough for strangers to kill? The Messerschmitt and the *Lazarus*, just two planes coming across each other and bullets flying in between. A snagged umbilical cord led to the boy in the Messerschmitt losing the battle. Mac in the forest. A knife to the throat. Kenway didn't even know the man. Man now? When did that happen? He didn't know any of them. Yet, the knife could cut regardless. Maybe he never left the hedgerows after all. Maybe he lived his whole life in the hedgerows. Maybe the world was nothing *but* hedgerows.

And then that night in the recreation tent at base camp. Boys playing cards and smoking cigarettes. *Boys* again? How easily people shifted from one thing to another in the course of dying. They played darts. Glen Miller jazzed it up from some unseen record player. *In The Mood. Kalamazoo. Serenade In Blue. American Patrol. Moonlight Serenade. Little Brown Jug. String of Pearls.*

Where was the common line? He drank root beer from Wisconsin while in France. He existed apart from it all. The boys gathered in groups put together by paperwork, but his original group was gone, killed in an ambush on a road to a town he never heard of that was full of box-shaped homes that held people he never met that ate, drank, laughed, loved, hated, and cried with desperation when all hope fled. People that didn't know him, didn't care about him, but would kill him. One minute they walked. The next minute they screamed and fell. Bullets filled the air—bits of lead, brass, sulfur, and potassium nitrate. Alone, none of the ingredients mattered, but in the strange combination equation of the world, they meant everything. And that was it. One second a unit, the next second a list with a sole survivor: Kenway.

Alone again, Kenway sat and drank root beer. It was good, tasty, and the fizz tickled his nose. That somehow made everything even worse.

Was that all there was to good? Sugar and water in a bottle?

It couldn't be. He remembered the wolves in the woods. How they looked. Their blue eyes filled with faith in their purpose and knowledge of the divine.

They weren't strangers. They belonged.

And then the Major appeared at Kenway's side like a conjurer's trick. He smoked a cigarette and looked clean enough to get real dirty, real fast. He spoke with a sly voice that neither offered nor asked, only demanded.

"You want a mission?"

"Is there a choice?"

"Free will's a bitch, isn't it?"

"What kind of mission?"

"The best kind ... personal."

"What do I get out of it?"

"Whatever you put in."

And away Kenway went on the *Lazarus*. And here he was: moving through the rain in Le Coeur. Kenway supposed the situation was ripe for a poem, something with weepy couplets that bemoaned the state of the world and the nature of man. Something that asked whose side are we on and why can't we all just get along?

But the hell with that.

The last good poem Kenway heard rhymed "cock" with "rock".

And the only time people got along was when they got something out of it.

Maybe it wasn't his war, but he was stuck in it—a stranger in a strange land.

CHAPTER

PRICE

THE RAIN FELL like a heavy curtain on the last act of a meaningless play. The Zombie Squad—a unit put together from the sole survivors of decimated platoons—slunk beneath it.

Each rumble of thunder brought a flash of lighting that knifed their shadows across crumbling buildings in hunchback shapes. They turned down a cave-like alley, goat-hoof boots clopping against cobblestones.

Clothes hung from twine strung between the cottages and flapped in the wind. The shirts and trousers looked ragged, like they hadn't been taken down in weeks. Their sound reminded Ritter of batwings. He put an ear between his teeth and chewed it with nervous tension.

Ritter was in his early twenties and already had streaks of gray hair. Hard lines etched his face, making him look like a weather beaten statue. He watched the shadows for

Nazi helmets or rifle barrels. If you saw them first, you had a chance. There were *supposed to be* no major German forces in Le Coeur, but reality and what was *supposed to be* rarely matched up in Ritter's experience. He learned that from his father.

✠　✠　✠

"GODDAMN 'EM ALL TO HELL!" Saul Ritter bellowed. He was a bull of a man who wore coveralls and held a bottle of whiskey. "This is not how things are *supposed to be!*" He slammed a hand down on the kitchen table for emphasis. Its centerpiece—a vase of tulips—tipped over under the impact, spilling water. "This is *supposed to be* my house, not the goddamn bank's!" He finished the whiskey and flung the bottle through the window. Glass tinkled across new linoleum and drought-stricken soil. "This is supposed to be my farm, not some bastard's who writes red numbers next to my name!" His impotent fists beat against the wall. The cupboard dishes rattled, and a picture of a sunrise slipped off its nail and landed on the floor with a broken crash.

Ritter—then only ten years old—cowered against his mother. She was a thin woman with brown locks and a pinched face. She held Ritter in tight arms. Her heart thudded against his cheek. The rabbit quality of its beats compounded Ritter's own fear. He always lived in awe of his father, regarding him the way natives regard a jungle idol who rules with the threat of wrath, but now he was terrified of the man.

"This is *supposed to be* our home!" Saul wailed to the ceiling. "How the hell is a man supposed to live if his work don't matter?" Then he collapsed to his knees and sobbed. The man's hopeless despair made the young Ritter even more uneasy. It's an ugly thing to see a grown man cry. It means the end of things.

Ritter's mother pried her boy away from her chest. Her face was an odd mixture of hard and soft—a foundation built on sand. Whatever resolve she managed to erect on its surface stood on the verge of sinking into futility. "William, go to your room."

Even at that young age, Ritter doubted the wisdom of the order. Should she allow herself to be alone with such a broken man? The landscape of a ruined man's mood is treacherous, wrought with potential hazards and pitfalls.

She gave Ritter a pained smile, trying to convince him—or maybe trying to convince herself.

"It'll be all right," she said.

Ritter wasn't fooled, but he left the naive optimism behind and went upstairs to his room. The risers still bled sap in some places. The house was only finished a month before. Then depression and dust did away with the family bank account. Calamity always waits until just the right moment to strike. It's not a matter of patience. It's a matter of cruelty.

Ritter lay on his bed. He tried to imagine the drama playing itself out in the kitchen. He supposed it was similar to when he scraped his shin on a rock and went to his mother for comfort. First she looked at the injury. Then she patted him on the head and whispered the same soothing balm words that all mothers knew:

There, there ... it's going to be just fine.

Did his mother pat his sobbing father's head right now? Did his father respond by throwing his shoulders back and facing a hopeful future he could pretend existed? That's how things were *supposed to be.*

The first shotgun blast galvanized Ritter with fear, and he jerked bolt upright. Did he really hear that? Or was he asleep and dreaming?

A second shot come moments later.

Ritter stared at the bedroom doorway. The sun went down and fiery shadows assaulted the hallway beyond. His ears rang, and his mind tried to assimilate the gunshots into nothing more than a strange occurrence. Like the time his father discharged a pistol in the house because he forgot it was loaded. Maybe he decided to clean the shotgun while he and his wife talked. Ritter's father liked to fidget, and maybe it was easier to talk about important things when you could distract part of your mind with some mundane task. Yes, he was cleaning the gun, and there was bullet in the chamber, and he mistakenly pulled the trigger … twice.

That's what happened. That's how things were *supposed to be.*

Ritter descended the stairs on numb feet. Irrational rationalization overloaded his senses and turned him into nothing more than a lump of flesh. That's why he didn't feel anything when he entered the kitchen. The sight of his mother sprawled in the corner, wearing an apron of blood awoke no emotion. It caused no sensation that her staring eyes didn't see him even though she looked right at him. What did it matter if his father laid in the middle of the floor with the smoking shotgun at his side and the top of his head blown away? Was it important that his brains dripped from the ceiling?

Of course not. Such things were not *supposed to be* …

But they were.

The episode taught Ritter that the world doesn't give a tin shit about what is or isn't *supposed to be*; it only cares about grinding people into dust and adding their remains to its mass. It's hungry and it eats … just like everything else. All you can do is bite back and hope you make it puke when all is said and done.

✠ ✠ ✠

THE LINES OF RITTER'S FACE grew deeper as he thought about such things. The set of his jaw turned adamant as he bit the world hard, refusing to be swallowed.

But that won't happen to me. The world won't make me scrap for a living like my father. It won't break my back with labor or ruin my flesh with calluses, blisters and sunburns. I won't be forced to watch everyone else gather more and more while all I gather is debt. I'll have means once this mission is over. I'll take. No more supposed *to be; rather, let there be—whatever I want.*

Ritter sniffed and smelled it on the damp air, growing closer: opportunity.

Strange that it should smell like that mingled odor of blood, brains, and buckshot that filled his nostrils on the day he discovered his dead parents.

CHAPTER

WISDOM

BERG'S ADAM'S APPLE stuck out almost as far as his nose, and his ears protruded from underneath his helmet like twin doorknobs. He had a thin chest, walked with a slight hop, and always looked on the verge of shaking to pieces whenever he moved.

His was an awkward body, and the mind that ran it was no well-oiled machine either. He came within an inch of getting 4F'ed because of low scores on his army entrance exam, and you really had to be a moron to barely make it into the army.

Nevertheless, it made him the most content man in Le Coeur. He didn't worry about the past; he couldn't remember it. He didn't worry about future; he couldn't imagine it. Finally, he didn't worry about being hurt; he trusted people. Ignorance is bliss, as they say.

A dead cat floated down the gutter in a maggoty lump. Ribs poked through the animal's torn belly, and it looked like it died screaming. The image triggered a rare memory for Berg, that of the corpses drifting in the tide during D-Day.

✠ ✠ ✠

ON JUNE 6, 1944, THE U.S. First Army and the British Second Army established beachheads in Normandy. Providence smiled upon the invasion. Not only did the weather cooperate by giving Operation Overlord a small window of opportunity, but the Nazis decided they didn't want to commit to an all-out defense.

Hitler was convinced the Normandy landings were a ruse, and the main assault would come north of the Seine River. Consequently, he refused to free up the divisions from that area to help repel the D-Day invasion force. By the end of June the Allies had eight hundred fifty thousand men and one hundred fifty thousand vehicles ashore, but it didn't come easy.

Berg was part of Doberman Company. They came into Omaha Beach split between seven box-shaped Higgins Boats. The coffin-shaped craft plowed through the water about as smoothly as a bowling ball rolls down a mountain. The motion made Berg seasick.

He vomited up the small breakfast they were fed on the transport before disembarking—toast, eggs and oatmeal. He tried to spew it over the side, but a large wave crested the steel wall and slammed into his face. The force of it knocked him to the floor of the boat where he swallowed vomit and seawater.

"Bail the bitch out!" the Lieutenant, a man who looked like he was formed from a lead mold, shouted, "or we'll never make the beach!"

The men threw the water overboard with their helmets. Part of Berg wanted them to flounder. What lay ahead caused his balls to shrivel up to the size of cashews.

A curtain of smoke covered the Normandy coast. Hundreds of corpses floated outside of the cloud. Their skulls bounced off the Higgins Boat as it passed through them. Berg was almost grateful when incoming artillery shells drowned out the funeral-bell sound.

Then the boat next to them took a shell dead center. It bucked into the air and broke apart—a ball of fire, debris and human limbs.

Berg blinked in disbelief. To go from a person to parts so quickly. Jesus. A trickle of warm piss ran down his leg.

The carnage gave the Higgins's driver doubts as well. His ashen face stared into the maelstrom from behind the controls as he quivered in his helmet and flak jacket like a wet puppy. "We can't go in there! We have to pull off!"

The Lieutenant couldn't abide such cowardice. He was the type of man who would send soldiers into a minefield until he ran out of soldiers or mines, whichever came first. Plus, he saw the very real possibility of earning himself a medal. He had visions of heroically leading his men all the way to Berlin itself and into Hitler's headquarters—all within twelve hours—sixteen at the most. He leveled a finger at the coxswain. "By Christ, you will take us in, or I'll paddle your dead ass to shore!"

The threat motivated the sailor to press on. Black smoke engulfed the Higgins Boat. The soldiers huddled on the floor of the craft, either crying or praying or both. Its ramp dropped with a high-pitched squeal of hydraulics, and machinegun fire barged in, ripping the front row of soldiers to shreds. Their blood joined the sea spray and drenched the men behind them.

Meanwhile, the mortar fire intensified. Blasts churned the water into a red foam. Shrapnel ricocheted around the interior of the Higgins and sliced flesh to ribbons. It was like being trapped inside of a meat grinder.

Berg froze amid the chaos.

What do I do now?

"Get out!" the Lieutenant shouted. "Go! Go! Go!"

Berg clambered over the side and hit the water. It made the screams, shots and explosions sound like what a child must hear in the womb—the steady beat and rush of mortality. The weight of his equipment dragged him down. Light rays shone through the murk and illuminated the bodies above. They looked like angels floating in a red sky. Bullets zipped through the surreal scene and left bubble trails. Whenever they passed through a man, they tugged out a stream of blood like a needle pulling thread.

Berg's lungs ached for air. He tried to swim for the surface and went nowhere—too heavy. He let go of his rifle, removed his helmet and maintained the presence of mind to draw his knife. He cut away his pack and two sections of a bangalore torpedo—a tube shaped explosive that troops could join end to end and shove through the sand toward German fortifications.

The discarded equipment lightened him enough to reach the surface. He erupted into the light with a great gasping breath. Soldiers floated around him like logs. Some screamed. Others had silent screams frozen on their faces.

What do I do now?

Berg looked for the Lieutenant but couldn't find him. He decided to follow the lemming-like movement of troops surging for the beach. Explosions shook the earth. Tracers whizzed by like angry bees.

The man next to Berg took a direct hit from a mortar shell. His guts streamed through the air like party favors.

Another soldier dove for the beach, and a machinegun burst blew his head into shattered-pumpkin shards. Berg reached dry ground and fell face first into the sand. One, two, three, troops trampled him.

"Don't quit on me, you yellow dog!"

The Lieutenant grabbed Berg and yanked him to his feet. A viscous snarl creased his face, like he was pissed that the Germans had the nerve to fight back and stymie his chances for glory. How dare the dirty motherfuckers! Berg almost gave the man a hug. Now someone was in charge again. All was right with the world.

"Where's your weapon?" the Lieutenant screamed.

Berg gave him an uncomprehending look. He wasn't expecting a test.

"And your helmet? Christ, man, how will you requisition a new one out here?"

A bullet took the Lieutenant in the throat. Annoyance crossed his features as he watched blood spurt down the front of his uniform. Surely getting shot was some sort of mistake that would soon be rectified. In the meantime, he still had that medal to win.

"Bangalores!" he croaked. "Hit the wire!"

But Berg ditched his bangalores.

The Lieutenant drew in a breath to rip Berg a new asshole, and then a burst of machinegun fire ripped a new asshole in the Lieutenant's stomach. The officer tumbled forward. Berg snagged the straps of the man's helmet and rifle. The rest of the Lieutenant slipped through Berg's fingers and dribbled to the ground with sickening plops.

What do I do now?

A mortar blast threw Berg into the air. He hit the sand hard. Men swarmed past him, and a machinegun scythe mowed them down. Berg crawled through the field of cut flowers—each blossom a dead face—and reached a line of soldiers strung out behind a dune. The shallow ridge of sand turned out to be anything but safe.

A German sniper was dug in on a forward cliff and had the perfect elevation to get a bead on any man on the beach. He happened to turn his attention to the line of soldiers behind the dune and began picking them off one by one, beginning with the side opposite Berg.

Blam!

Brains exploded from the back of the target's skull.

Somehow, impossibly, even over the screaming, exploding, and shooting, Berg heard each of the sniper's individual shots.

Blam!

Blood gushed from the neck of the next GI.

The soldier beside Berg prophesied doom: "Goddamn it! We're all going to die!"

Berg tried to wrap his mind around the concept of death and failed. For once that wasn't a sleight on his limited intelligence, however. Even many geniuses can't comprehend the concept of their own inevitable end.

Blam!

The third trooper shrieked for his mother. A second bullet silenced him.

The Doomsayer beside Berg tried to find cover at another location. He pushed himself to his knees to run. A buzzing line of bullets ripped his helmet off. *Chink!*

"Son of a fucking bitch!" He flopped back to a prone position.

Blam!

Another soldier rode a bullet into the afterlife.

The fifth trooper tried to burrow into the sand. His lips moved in prayer: "Forgive us our trespasses as we forgive those who trespass against us and—"

Blam!

The Doomsayer uttered a broken scream of terror as gore from the praying man dripped off his face. "Goddamn! Fuck! Ah! Ah! Ah! Ah!"

Berg tapped the man on the shoulder, clinging to the only foundational truth that he could think of amid the chaos. "You shouldn't say that, you know."

"What the fuck are you talking about?" the Doomsayer screamed, momentarily forgetting about the sniper in the moment of absurdity.

"Saying 'goddamn' is blasphemy."

"Are you fucking shitting me!?"

"Fuck's a bad word, too."

"You've got to be fucking shitting me!"

Something else occurred to Berg. "You think I should take out that sniper?"

"Fuck YES you should take out that goddamn sniper! NOW!"

Despite the harsh language, Berg gratefully accepted the order. Purpose and direction existed again. He put the Lieutenant's rifle to his shoulder. He was never confused when he looked at the world through gun sights. The view made him brilliant.

The sniper was on top of a cliff, fifty yards away, shooting through a foot-wide hole in a wall of sandbags. Berg watched him draw a bead on the Doomsayer, and—

Blam!

The Doomsayer screamed, simultaneously wetting and shitting his pants, thinking that the gun blast severed his silver cord. Then he realized that he wasn't dead.

Berg waited for the Doomsayer to open his eyes and then smiled a vacant grin.

"Got the sniper! What do I do now?"

✠ ✠ ✠

STEVE RUTHENBECK

BERG KNEW EXACTLY what to do as the Zombie Squad took up position along the outer wall of Le Coeur's courtyard. The Major's orders were clear—*do as I say and all your dreams will come true.*

The group moved toward the bank, passing the Michael and Dragon statue. Ritter, Kenway, Jacobson, and Chaplain took up position on either side of its double doors. Cain placed an explosive charge at their base and awaited the Major's signal.

CHAPTER 11

CONVERGE

THE BANK WAS DECORATED with dead plants, still photographs, and paintings of men hunting dangerous prey. Light fixtures dangled from the ceiling. A counter ran along the back wall and a marble staircase led to second-floor offices and storerooms. A small phonograph squeaked out the muffled voice of a female singer. She sounded sad.

Fireplace flames lit Stark, Gunther, Verning, and Hagen as they played a disinterested game of Hearts. None of them could concentrate on the cards they were dealt. Part of it was the threat of the impending attack. The other part was just being around *it*.

It sat on a table in the corner of the room, covered with a dun-colored tarp. Its square shape was plain and innocuous, yet it drew one's eye with the strange magnetism of somehow alien lines. The thrill of possession was gone. Now the air was heavy with nothing but its peculiar influence—*living in the past, dying for the future.*

Stark stared into the fire and thought about Elsa.

Gunther ran a shaky hand through his gray hair and re-lived the day his brother fell off a horse and fractured his skull. His older sibling lingered for three days, shouting at unseen people and cursing family members in a demonic voice. Gunther whistled a tuneless song to drown out the phantom screams ringing through his head.

Hagen remembered the day he fell down a well. The bottom of the shaft was dank, pitch black and littered with the corpses of small animals. Their rotten smell saturated his clothes, and their bones poked him whenever he moved. Since he couldn't call for help, it was two days before he was rescued.

Verning drifted back to when he was forced to stand barefoot in the snow for stealing bread from the orphanage kitchen. He lost two toes to frostbite. His right cheek ticked. The effect was disturbing in the shadowy light. Half of his face was that of a handsome man. The other half looked insane. He licked his lips and touched the tip of his nose with his tongue. His nostrils flared. "I smell something."

Stark nodded. "They're here."

Their eyes swiveled to the covered object. The bad memories stopped—for the time being—and were replaced with the desire to kill.

Then the bank doors exploded in a cloud of fire, smoke, and shattered brick. The shock wave knocked Stark and his comrades to the floor. Playing cards fluttered around them; the ace of spades landed in front of Stark's nose as soldiers poured through the smoking hole. Stark tried to get to his feet. Staccato machinegun bursts rang out. He twitched under the bullet impacts like a marionette being jerked by its strings. Blood spouted from many wounds.

Then he slumped back to the floor, joining the prone and tattered bodies of Gunther, Verning and Hagen.

The singer on the phonograph wavered and then clicked off.

"Clear!" Ritter shouted.

Kenway, Jacobson and Chaplain echoed the cry.

The Major and the remaining troops entered the bank. They looked from one to another, wordless, faces flush with success and the realization they were about to discover if it was all really worth it. They gathered around the tarp-covered table in a half circle, like Druids gathering around a sacrifice. Sweat glistened on brows. Teeth gnawed lips. Hands twitched. Eyes looked feverish.

The Major pulled the tarp away.

CHAPTER

DESIRE

THE ACACIA-WOOD BOX was polished to a mirror sheen. Its rich laminations distorted the Zombie Squad's reflection into screaming ghosts.

The box was two cubits long, one cubit wide, and half a cubit deep. It had gold-plated corners and an odd design carved into its cover. To some of the men it looked like a serpent, to others a goat; some even saw a lion, a sword, a rose, a heart, or a gaping slit.

Awe and disbelief mixed into an oppressive silence. Even the storm seemed to pause in the moment. Then ringing filled their ears, like the song of a distant celestial choir harping evil incantations.

The soldiers' stark faces grew drawn and haggard in the flickering firelight. Until that moment, none of them really believed they were going to find it. When the Major came to them and told them the object of the mission, they could not resist participation—the temptation was far to great—but deep inside, they scoffed at the notion of its existence and acquisition. Yet, there it was, right in front of them.

"The Big One," the Major whispered.

Berg's face turned hard. His soft look of idiocy disappeared. For the first time in his life he knew exactly what to do: *possess.*

"Beautiful." Mac grinned like a man offering candy to a little boy. He wanted to reach out and caress the box, to hold it close and cover it with soft kisses.

A high-pitched giggle escaped Ritter's lips. It grew into a genuine laugh and then degenerated into a hoarse cackle. Nobody would ever own him again.

Cain couldn't stop licking his lips. The sight made him hungry.

Pain grew in Jacobson's chest. It constricted his organs, like he was caught in a vise. His head went light. *Is this a heart attack?* Then he realized the problem: he stopped breathing. He sucked air into his lungs and promptly forgot all about living once more.

Kenway's eyes grew wet and shiny. Tears spilled over his lower eyelids and ran down his cheeks, leaving gleaming trails. He would never be alone again.

Only Chaplain seemed unaffected by the sight. He examined the box with cold appraisal, assessing whether or not it contained enough to make up for all he lost. His teeth ground against each other, and his hands clenched into fists.

"Open it," someone—*everyone*—said.

The Major drew his knife. The sound of leather on steel was very loud in the stillness. His hand trembled as he lowered the blade toward the box, like he expected an electric shock. Tentatively, he levered the tip under the box's cover.

The men flinched unconsciously, like their own flesh was penetrated. The cover rose a fraction of an inch. Its creak sounded like a groan of pain. A cold glow spilled out of the crack.

The Major returned the knife to its sheath and placed his hands on the box. It was warm and seemed to throb under his touch. He tensed his muscles to lift the cover away.

Chaplain noticed an odd shuffling sound. He tore his eyes away from the box and its contents with a grim effort of will that caused him pain. What he saw should have sent his brain reeling, but seeing the box had already altered his perceptions.

The blasted Germans rose to their feet like old men rising from chairs. Their bloodstained clothes glistened. Sly smiles creased their lips.

The hairs on the back of Chaplain's neck rose. He cocked the bolt of his Thompson by reflex. The metal snap startled the other GIs out of their box-induced fugue. They turned and saw what Chaplain saw.

"What the hell?" Mac gasped in disbelief.

The Germans swelled inside their clothes, like someone hooked them up to air compressors. Clear complexions turned mottled. Blond hair darkened and grew shaggy. The sound of tearing cloth filled the air. Black fur sprouted through burst seams. Muscles ballooned. Fingernails grew into claws. Bones cracked and tendons snapped. Mouths and noses elongated into canine snouts. Fangs distended from jaws and ears tapered into sharp points. Blue eyes turned bloodlust yellow. Lips curled back into lupine snarls.

"What the hell?" Mac repeated. "*They're dogs!*"

The beasts howled in rage and loped across the room on all fours.

CHAPTER

13

CONFLICT

THE SOLDIERS OPENED FIRE. A wall of .45-caliber slugs filled the air. Muzzle blasts illuminated roaring faces with flashbulb bursts.

Some bullets struck the floor, chewing up slivers of wood. Others peppered the wall, puffing out clouds of plaster. Many struck the charging monsters and tore out tufts of bloody fur.

The dogmen yelped in pain, the momentum of their charge broken. Then bolts clicked on empty chambers. The beasts shook themselves of their wounds the way wet dogs shake themselves of water. Deep growls emanated from their chests as they gathered themselves for another attack.

"Oh, shit!" Jacobson cursed. He fumbled with the Thompson's magazine release button and tried to extract another clip from his belt. The rest of the Zombie Squad went through similar frantic movements. None of them took time to disbelieve the situation; survival dominated all thought as the monsters leapt into their midst.

Three-inch claws swiped at Jacobson's face. He ducked. The furry hand whisked over his head. He straightened up and slammed the butt of his Thompson across slavering jaws. The empty clip dropped from his weapon. He slapped a fresh one into place. The dog-man darted in to rip out his throat. Jacobson shoved the Thompson into its chest and pulled the trigger. The heavy slugs blew it backwards with sledgehammer force.

Screams, gunshots, growls, flashing teeth, and claws—Berg was frozen by it all, his limited brain capacity jammed up by the excess input. Then the situation simplified itself down to something that he could deal with—one on one.

A burst of lead slammed one of the beasts into a nearby wall. Berg took in its details with stupid awe—seven-feet-tall, slender but very muscular, covered with coarse black hair, long claws on the hands and the feet, backward-bending knees, a snout full of razor teeth, and burning yellow eyes—burning yellow eyes that now focused on him. He deemed that as a bad sign.

The monster snarled and launched itself through the air with outstretched talons. Berg turned to run, and a table took out his legs. He sprawled across its top. The dogman sailed over him and crashed into the counter. It regained its feet with savage quickness. Berg rolled off the table. A furry fist smashed it in two. Berg tried to raise his weapon. A steel-strong paw grabbed him by the neck and threw him across the room.

Ritter had his back against the wall and his gun against his shoulder while he tried not to die. He watched the nightmarish chaos through gun sights, picking out targets and firing short bursts.

The monsters moved with lightning speed. It was hard for him to draw a bead on them and avoid shooting his comrades.

One of the beasts closed on Kenway, who had his back to the monster while trying to blast a different creature. Ritter tagged it with several rounds from his Thompson. The force of the bullets barely slowed it down.

Another black blur reared up in Ritter's peripheral vision. He whipped his head around and saw furry lips pull back over glittering fangs; a pink tongue lolled over the bottom row of teeth.

Ritter twisted away from a swiping paw that punched a hole in the wall. He cursed and backpedaled toward the center of the room. The monster lunged again. Its claws raked across his chest, shredding his jacket and drawing blood.

Ritter shrieked as the furry buzz saw closed in for the killing blow. Then a great weight slammed into him. He got knocked to the floor and opened his eyes to discover Berg sprawled on top of him.

"Get the fuck off me!"

Berg groaned, dazed.

The beast loomed.

Ritter struggled to free his weapon.

"Got you, bastard!" Jacobson screamed as he strafed the monster threatening Berg and Ritter. It bounded away with a howl of pain. Then a wet growl rumbled behind him; hot breath steamed his neck.

Oh, God.

Jacobson turned around just in time to take a powerful forearm across the chest. He flew through the air and slammed into the wall, smashing his head against the plaster. He slumped to the floor in a boneless heap.

Mac shot a beast in mid-leap. The barrage of lead knocked it out of the air. The creature tumbled onto a table and smashed it to pieces.

Mac's gun clicked empty. He grabbed its barrel in tight fists and charged, catching the dogman upside the skull with a baseball-bat swing. The force of the blow spun the monster around.

Mac bellowed and brought the Thompson's down on top of its head. Something snapped. Violent glee lit up Mac's features. Then he realized the sound wasn't broken bone. The stock of his rifle had cracked.

The beast improvised a club of its own. It swung a chair with savage strength. The piece of furniture caught Mac across his right side and shattered into fragments. He stumbled backwards and tripped over Ritter and Berg.

The dogman closed on the three prone men.

Mac and Ritter drew their pistols. Berg took an extra second to think of the same thing. The three of them opened fire, popping off twenty-four slugs at the beast.

Kenway ran across the room with a dogman at his heels. His gun was empty. No time to reload. He found himself heading for a wall—the end of the line. The pursuing thing would catch him and shred him.

Kenway leapt on top of a table for lack of any other remaining course. The monster swiped at his legs. He jumped. The claws passed beneath his feet. He wasn't so lucky the second time. The talons raked across his shins. Molten pain shot up his legs. He screamed and kicked out with a size-twelve combat boot. The steel-toed clodhopper caught the beast square in the chops. It howled in rage.

Desperate, Kenway noticed the light fixture dangling from the ceiling. He leapt, snatching its chain in midair. Momentum swung him across the room like Errol Flynn. Ominous cracks sounded. The beam holding the fixture snapped.

Kenway hung in the air for a split second, weightless, then gravity ripped him to the floor. He landed with painful force but maintained the presence of mind to roll into a ball before the fixture, beam and a shitload of plaster crashed down in a billowing cloud of debris.

A chunk of ceiling hit Cain on the head. Stars danced before his vision. He coughed and gasped in the thick cloud of dust. The firelight and lightning did nothing to penetrate the pall. He heard the sound of others moving and coughing within its depths, along with the sound of furious snarling. A vague shape appeared to his left. He figured that it was Chaplain. They had been back-to-back and shooting the hell out of the place when the sky fell. He reaching out and grabbed the soldier's arm.

"Chaplain! Let's get the hell out of here!"

Cain's hand closed on coarse fur. A fang-filled face broke through the cloud of dust and growled at him eye-to-eye.

"Jesus!"

A heavy body the consistency of concrete covered with carpet took Cain to the floor. Cain screamed like a woman. Claws ripped his clothing. Teeth snapped at his face. He pushed and beat and pounded at his assailant with panicked fists. Sharp pain sank into his forearm. He screamed even louder. The beast shook its head from side to side, mangling Cain's arm in its powerful jaws.

"Help! Jesus! God! It's eating me!"

Chaplain wiggled out from underneath a pile of lumber. A six-inch sliver of wood stuck out of his shoulder. He reached up and tore it out. Blood coursed down his arm. The wound would have to wait. He had things to kill. Cain's scream pierced his ears. Through a break in the wispy dust, he spotted a dark bulk perched on top of the struggling soldier, savaging him.

Chaplain hit the beast like a linebacker plowing into a quarterback and stabbed the wood spike into its face. The dogman screeched a yelp that damn near burst his eardrums and threw him off its back. He landed beside Cain.

Cain held his shredded wrist to his chest. "My arm!"

Chaplain grabbed the neck of Cain's jacket and yanked. "Get up!"

"It ate my arm!"

"Get the fuck up!"

"My arm! It huurrrrrrrrrrrts!"

The Major ended up sprawled out at the base of the stairs. The barrel of his Thompson was hot to the touch. His uniform was torn and claw marks striped his face. He looked out on the cloudy melee and cursed. Of all the godforsaken shit that could happen.

He suddenly realized what Franz said with his last words: *Das Wolfsrudel*—the wolf pack. Well, whatever the hell they were, he'd have their heads on his wall before he was through, and you could take that to the fucking bank—even though they were already in one; that was the problem. They didn't stand a chance in the enclosed space.

The Major cast one last glance at the box—the lone spectator. *I'll come back for you.* Then he jerked a grenade off his vest and shouted.

"Withdraw! Regroup at base camp! Now!"

The Major tossed the grenade in between the two closest beasts. It blew with a flash of smoke and flame, raising a second cloud of dust. A dogman sprang out of the veiled destruction. Bloody wounds smeared its pelt. Smoke rose from its flanks. It stood up on two feet and marked the Major with bloodshot yellow eyes.

"What the hell are you looking at?" The Major lobed a second grenade at the monster and ran up the stairs. The detonation shook the steps. The dogman bounded after him. He reached the stairway landing, turned and fired.

Bullets stitched their way across the beast's chest. It tumbled down the stairs with sickening crunches of organic impact, hitting the floor on its back. The Major watched its eyes narrow into slits and its jaw clench in concentration. Three of the four wounds in its chest closed. The fourth shrank down to a mere buttonhole. The monster rolled back to its feet, panting with fury.

"Interesting," the Major commented.

The beast snarled—the sound of it almost like an expletive—as the hair on its back bristled. It leapt halfway up the stairs. The Major shot off the rest of his clip, turned and ran. A hallway stretched before him. There were three doors, one on each side and one at the end. The Major tried the first. The knob went nowhere in his hand—locked.

"Shit!"

The sound of claws scrabbling up steps reached the Major's ringing ears. The beast appeared over the stairway's edge like it rose from a grave—pointy ears, yellow eyes, snarling snout, powerful arms and chest, clawed hands —

The Major tried the next door. Same result.

"Fuck all!"

A *thump* sounded as the dogman leapt to the landing and stood on its hind feet. It raised a paw. The clawed fingers wiggled at the Major. It seemed to grin. *I see you.* Then, it launched forward. Its hind feet tore up the carpet like a car peeling out on gravel.

The Major sprinted down the hall. The closed door loomed ahead. In his mind's eye he saw the monster chew up the distance between them. He saw its lips pull back over fangs as it tensed its haunch muscles to spring. Then, it would land on his back and tear out his spine.

The Major hit the door, grabbed the knob and turned. The door fell open. He tumbled inside, slammed it shut and threw his weight against it.

Wham!

The door rattled in its frame. A growl of rage rose behind it. The Major turned and felt for a bolt. His hand found it and shot it home just as the beast tried the knob. Finding it locked, it resorted to strength. It hit the door again, with greater force than before. A sliver of wood popped out and into the Major's face.

He guessed he had a minute—maybe. He spun around and searched for an escape. He was in a storage room. Stacks of boxes went from the floor to the ceiling. The place smelled like moldy paper. A window was set into the back wall.

"Move, goddamn you!" Chaplain shouted as he half-carried, half-dragged Cain out of the smoke-filled bank. They stumbled left, more by the physics of objects in motion than design—Cain's dead weight pulled them in that direction.

"My arm!" Cain screamed like a broken record. Blood soaked the shredded sleeve of his jacket. His face was a tragedy mask of pain, and tears washed clean streaks in his black greasepaint. "It ate my arm!"

"And it's going to eat your ass, too, if you don't move!"

Howling wavered in the night air behind them. Chaplain spun the two of them around, bringing his gun up at the end of a shaking arm. Nothing was there. Biting rain dimpled the water in the street and sent out an infinity of ripples. Another howl sounded, closer this time. A ghastly smile split Chaplain's lips—the look of a man who finally found something other than the abyss to stare into.

Two eyes staring out of a dollhouse.

"My arm ..."

Cain's weak cry snapped Chaplain out of his revelry. He guided the wounded man around the back of the bank. Lightning revealed a small Nazi motor pool that consisted of a Krupp Truck, a Kubelwagen, and a Panzer Wolf. The tank looked like a giant bullfrog sitting on a lily pad. Chaplain headed for the Kubelwagen. The jeep-like vehicle was built by Volkswagen and was a sturdy construction of straight lines, rivets, and cookie-cutter steel. It was anything but pleasing to the eye, but it was still better than trying to carry an injured man. Chaplain jerked its door open and threw Cain inside.

"My arm!"

"Shut up!"

Chaplain stomped in the clutch and pressed the starter button. The engine rolled over with a cough-chug. Chaplain gave it some gas and tried again. The engine fired into life. The Kubelwagen's headlights speared the darkness. A dog-man stood in the middle of the street. Raindrops cascaded around it like a curtain of jewels.

"Go!" Cain screamed. "For the love of Christ, go!"

Chaplain wrestled with the stick shift. Gears groaned and clashed. The dogman advanced on all fours. Its teeth gleamed white and sharp as it snarled, and its yellow eyes reflected the Kubelwagen's headlights. The Volkswagen finally slipped into drive. Chaplain stomped the gas pedal down and popped the clutch.

The vehicle shuddered and died.

Mac tailed Ritter and Berg through the twisting streets. The three of them ran all out, arms pumping and legs scissoring. Heavy rain obscured the surrounding buildings.

All of the structures looked the same—rundown and crumbling, like forgotten gravestones in an overgrown field. Trees sprouted between them like giant weeds.

None of the streets appeared familiar. Were they going the right way? What if they got cut off—stragglers separated from the herd? Distant howling echoed through the night.

Stragglers got eaten.

"Hold up!" Mac shouted. "You sure this is the way to the church?"

Ritter came to a stop. "Why you asking me? I'm following Berg."

Berg blinked with bewilderment. "We're supposed to go to the church?"

"Yes, we're supposed to go to the church, you stupid shit! Didn't you hear the Major?" Mac turned in a frustrated circle. A gathering fog made it even harder to establish direction. "So which way do we go, assholes?"

Ritter pointed out at an alley. "That way."

"You sure?"

More howling, only a block away this time.

"You got a better idea?"

Mac ground his teeth and said nothing.

"That's what I thought." Ritter headed for the alley.

Berg turned to Mac, back to Ritter, indecisive on whom to follow. The howling drew closer and helped him make up his mind. He bolted after Ritter.

Mac swore and followed Berg into the alley. It was narrow and smelled like rotten vegetables. Broken flowerpots littered the cobblestones. Vines covered the walls like strange parasites. The alley took a left turn … straight into a dead end.

"What the fuck?" Mac cursed. "I thought you knew where you were going!"

"I do know where I'm going!" Ritter pointed at the blockage. "I'm going that way! How was I supposed to know there'd be a fucking wall in the way!"

Mac turned to retrace their steps. "From now on I lead, you shit sticks follow."

A dogman prowled around the blind corner. Its eyes glowed in the dim light, and a low growl bubbled up from its chest. The wind carried its wild odor to the three soldiers. That more than anything clarified its reality.

"What do we do?" Ritter whimpered.

Mac eyes slid to a door in the alley wall. "Like I said, I lead, you follow." He slammed a shoulder through the wooden portal and burst into a living room. Ritter and Berg trailed close behind.

The beast barreled through the door after them. Mac fired from his hip. The monster backpedaled. A dark blot of its blood splattered the wall. Mac turned to run. Ritter and Berg were already through the living room and into the kitchen.

Berg arrowed for the front door and aimed to put his shoulder through it in imitation of Mac. He hit the entrance and bounced off it, careening into Ritter.

"Get the hell out of my way!" Ritter shouted.

"Fucking idiots!" Mac squeezed past them and shot off the door's deadbolt. Empty shell casings tinkled off the wall. Before they hit the floor, Mac spun around and emptied his clip at the dogman as it charged through the living room.

The beast darted out of Mac's line of fire. Mac turned and smashed through the door. He skidded down rain-slick steps and somehow kept from falling. Ritter and Berg untangled themselves and followed. The dogman crashed through the house in pursuit.

Mac slapped a fresh clip in and sprinted for the cottage across the street. He dove through the window, landed in a bedroom, rolled to his feet, and lunged back to the casement. Ritter jumped through. Berg brought up the rear. The dogman loped at his heels.

Mac raised his Thompson. It was a tricky shot with Berg right in front of the target like that. Mac figured there was a very real possibility he'd blow the man's brains out. Fuck it. Like there were any to blow out anyway. He pulled the trigger and winged the dogman's shoulder. Berg jumped for the window and got hung up on the frame.

"Help me!"

The beast dove for Berg's struggling feet. Mac grabbed the back of his pants and yanked. Berg tumbled inside. The monster slammed its head into the wall below the window. Mac leaned out and hosed it with his Thompson. He didn't wait around to see if it did any good.

"Move it!" Mac shouted and shoved Ritter and Berg through the bedroom doorway. They hustled down a short hall. Mac booted the front door open. They beat their way across the street. Mac looked over his shoulder for their pursuer.

The beast scrabbled along the cottage roof. It crouched beside the chimney and met Mac's gaze. Its eyes contained brutal intelligence and cunning.

"There!" Mac raised his rifle. "Shoot the son of a bitch!"

Bullets turned the tile roof into a maelstrom of ceramic chips. The dogman bolted under the hail of lead and dashed across the roof on all fours, leaping for the next cottage. It easily cleared the twenty feet of open space and landed on the peak of the abutting roof with uncanny balance. Flames jetted from the muzzles of Thompsons as they tracked its progress. Then their clips ran dry.

The dogman stopped running and turned back to mark them with baleful eyes. It knew they were empty. Growling in hate and rage, it jumped down into the street and charged with liquid speed.

"Go!" Mac bellowed. The three of them sprinted for another cottage. The thing would run them down in the open. This time Berg had better luck with the door. It was unlocked.

The three of them pushed inside with the monster hot on their heels. They slammed their backs against the wall and prepared to fire at—nothing. No dogman burst through the door. Rain whispered across the roof like God telling secrets. Thunder rumbled. Lightning illuminated their frightened faces. The seconds ticked by.

The wait reminded Mac of when he was ten years old and sitting in his room on rent day. The moments before his mother returned home with the verdict—how he went to the bathroom, brushed his teeth, combed his hair and put on a dash of the perfume that Mr. Webster liked. Then he would hear the door open and meet his mother in the living room. She was a tall, large-boned woman who wore too much lipstick, which was usually smudged so badly she looked like a clown.

"Not enough," she said every time. "I didn't make enough. You'll have to work off the rent with Mr. Webster again."

And then Mac went out the door and up the stairs. It got easier each time. It wasn't so bad if you made the best it. He knocked on Mr. Webster's door and Mr. Webs swered. He wore a bra and panties and ushered Mac inside, the wait over for another week.

"Where did it go?" Ritter whispered.

A hairy arm punched through the wall and grabbed his shoulder.

Eyes probed the Thompson's field of fire. A nose sniffed the air for the tang of animal musk. Ears strained to hear the sound of stealthy pursuit. Skin tingled, sensitive to the currents of approaching danger. A tongue tasted the wind. Its flavor was blood.

Kenway stood next to a graveyard. The soil rose in humped mounds. Crosses and tombstones tilted this way and that. A fog wormed out from among them. Lighting painted their shadows through it in inverse rays.

The mist looked like someone ripped a gash in the earth and stuffing bulged out. It crept forward like the searching tentacles of a Lovecraftian monster's ghost as it pooled around Kenway, rising to his chest—an ocean of obscurity and veiled threat.

Sweat dotted his brow. His gun swiveled between every hint of potential danger—the tapping that turned out to be a branch blowing against a house, the hiss of rain drumming against a barrel and the twisted shadow that was nothing more than a fissure in a rock wall. The hairs on the back of his neck stood at stiff attention. It was exactly how he felt in the grove after the jump—hunted. Something was out there then. Now he knew what it was—one of them.

And he was on his own. He was always on his own.

The mist surged in like the tide. It made the buildings across the street look like they floated in a cloud. Kenway bent at the knees, sinking into the fog until it swallowed him whole. He huddled in the dark white, ears attuned to the inevitable sound.

"Come on in," he whispered. "Come on in."

It came fast: claws on the cobblestones. They ticked past Kenway in the fog off to his left. He crept into the path the creature took. His boot scuffed the ground with a raspy noise as he fell in behind the beast. He froze, holding his breath. The dogman stopped, too.

Kenway knew what it was doing: listening. He stayed silent, eyes trying to pierce the shifting mist. At last the claws moved again, further away, turning, doubling back along a different tangent, running a search pattern through the fog. Kenway pondered his next move in the game of cat and mouse. Then, the rules changed. The clicking claws stopped once more, and Kenway heard another sound: sniffing.

The Major dangled from the bank roof. Cold stone numbed his fingers. They started to slip. He watched raindrops sail toward the street and splatter their guts on the sidewalk. Vertigo churned his stomach and spun his brain. He closed his eyes, willed the sensation away and braced his legs against the bricks.

A door shattered on the other side of the wall. The beast was in the storeroom. The Major executed a frantic chin up and tried to swing a leg over the roof edge. Something grabbed his ankle. He looked down. A snarling canine face leaned out of the window. Irresistible strength yanked the Major back into a straight-arm hang, putting his groin even with the dogman's teeth.

"Son of a bitch!"

The Major caught the beast under the jaw with his knee. A broken fang tumbled through the air. The grip on the Major's ankle loosened. He wrestled free and jackknifed both legs into the dogman's chest. It stumbled backwards. Before it could recover, the Major dragged himself onto the bank's flat roof. He rolled to his feet and saw the beast's hand grip the roof edge; its talons scratched the stone.

The Major slammed the stock of his Thompson into the monster's fingers. "Fuck off!"

The dogman retracted its hand with a sharp yip of pain.

The Major searched for an avenue of escape. His brain assessed the options and gave him the recommended course of action. Unattractive as it was, he had no choice. He ran.

The beast exploded over the roof edge and landed behind him. The Major put on a burst of speed. The other side of the roof drew nearer. He jumped onto its lip like a steeplechase hurdler and threw himself into the void with a shout of effort. He sailed through the air and slammed into an inclined cottage roof. The impact knocked his wind out. His face smashed into the tiles. Pain burst in his nose, and tears filled his eyes.

The dogman followed, loping across the bank with lithe grace.

The Major rolled onto his back. The beast leapt. The Major aimed his Thompson. The monster flew through the space between buildings. The Major pulled the gun's trigger.

Six rounds caught the dogman in midair. It crashed into the roof at the Major's feet. Its claws skittered for purchase on the tile slope. The Major booted it in the face. It seemed to hang in space for a moment; then it disappeared.

A distant crunch and an agonized screech brought a smile to the Major's face. He crawled to the roof's skylight and smashed it open with his gun butt. He dropped into an attic stuffed with boxes and racks of old clothes. He reloaded as he went to the window.

"Time for another dose, asshole."

The Major shoved the gun through the glass and pointed it down into the street. No dogman lay in a broken heap. The

Major was disappointed but not surprised. He burst through the attic door and into a short hall. He reached a set of stairs and descended, gun sweeping back and forth, searching for targets. None showed themselves.

The Major spotted a backdoor, hit it in full sprint, and blasted into an alley. He raced down it and came out on a dark street. The Major hated running, but he'd be back. No way in hell he'd leave town without that box. The street led him to the river. He dove in and swam for the church.

The dogman approached through the cone of the Kubel-wagen's headlights. Its fur was so black it absorbed the glare, making it look like a hole cut into reality.

"Go!" Cain screamed. "We've got to go! Now!"

"No shit!" Chaplain hunched over the steering wheel. He pressed the starter button, pumped the gas and worked the choke. The vehicle's headlights waxed and waned with each cycle.

"Come on, bastard!"

The engine roared into sudden life. The Kubel's tires squealed as Chaplain headed straight for the dogman. The beast leapt out of the way at the last moment. Chaplain slammed the vehicle into second and wrestled it around a corner so sharply its inside wheels came off the ground.

Cain cried out as they bounced over a curb, cradling his wounded arm. Chaplain whipped the Kubel around another corner. Centrifugal force threw Cain against the side window. A furry face looked in; its breath fogged the glass.

"Faster! It's right here!"

Chaplain found third gear. The Kubel neared thirty miles per hour. The beast swung a huge fist through the window. Cain screamed. Swiping claws missed his face and latched onto the door's lip. The monster tried to pull itself inside.

"God! Jesus H. Christ!" Cain climbed into Chaplain's lap to escape.

"Get the hell off me!" Chaplain shoved Cain halfway into the backseat. The dogman strained to reach him. Chaplain leaned over and yanked on the passenger door latch. The weight of the beast pulled the door open. The monster held on, feet dragging in the street. Chaplain took another corner. The door swung shut. The dogman's teeth snapped inches from Cain's quivering form.

"He's going to get me!"

Chaplain took his foot of the gas and booted the door back open. The beast refused to fall.

All right you son of a bitch, you asked for it! Chaplain drew his pistol and pulled the trigger until it was empty. The dogman howled in pain and tumbled into the street.

Chaplain reholstered his gun and whipped the Kubel around a corner before it plowed straight through the front door of a flower shop.

"He's still coming!" Cain screamed. "He's still coming!"

Chaplain looked back. The beast charged down the street, veered to the side and leapt onto the roof of a cottage. It loped along the peaked gables like a deer running across a field. While they were confined to the twisting streets, the dogman cut across the roofs and gained on them by taking straight angles of pursuit.

"He's going to get us! He's going to get us, and he's going to eat us!"

"Shut up!"

"He's going to eat us!"

"I said shut the fuck up!" Chaplain grabbed a handful of Cain's hair and slammed his head into the dash. Cain flopped back into his seat, dazed.

A great weight landed on the Kubelwagen's roof. A hand punched through the canvass. Razor claws waved in Chaplain's face. He grabbed the monster's wrist and tried to keep the claws from cutting his throat.

The Kubel weaved drunkenly down the street. The VW chassis bounced up and over a curb, ran down the sidewalk and scraped the sides of buildings. Sparks flew. The sound of tortured steel filled the air. The dogman's claws ripped away the front of Chaplain's shirt. He screamed in pain as the talons dug bloody furrows across his sternum.

The Kubel careened from one side of the street to the other, bouncing off the buildings like a ball in a pinball machine. Flash cut glimpses—claws, street, buildings, crashes, pain, snarling face, vibrating wheel, sparks, rushing wind, Cain whimpering in the passenger seat.

"Shoot the son of a bitch!" Chaplain shouted.

"Don't let him get us!" Cain screamed.

"You goddamn worthless fuck!" Chaplain replied.

The Kubel bounced off a cottage wall with a vicious crunch. Bricks flew. The wheel lurched in Chaplain's hand. The impact threw the monster across the hood. It sank its claws into the spare tire, deflating it.

Yellow eyes found Chaplain through the windshield. It snarled. Chaplain snarled back. He hit the gas. The beast's snout slammed into the windshield. Chaplain stomped on the brakes. The monster rolled toward the end of the hood. Chaplain hit the gas again.

Fall off, bastard! No such luck. The dogman's claws punched through the thin metal of the Kubel's hood, anchoring it in place.

"Motherfucker!" Chaplain screamed in fright and frustration. One of his hands went to the floor of the Kubel, searching for his rifle. His fingers brushed against its stock. The dogman scrabbled over the hood like a giant spider and punched a clawed hand through the windshield. Chunks of glass sprayed Chaplain's face.

"He'll eat us! He's going to eat us!" Cain yelled.

A hairy fist slammed into Chaplain's temple. The wheel shimmied in his hand. The Kubel slewed into a three hundred sixty degree turn. Its tires squealed and screamed against the surface of the street. One of them exploded.

Chaplain fought the spin, pulling the Kubelwagen back on course with gritted teeth. The beast was no longer on the hood.

"Where did it go?" Chaplain wheezed. "Did we lose it?"

A tearing sound filled the air. Chaplain looked up and saw half the roof get ripped away. The beast raged and gibbered through the slit.

"Christ!" Chaplain tried for his Thompson again. It was caught between the seat and the gearshift. He yanked it free. The barrel knocked the shift stick into neutral. Chaplain's foot remained on the gas. The engine torqued up to an eye-watering scream. Chaplain stomped in the clutch and jammed the stick back into second. It went with a tremendous clash of gears. The engine clunked into motion with a steel spasm that rattled Chaplain's teeth and the Kubel's frame.

The dogman was thrown about so that its lower body hung over the windshield. Its head and shoulders squeezed through the hole in the roof, teeth and claws straining to reach its prey. Chaplain wrestled his rifle above the seat, shoved the barrel into the beast's face and pulled the trigger.

Chaplain guided the wheezing Kubel to the church. The blown tire made the vehicle limp as it *whumped whumped whumped* along the cobblestones. Chaplain ran it onto the building's steps where the engine died with a final rattle of pistons.

Chaplain opened his door. It fell off its hinges. His shirt hung in rags, revealing old scars and fresh wounds inflicted by the beast. He left Cain crying in the passenger seat and entered the church.

Christ watched from His crucifix, weary and in great pain. Chaplain ignored him. He went behind the altar and opened its storage doors one by one. There were vases, rectory cloths and hymnals. He finally found what he wanted—a bottle of communion wine. He took it to the pews, sat down and drank.

"Get it off me!" Ritter screamed. A clawed hand protruded through the wall and gripped his shoulder, drawing blood. He squirmed and kicked but couldn't get free. His face was a twisted visage of fear and pain.

Berg stepped forward and beat on the hairy arm with an ineffectual fist. It was like trying to chop a tree down with the edge of his hand.

"Out of the way!" Mac shouldered past Berg and stabbed the arm with his bayonet. The dogman howled on the other side of the wall and retracted the injured limb. The blade ripped free, splattering dark blood across the wainscoting.

"Fucking bastard!" Ritter twisted around and sprayed the wall with .45-caliber slugs.

Once the smoke cleared, the silence hung heavy, like a muddy sheet.

"I think we got him," Berg whispered.

The dogman exploded through the perforated wall in a storm of plaster and wooden slats. It plowed through Mac, Ritter, and Berg like they were tenpins.

Mac found himself thrown on a couch. The dogman swiped a handful of claws at his guts.

"Jesus!" Mac dodged the attack and rolled head over heels off the sofa.

The sound of ripped upholstery filled the air. Stuffing billowed around the beast like snow. A burst of bullets caught the monster in its side and knocked it over the back of the couch. Mac got to his feet and joined Berg and Ritter while they reloaded.

Springs creaked. Wood groaned. Furry muscles bulged. The three men watched as the dogman lifted the sofa over its head. Its snarling face glowered in rage.

"Christ," Mac said in disbelief.

The monster hurled the couch across the room. The three soldiers dodged. The piece of furniture slammed into the wall, denting the plaster and cracking studs.

Ritter and Mac pushed themselves off the floor. Their blood was up to the point where brains stop weighing odds and instinct takes over. Their faces looked as ferocious as the beast's. Primal yells roared from their throats. Their chests heaved. Lungs fueled muscles with bloodlust and hot oxygen. A single thought pulsed through their heads: kill the bastard!

The dogman mirrored their state. It stood on two legs, lips curling over fangs and yellow eyes burning with violence. Its hair bristled, and its entire form seemed to vibrate with volcanic fury on the verge of being unleashed. Long tendrils of drool distended from its jaws while its claws clicked in anticipation of shredding.

Something clunked on the floor between men and monster. The three of them looked down. A grenade rested on the carpet. Ritter and Mac's incredulous eyes fell on Berg simultaneously. He stood against the far wall, white-faced and unsure of himself.

"What the fuck are you doing?" Ritter shouted.

"I … I'm helping you!"

Mac dove for the floor. "Get down!"

The grenade exploded with a terrific boom, blowing up chunks of carpet, knocking over chairs and charring the ceiling. Mac coughed and gagged on the acrid fog that filled the room. A hand pulled him through a doorway. He found himself in a kitchen with Berg and an equally dazed Ritter.

"I'm sorry," Berg babbled. "I just … it seemed like a good idea. I—"

The dogman burst through the door in a tornado of claws and teeth.

Berg got knocked to the floor hard enough to black out. Mac and Ritter lost their rifles in the grenade blast. They grabbed whatever they could find and pelted the beast with pots, pans, plates and dishes.

The monster whirled and slavered as ceramic missiles bounced off its chest and shattered against the walls. It caught Mac with a glancing blow. He slammed into a cupboard and knocked it off its mounts. It crashed to the floor and spilled utensils across the tiles. Mac ripped off one of the cupboard doors and broke it over the beast's back.

The monster spun and hit its head on the light fixture. Berserking, it ripped the globe from the ceiling and flung it to the side where it shattered against the stove.

Ritter ducked out of the way, grabbed a frying pan and hit the beast upside the head. The dogman swatted him across the room. He landed on top of the counter.

Mac flipped up the kitchen table and held onto its legs. He used it as a shield and charged the dogman, pinning it against the wall. Then he drew his pistol, stabbed the barrel into the back of the table and pulled the trigger over and over and over.

"Die, asshole!"

The enraged beast howled in agony and tossed Mac and the table aside. Bloody wounds dotted its chest. Its eyes fell on Ritter. His frantic fingers scrabbled across the kitchen counter, looking for a weapon. One hand closed around a peppershaker. He ripped its cap off and threw the contents in the dogman's face.

For an absurd moment, an almost comical look of surprise crossed the beast's features. Then, it sneezed. A great gob of snot splattered Ritter's face.

"Goddamn fuck!"

Berg sat up and shook his head clear. Then he sighted in on a black blur and pulled the Thompson's trigger. The rounds blew the kitchen's wood stove to pieces. Creosote filled the room as its chimney clattered to the floor in broken sections.

Mac, Ritter, and Berg stumbled out of the kitchen, coughing and covered with soot. The dogman bulldozed through the wall behind them. Mac grabbed a fireplace poker and aimed to put the steel pike through the monster's skull. The beast blocked the swing, grabbed Mac's wrist and threw him to the floor.

Ritter picked up the throw rug lining the hardwood and yanked it out from underneath the dogman's feet. The monster slammed onto its back.

Mac roared, eyes wild, mouth foaming and stabbed the poker into beast's guts. He leaned on it and twisted. The impaled monster screamed through sharp fangs.

"Come on!" Mac shouted. "Let's go!"

The three soldiers spilled through the front door. Mac and Ritter managed to snag their rifles on the way out. Mac stopped at the end of the sidewalk.

"*Now* would be a good time for grenades!"

They each lobed a pineapple explosive into the cottage. Flames blasted through the windows. The entire structure shook and wobbled like it was caught in an earthquake. The front wall pitched out and crashed to the lawn. The roof came down next and collapsed the remaining walls. Dust flew into the sky.

Mac, Ritter, and Berg stood before the twisted pile of bricks and lumber, exhausted. They looked like cadavers held up by wires. The wind rippled their torn and bloody clothes while the rain washed soot and dust from their backs. Their eyes were wide and burned out, like they were victims of starvation. They became wider still when a hairy arm shot out of rubble like a zombie rising from its grave.

"We have to keep moving," Mac wheezed.

They ran down the street on numb legs. Ragged breaths flapped their lips, and cramps stitched their sides. Mac noticed a steel plate set into the street—a sewer cover.

"Here! Help me!"

They hunkered down and heaved with gritted teeth. The metal disc flipped over and clattered against the cobblestones with a sharp clang that made the men wince.

Behind them, the beast entered the street in pursuit. It limped and hobbled but still came on, relentless. Its breath hissed like a locomotive building up steam.

"Inside!" Mac ordered.

They dropped into the hole one by one. The pipe was about four feet tall. Foul water ran over their boots. It smelled like dead fish and sun-baked shit. Mac took out his flashlight and shined it down the tunnel.

"Go!"

Ritter and Berg sloshed through the pipe ahead of him, their backs scraping the ceiling. Slime coated the walls and felt like cold snot under their fingertips.

The dogman's low growl reverberated through the tunnel behind them. It stood in the small cone of dim light shining through the pipe's opening. Its eyes glowed.

STEVE RUTHENBECK

Mac pulled another grenade and threw it as far back as he could. "Get down and cover your ears!" The three soldiers threw themselves onto the floor of the pipe.

The grenade blew with a tremendous *crump*! The concussion battered Mac, Ritter, and Berg like a cloth-wrapped baseball bat as the tunnel collapsed.

Kenway crouched behind a tombstone. Thick fog walled him in on all sides. Somewhere in its depths, the dogman followed his scent. He tried to stay calm. He didn't want to sweat. That would increase the strength of his spoor. He also tried to confuse the beast by running a twisted path of double-backs and crisscrosses. His boots hung around his neck so that he didn't make a sound when he moved. The dogman made no such attempt at stealth. Kenway periodically heard its claws on the cobblestones; sometimes it even growled with frustration.

The longer the hunt went on, the less chance it would remain frustrated, however. Kenway couldn't avoid it forever. He had to get out of the graveyard, or he'd end up being one of the dead.

Kenway stood up. His head broke through the shifting mist. Some of the taller grave markers poked out of the white-fog swamp like half-sunken artifacts. He thought he saw the lean skull of the dogman in the distance, cruising through the vapor like a crocodile stalking prey. If it was the beast, it was heading right for him.

Kenway moved away from the tombstone. He considered climbing a tree; then he imagined being trapped in its branches while the dogman climbed up after him, claws sinking into the bark. No good. Maybe he could strip naked and scrub himself down in the rain. He read that a dog couldn't smell a person if they came straight from a bath. No, no time.

Besides, the beast could hunt on sight, too. Running was the only option.

A sharp pain stabbed Kenway's foot. He bit his lower lip to keep from crying out and flopped to the ground. A broken stick protruded from the arch of his left foot. He gritted his teeth and pulled it out. Blood flowed—a predator's favorite scent. Panic sweat soaked Kenway's brow, adding another pungent odor to the mix. He may as well just shout *'I'm over here'* at the top of his lungs.

Were those padding paws coming closer? And the sound of panting?

Kenway pulled the clip from his Thompson and ejected four shells into his palm. He rubbed them with blood and flung them as far as he could. They clattered in the street, the sound amplified by the fog.

Kenway listened to the clicks of the dogman's claws as it darted toward the noise. How long before it realized it was fooled and came back?

Not long enough.

Kenway used his handkerchief to bandage the wound the best he could. Blood soaked through the thin material like blooming roses. Doom overcame him. Then he saw it through the shifting mist—a small building with a half moon cut into one wall.

"Thank Christ!"

The stench of the outhouse hit Kenway as he neared it. He entered the small building and flipped up the shitter lid. He reached inside, pulled out a handful of cold muck and smeared it across his chest, under his arms and over his wounded foot. The smell made him want to puke, but the excrement would cover his scent.

He exited the outhouse and ran through the graveyard as fast as his wounded foot could carry him. He could see the church steeple in the distance. He had a chance.

A thwarted howl wavered on the wind behind him.

The Major crawled from the river on his hands and knees, beaching himself near the bridge. Water dripped off him and splattered on the rocks as he made his way up the steep bank. He was back where they first entered town. The carved up corpse still stood on the bridge. *Hölle.* Its gray face looked up at the storm clouds like it cried out for divine help. Raindrops ran down its cheeks, making it look like it wept.

"Fucking crybaby," the Major muttered. He left the corpse behind and made his way to the church through the dark streets and alleys. He stopped when he saw the Kubelwagen sitting on the cathedral's steps. How the hell did that get there? He dismissed the question as irrelevant and paused at the church doors. A prickling sensation tickled the back of his neck. He spun around.

A dogman crouched in the middle of the street. Its ears pricked upright while its yellow eyes glowed with an interior flame. As the Major watched, it raised a leg and pissed on the cobblestones. The gesture was full of disdain and meaning.

Once finished, it rose up on its hind feet and began to shake. Coarse hair retracted into its body and revealed white skin. Its muscles deflated. Claws sucked back into its fingertips. Its snout flattened and sank into its face. At last, a naked blond man stood there, grinning.

The Major stared back, his face hard and defiant. He reached down, opened his trousers and pissed on the church steps, marking *his* territory.

The naked man's smile widened. Then he slunk away into the shadows.

The Major turned his back on his opponent and entered the cathedral. Mac, Ritter, Berg, Chaplain, Cain, and Kenway passed around a bottle of wine. They watched the Major approach with tired eyes. Most of them had cuts and bruises. Cain held his wounded arm against his chest and rocked back and forth on waves of agony as he bandaged it the best he could. Ritter played with one of his lucky ears.

"Where's Jacobson?" the Major asked. The men shrugged. The Major wrote the soldier off as a loss and snatched the bottle from Kenway.

"You smell like shit," he said matter-of-factly. Kenway said nothing. None of the men did.

The Major emptied the bottle, climbed into the pulpit and faced them. "So … morale is low, and motivation is waning. Well, what do you want to do about it? Do you want to piss, moan, and cry and say you don't believe what just happened? Well, fuck that. We saw what we saw. To believe it or not to believe it doesn't mean shit. We still have to deal with it. And you know what? It doesn't change a thing. Close your eyes."

The men stared blankly.

"I said close your fucking eyes!"

The men startled and shut their eyelids one by one, as if in fervent prayer, while their domineering priest stood over them. "What do you see?"

Knowledge. Satisfaction. Wealth. Contentment. Companionship. An end …

"I know what I see," the Major said. "I see a box full of power just waiting to be taken. I know you see the same thing. There's no unseeing something like that. And how can you go back to your regular lives after seeing the Big One anyway? What are you going back to that is worth a tin shit compared to what's in that box? Love? Family? Country? Do you think you'll ever have a chance like this again? Do you think hard work is going to get you anywhere? Perseverance? Doing the right thing? Bullshit! It's a dog-eat-dog world. The only people who get anything that matters in life are the ones who inherit it or the ones who take it. And we can take it, here, tonight. That box is our destiny. No one can keep us from it. Not a bunch of hairy assholes, not even the goddamn devil himself. It's *ours*. Now ... are you men or are you pussies who want to quit?"

Silence greeted the question. The men sat like corpses.

"No answer? That's fine. Actions speak louder than words anyway. Whoever's with me, stand up."

The men remained sitting.

"What's wrong? Are you afraid that you're going to die? Well, guess what? *You're already dead.* Everyone is an end waiting to happen. Or do you think that you'll live forever? Maybe you even think that you can lead a life free of bitterness and hate? That you can be happy? Fuck you for your stupidity. That never happens to anyone—*unless they have what is in that box.* So make your choice. Live worthlessly or take something that makes life worthwhile."

Silence pervaded the church. At last a pew creaked. It sounded like the trapdoor of a hangman's gallows swinging open. More creaks followed.

The Major exited the pulpit and joined the standing men. He drew his bayonet. "We're in this to the end—blood, sweat, and tears." He sliced his palms with the same blade that pierced the box and then passed it to Ritter. Ritter cut his hands and gave the knife to Mac.

Mac slashed his skin and passed it on to the rest of the Zombie Squad.

They joined hands. Blood ran from their stigmata-like wounds while they stood in the shadow of Christ. The storm outside grew in intensity.

"That's our fucking box," the Major said. "We'll have to go through those things to get it, but I've got an idea. *Silver.*"

CHAPTER

HUNGER

JACOBSON DREAMED a childhood memory.

He was a city kid from Los Angeles and grew up in a crowded neighborhood on a crowded street in a crowded apartment with five siblings and two parents. The place smelled of cabbage and feet. Cabbage soup was the centerpiece of nearly every meal, supplemented by bread, noodles and the occasional orange. Baths were as infrequent as meat. When the once-a-week wash came, Jacobson damn near needed a jackhammer to get through the grime on the back of his neck.

Jacobson spent most of his free time outside due to the smell. He often played soldier in the abandoned lot behind the apartment building. It was a rat's nest of weeds, broken glass and other assorted junk.

Within that barren wasteland, Jacobson and the neighborhood kids relived the great battles of World War I, stopping the advance of the bloody Hun and kicking the Kaiser's ass, as they put it.

The junkyard was appropriate for such games. It was almost as desolate as the no man's land between trenches where artillery shells mixed blood, guts and mustard gas into a quagmire.

During one such adventure, Jacobson hunkered behind a large tire. Where it came from, he had no idea. It was six feet tall and two feet wide. He imagined it came from a giant car; kids are stupid after all.

Frankie Dean sprawled behind the massive tire with Jacobson. He was a skinny boy with so many moles that he looked like he was covered by a single giant mole that exploded. He had thick glasses, an annoying donkey laugh, and a personality about as grating as chewing on tinfoil. Nevertheless, Jacobson still hung out with him for one important reason. Frankie also had a good-looking sister for whom he had no qualms about trying to see naked. It was a quest for the two of them. They spent six months trying to peek through keyholes and under doorjambs. They even went so far as to hide in her closet (she discovered them and beat them with her shoe until they fled) and planned to lower each other off the apartment building's roof and down to her bedroom window by a piece of rope. In fact, they were searching the abandoned lot for a hank of discarded rope when they got sidetracked into playing soldier.

"They're going to flank us," Frankie whispered. He gripped his stick-rifle and scanned the trash heap through his pop-bottle lenses.

They, in this case, meant the Alten twins. They were okay playmates but had the annoying habit of crying "cheater" when shot, or even worse, "I'm bulletproof", after seeing the *Superman* serials.

"What do we do?" Jacobson asked.

"We have to get to the pillbox."

The pillbox was an old boxcar that stank of cat piss.

"Right," Jacobson agreed. "I'll cover you."

Frankie gave him a solemn salute and took off running. Jacobson followed him through the knee-high ragweed. Broken bottles glittered in the sun. Piles of crumbling bricks teetered like broken monuments. They passed a rusted refrigerator, a twisted bed frame, and a worn-out pinball machine that kids pretended still worked when bored.

The boxcar rotted in the middle of the lot. Its cargo door blew off in a recent storm and lay on the ground. Several of its boards jutted up like sharp dragon fangs.

"Made it!" Frankie grinned. His tone carried a distinct we-sure-foiled-those-bastards-this-time timbre. The floor of the car was four feet high, quite a step for boys their age. Frankie threw himself at the summit with fearless childhood enthusiasm.

Jacobson eyed the sharp boards of the door. "Be careful."

"Careful is my middle name!"

"*Bang! Bang! Gotcha!*"

Bobby Alten popped out of the boxcar and jabbed his stick-gun into Frankie's chest. The cunning twerp was hiding in the pillbox the whole time!

"Wha—" Frankie squawked in surprise. He pinwheeled his arms, lost his balance and fell. He hit the door on his back. One of the boards punched through his chest with a sickening crunch. Blood sprayed across his face. "Tuh."

Jacobson realized that the two sounds formed a question: *What?*

Jacobson saw many dead bodies since then, but he always remembered Frankie's the best. They way he lay in the sun, the wind playing with his hair like he still ran, blood oozing from the corner of his mouth, and his eyes wide and surprised behind his thick glasses, glazing over without so much as a single answer to his final question or even a quick glimpse of a naked sister in his short life.

It was so damn easy to die.

✠　✠　✠

JACOBSON OPENED HIS EYES. The box came into grudging focus. The firelight gave it a mellow glow. Jacobson forgot about the pain in his head and remembered what he thought when the Major pulled the tarp away: *I could live forever if that belonged to me.*

A naked man blocked his view. Jacobson blinked up at him, still bleary and not entirely aware of what was happening. The man's blue eyes were as sharp as his face. He gestured at the box with a muscular arm.

"Beautiful, isn't it? But it's rude to show more interest in a host's trinkets than in the host himself. I am Erick Stark." He pointed to Jacobson's left. "These are my brothers-at-arms, Fritz Gunther, Hans Verning, and Stefan Hagen."

Jacobson turned his head. Three more naked men sat around a table littered with sausage, bread, cheese, and wine. They stuffed the food into their mouths until their cheeks bulged. Wounds marked their skin—bullet holes, scrapes, bruises and cuts. One of the men looked like someone tried to cut off his arm. Another had bones sticking out of his legs, like he fell from a building and the impact shattered his shins.

As Jacobson watched, the wounds healed. Flesh closed up. Scrapes morphed into clear skin. The process was slow, like a minute hand revolving around a clock face, but unmistakable.

"Our metabolism can deal with just about any injury," Stark explained, "but it takes a lot of food when the damage is particularly bad."

Everything came flooding back to Jacobson—the bank, the battle, the beasts. He finally realized he was tied to a chair. He tried to move his arms and legs.

The rope was without slack and would have worked great for, say, lowering a buddy off a roof so the he could spy on a naked sister. Jacobson turned to Stark with terrified eyes.

"What are you?" he stammered.

"I told you, I'm an Erick Stark. What are you?"

"Juh-Juh-Jacobson... Private ... U.S. First Army ..."

"Well, Juh-Juh-Jacobson, what brings you to our so fair town?" Stark glanced at the box. "As if I can't hazard a guess ..."

"Serial number four, eight, four, seven..."

Stark rolled his eyes. "You're not a prisoner, Juh-Juh-Jacobson."

"I'm not?"

"Oh no," Stark shook his head. "*You're worse.*"

The box sat on its table—beautiful, imperious and as silent as the stone walls of Wewelsburg to the shrieking pleas and smacking jaws.

CHAPTER

BIRTH

WEWELSBURG KNEW WAR. Bishops took over the Paderborn region in 805 and built the triangular castle as their stronghold. German tribes destroyed a Roman army in the nearby Teutoburger Forest a century later. Rome subsequently lost all territory east of the Rhine River, and the area became part of the Holy Roman Empire. Eventually, the Thirty Years War broke out. The religious battle encompassed most of Western Europe and killed roughly twenty percent of Paderborn's population.

Like a dark idol, Wewelsburg sat on its hill and oversaw all the bloodshed and fear. It became a sagging ruin, perhaps weighted down by the horrors it witnessed throughout the centuries— and there were more horrors to come.

Unlike most conflicts, World War II was not about money or gaining territory. At its heart, it was about the nature of man.

Everything the Nazis did was dominated by a single ideology: that Germany would lead humanity to the next stage of evolution and create a race of supermen—the *Übermensch*.

According to Nazi philosophy, only one thing prevented mankind from maximizing its potential: blood. They believed that man's blood was polluted by inbreeding with the subhuman races—the *Untermenschen*—most notably the Jews, but also the Negro, Slavs, and Mongoloids.

The ideal human specimen was the Aryan: white, blond, blue-eyed and possessing a clear mind.

Thinkers of the time helped clarify Nazi ideology. Charles Darwin observed that animals were not identical to their parents. The differences were due to more than the environment; they were often inheritable. Breeders could change offspring characteristics by mating parents with the most desirable qualities—strength in workhorses, tracking in dogs, etc. He called it "artificial selection" and reasoned the same principle applied to nature. The stronger animals had higher reproductive rates due to their greater fitness while the weaker animals perished. He called the phenomenon "natural selection"—survival of the fittest.

It didn't take long for someone to apply Darwin's theories to human beings and society. That person was Darwin's cousin, Francis Galton. Galton theorized that medicine and civilization acted against natural selection by promoting the protection of the weak and retarding the evolution of the strong. He proposed human breeding be guided to favor the better stock, a practice he called Eugenics.

Darwin's theory also assisted in removing God from the equation of human morality, which was based on Judeo-

Christian models. If God didn't create the world, did he really exist? And if he didn't exist, what was morality?

Friedrich Nietzche ran with the concept and became one of the most provocative thinkers of the nineteenth century. He reasoned that the traditional ideas of Christian morality were a set of myths designed by the weak to protect themselves against the strong—a slave morality that tamed, weakened, and emasculated the natural impulses of man.

God is dead, he proclaimed. Nothing is true. Everything is permitted. Thus, he redefined truth and inserted the *Übermensch* in place of God.

Darwin, Galton, and Nietchze weren't the only thinkers to influence the Nazis. Self-proclaimed psychics and mystics flourished in Post-World War I Germany.

Jorg Lanz wrote an occult newsletter, *Ostara*, which was read by over one hundred thousand people. Lanz claimed that many legendary figures were Aryans fighting the racial battle. He believed that the Knights Templar, who searched for the Holy Grail and fought in the Crusades, did so to defeat the *Untermenschen*. He also wrote that the Holy Grail contained racial purity.

Lanz's distorted view of mythology helped contribute to Hitler's interest in obtaining ancient relics, such as the Staff of Annubis and the Crucifixion Cross. He believed possessing such artifacts guaranteed him success.

Madam Helena Blavatsky was another originator of the Aryan Myth. She claimed ancient beings communicated with her via telepathy. They told her that six root races existed throughout history, such as the Hyperboreans, Atlanteans, and Greeks. The Aryans were to be the seventh race. They would rise up from the darkness of the present day and bring light to the future by defeating the subhuman peoples.

Guido Von List took Blavatsky's ravings even further and stated that Germany's loss in World War I was a result of an *Untermenschen* conspiracy to prevent the Aryans from gaining their rightful place as masters of the world. He even invoked the prayer of the German heretic Giordano Bruno in his prolific writings: *Oh Jove, let the Germans realize their own strength, and they shall not be men, but gods.*

This mishmash of science, philosophy, and occultism formed the basic tenants of Nazism. The SS then became the primary instrument used to indoctrinate the German people into the ideology. The architect of the system was Henrich Himmler.

Himmler grew up in Bavaria, the son of a strict Catholic professor. He was uncoordinated, nearsighted, and clumsy around girls. He served a stint in the military and then embarked on a series of failed business ventures, including chicken farming and selling fertilizer.

Himmler joined the Nazi Party in 1925. Due to his shrewd nature and ability to be perfectly rational about irrational things, he rose through the ranks and gained Hitler's trust. In 1929, he was promoted to chief of the SS.

Himmler believed in the Aryan Myth and formed the Race and Resettlement Bureau to record the racial history of everyone in Germany. This led to strict requirements for SS members, who had to prove family racial purity back to 1750 and could only marry women of similar quality.

So serious was Himmler's vision that he founded Lebensborn in 1935. The Fount of Life Society was meant to care for unwed mothers of good blood who were impregnated by SS men. This prevented abortion and the loss of valuable racial stock.

In reality, Lebensborn ended up a stud farm where SS men could find suitable girls to breed. The installations became virtual baby factories where midwives powdered and changed entire tables filled with squalling infants.

Himmler also believed he was the reincarnation of King Henrich I. Himmler claimed that King Henrich sent him psychic messages to prepare him for his divine purpose, which was to defeat a subhuman invasion from the East. This contributed to Himmler's interest in ancestor worship and other occult practices, which led to strange rituals being performed deep inside Wewelsburg.

Himmler made Wewelsburg the seat of the SS organization in the early 1930s and began renovating it to suit his grandiose dreams. He hoped the castle would eventually become the Vatican City of the Thousand-Year Nazi Reich, a monument to the evolution of mankind into gods.

But God had nothing to do with what happened to Stark, Gunther, Verning, and Hagen in the castle's darkest chamber.

✠ ✠ ✠

THE WALLS OF WEWELSBURG closed in on all sides. It was like standing at the bottom of a giant grave. Hammers and chisels rang out as carpenters and masons beat the castle back into relevancy. They made the crooked straight and the weak strong.

Stark's breath puffed out in the chill evening air. His withered leg and twisted back wanted to collapse after the long truck ride, but he refused to fall.

"Why did they bring us here?" Gunther whispered. His gray hair and thin overcoat flapped in the cold wind. Arthritis turned the joints of his fingers into salt-dome knobs as they curled around the handle of his cane.

Stark had no answer, but their location made him uneasy. He regarded the SS with superstitious awe. They were the cleaners who removed the stains from society. Bullets were their bleach and ruthlessness was their soap; heaven help you if you had a blemish.

None of the guards paid him, Gunther, Verning, or Hagen any attention, however. Their eyes scanned designated sentry zones like buzzards watching for road kill.

A shiver ran up Stark's spine. Suppose he was there because of what he did to Mr. Leberwitz? But the old man was only a Jew, he reasoned. The SS did much worse to his kind. Stark's breath hitched in his throat. What if they knew about Elsa and Emil? They were not Jews; they were fine upstanding German citizens.

The castle opened, and a man in black exited. His leather jacket creaked as he approached with birdlike steps. He wore an officer's hat with a silver death's head pinned to it. Small round glasses glinted on his schoolmaster face.

"Greetings," he gave them a curt nod. "I am Henrich Himmler." He consulted a handful of index cards and moved down the line. "Fritz Gunther," he read. "Sixty-two. Born in Munich. I have visited there often. Do you know the Fliesse Flower Garden?"

"Yes," Gunther's voice cracked.

The presence of the Reichsführer was an unsettling thing. Death dealing was the man's business. People disappeared with a snap of his fingers. One expected him to have horns, but he looked like an accountant.

"The garden's roses are exquisite in the spring. Roses are my favorite flower. Their thorns give them a will to match their beauty. We ourselves could bloom into such magnificent forms if we were so rooted in the earth. Man is not meant to walk on concrete but on fertile soil. Your wife is named Gisela, I understand."

Gunther nodded, surprised by how much information the card contained and unsure how to handle Himmler's disconnected way of speaking.

"She is a good woman," Himmler went on, "very Aryan, I see, blond, blue-eyed. The lines of her nose indicate fine breeding. It's a pity she is barren and unable to produce stock for the Fatherland. Children are the seeds of the future. We cannot change the old, so we must mold the young. You have my sympathies."

"Thank you," Gunther replied uncertainly.

Like a clerk switching from one completed form to the next, Himmler flipped Gunther's card to the back of the pile and moved on to Verning. "Hans Verning, your parents abandoned you at birth, correct?"

"Yes."

"You were found on the streets of Dresden in 1915 and put in a foster home. You were adopted twice. The adoption failed both times due to antisocial behavior. You even stabbed your second stepfather in the stomach. How come?"

Verning's face hardened enough to stop his cheek from ticking. "I got tired of him visiting my room every night. So did my ass."

"Ah, yes, in that case, your behavior is excusable. Homosexuals deserve to be gutted, and they will. They are an affront to decency. A man must not let emotions dictate his actions, however. Can you control your temper, Verning?"

"My temper kept me alive."

Himmler's face softened. "Orphans do not exist in Germany, Hans. You're a child of the Reich now, and you will have a chance to make your father proud."

Himmler moved on to Hagen. He spoke with exaggerated enunciation so Hagen could read his lips. "Stefan Hagen, you are deaf and dumb, yes?"

Hagen nodded.

Himmler shook his head with genuine remorse. "It's a tragedy that someone of such excellent physicality is so afflicted. Nevertheless, it's your imperfections that allow you this opportunity. Investigations reveal you all come from fine Aryan stock. Regrettably, the latent impurities in your blood have rendered you unfit for conventional military service, yet you are not unfit for other … special duties."

Stark perked up at Himmler's statement, his earlier unease swallowed by excitement and hope. Could it really be he was there for some special purpose? If only all those who doubted, put down and patronized could see him now. The Reichsfuehrer of Germany addressed him next, personally, like a man.

"Erick Stark, from Berlin. Have you seen the Führer speak there?"

"Yes," Stark answered, remembering the night of Elsa and Emil. His excitement was momentarily lost in … guilt? No, it was far too late for that.

Himmler's eyes turned worshipful. "Such a great man. Do you believe in him?"

"I believe."

"Belief is one thing, but actions prove faith. I know what you did to a certain Mr. Leberwitz."

Stark stiffened, but Himmler's crooked smile reassured him. "Tell me, what did you find in his skull after you cracked it open? Air or worms?"

"Shit," Stark answered with a twisted smile of his own.

Himmler barked a derisive laugh. "Shit! That's good. That's very good."

He chortled to himself and then addressed all four men at once. "Well, gentlemen, it's pleasant to talk, but work must intrude. Now is the time for you to make a choice. Will you give all that you have for the Führer?"

Answering was easy. None of them had anything to lose.

"Yes."

"Even your life?"

"Yes."

The setting sun gave them skeletal shadows. Himmler's glasses reflected the red light and made him appear to be filled with the fires of hell itself.

"Your soul?"

"We're still remodeling the interior, but the end result will be glorious."

Some of Wewelsburg's walls were unpainted. Tarps covered tapestries and scaffolding blocked sculptures. Nevertheless, the potential splendor of the place glowed with a near blinding light.

All of the woodwork was polished oak. An elegant teak staircase spiraled to higher levels. The floor was shiny marble. Chandeliers made wind chime noises as air eddied around their crystals. A phonograph played in some side room; the powerful strains of Wagner drifted through the opulence.

Himmler led them into a dining hall that was dominated by a circular table with twelve chairs.

"The SS Round Table," Himmler beamed, "with seats for the senior Gruppenführers, just like King Arthur and his knights of old."

The next room contained an arsenal of medieval weapons. Suits of armor stood in the corners. Ancient weapons—swords, crossbows, spears, and spiked clubs—hung between romantic paintings of battle. A torture rack took up an entire wall. Its hooks and pulleys gleamed with wicked light. It had been well restored. It seemed to smile at them and whisper: *Go ahead, touch me. Pain is the universal language. I will listen to what you have to say very closely and with great interest.*

"Let the bleeding hearts speak of peace," Himmler said, "but war changes the world. Peace makes people dull and lazy while war tempers the spirit and encourages growth. The human race would still be squatting in caves if not for war."

A variety of stuffed animals filled the following room. A lion stalked unseen prey, an eagle spread its wings from atop a bookcase, and a wolf prowled between two rocks. Himmler paused and ran his fingers across a zebra's hide.

"Black and white," he said. "Everything serves one or the other in the end. Many labor under the delusion that they are for white when they're actually for black, however. Lucky for us, we need not have any doubts about our shade."

They passed into the next chamber.

"Ah," Himmler smiled with great aplomb, "this is the room that I am most proud of, my little museum of relics." He gathered them around a knife in a display case. The weapon was very utilitarian, eight inches long and possessed a thirty-degree angle halfway down its cutting edge. "If you know your Bible history, this is the blade which Abraham almost used to sacrifice his son, Isaac. Imagine the will of such a man, to be so zealous as to kill his own child. That is the type of devotion we must show as we fight the good fight."

Next in line was a tarnished spearhead on a pillow of red velvet. Himmler let his fingers play along its edge.

"Just think, the metal I now touch pierced Christ's flesh nearly two thousand years ago. It's flecked with some of the purest blood to ever flow upon the Earth. Many scholars believe that Christ, Abraham, and all the heroes of the Bible were Jews, but that is a blasphemous lie. They were Aryans, though and though. Our records prove it. Legend says that the ruler who possesses the Spear of Destiny will be invincible in battle. Soon I will present it to the Führer himself."

They passed on to an ornate altar surrounded with purple curtains. The altar's sandstone was carved with great detail, depicting animals, men, moon, and stars. Himmler rested a hand on its surface and spoke with a hint of apology tainted with anger. "The Ark of the Covenant was supposed to be displayed here. We had it in our possession, but it was liberated by a freelance archaeologist. I understand it is now in some American warehouse. My men are working to ascertain whether or not that is true. If so, I hope to reacquire it soon. In the meantime, I have another treasure to show you."

The last exotic object the room contained was a massive stone tablet. Faded runic symbols covered its surface.

"This rock is from Atlantis," Himmler explained. "We haven't been able to decipher all of it, but it speaks of a race so advanced they could capture dreams and put them in a box ... or something to that effect."

A small man in an SS uniform entered and interrupted Himmler's lecture. He didn't look like he belonged in the black cloth. He was old, with thinning white hair and a stooped stature. Thick glasses perched on his nose. He carried an armful of notes and had a bird-shaped birthmark on one cheek that gleamed dull red.

"Ah, Franz!" Himmler greeted him. "How goes the research?"

"Passing," the man said absently. "It is passing." He shouldered his way between Stark, Gunther, Verning, and Hagen and stood before the tablet. He stared at it with deep concentration. "Location," he muttered. "Where? Where?"

"Pay him no mind," Himmler apologized. "Come, I will show you to your rooms so you may rest and refresh yourselves. You will find food there, as well. Good food is a must for a healthy life. The English upper classes have such fine physiques because they eat porridge for breakfast. That's why I make SS men eat porridge every day."

Himmler led them down a corridor until they reached a hall of doors. "Each guest room is dedicated to a Germanic hero," Himmler said and opened one for Hagen. "The Attila Room. Attila made the Huns the terror of Europe and Asia in the 400s. He invaded the Eastern Roman Empire, passed through Austria, across the Rhine into Gaul, and then down into Italy, plundering and devastating all that lay in his path."

Himmler opened another door for Verning. "The Giselher Room. He and Wolfhart killed one another in single combat. Giselher mortally wounded Wolfhart, but Wolfhart delivered a killing blow with his last breath."

Himmler ushered Gunther to the next room in line. "The Witege Suite. Witege was one of the few men to defeat Dietrich in single combat. He did so because he was armed with Mimung, a magnificent sword created by his father."

"And this is your quarters." Himmler opened a door for Stark. Tapestries hung from the room's walls. A roaring fireplace crackled. There was a bookshelf, a black oak desk, a harpsichord, fur chairs, and a feather bed. A mural depicted a muscular blond man wrestling with a hairy beast. "The Beowulf Room. Beowulf was —"

146

"A Scandinavian Prince," Stark interrupted, "who rid the Danes of the monster Grendel, half-man and half-fiend. Years later, Beowulf became a king and fought a dragon. They killed each other in battle."

"As you say," Himmler smiled a thin smile. "We will come for you when the time is right." With that, he shut the door and left Stark to himself.

Stark went to the table and made a meal of sausage, bread, cheese, fruit, and wine. It made him drowsy. That was fine. He would lie down and have a nap.

For the first time in a long time, Stark was content. He had a purpose and comfort. How long had it been since he experienced such things? He was too tired to remember. He struggled to keep his eyes open. To sleep and dream.

Poe wrote, *For the moon never beams without bringing me dreams ..."* Dreams ... dreams ... such a funny word the way it rolled off the tongue.

A race so advanced that they could capture dreams and put them in a box. A jangled laugh escaped Stark's lips. He tried to stand up, but his legs felt far away. The room swam before his eyes. As Stark pitched to the floor, he realized that the food was drugged.

The last thing he saw was the man beast snarling on the wall.

There he stood with Elsa, under the moon, in the park, beneath the trees, near the stream. The wind throws dimpling shadows over them.

Torchlight flickered, barely holding back the dark.

Were they holding hands?

Of course they were! What else would two lovebirds have done on such a lovely night in such a lovely place?

He whispered something. Something clever? Something romantic? What did it matter? Wasn't everything that is said in such a situation one or the other?

Chanting—a continuous low drone in an alien language. It sounded like lunacy dispensed with utmost control—the utterance of a committed madman as he raved in emotional agony and tried not to wake the person in the next bed.

"Golarom Beelzebub, r'lia yog soggoth m'li mene tiki la'lia Beelzebub ..."

Did she laugh? Did she smile? Did her pupils dilate, her breath quicken and her pulse race? Did her cheeks take on a rosy glow?

Yes, yes, and yes to all that and more—because things were perfect for them. The wind blew stronger right on cue, billowing her dress, waving her hair out in a shining fan, and chilling them both, just enough to make them draw closer together as they looked out on the water and leaned against the waist-high brick wall.

His cheek rested on cold bricks. He tried to move and discovered that his arms and legs were weighted down with chains. The heavy links were attached to a steel ring sunk into the stone floor. It looked strong enough to hold an elephant. With slow dawning, he realized that he was naked.

"Tekeli-li! Tekeli-li!"

He managed to turn his head. The room was a circular crypt with damp stone walls. He lay along the edge of a round depression in the floor. Gunther, Verning, and Hagen were similarly situated around the sunken circle. They were also chained and naked. They seemed dazed, as if caught between the real world and a dream.

Was she soft? Did her clothes contain willing compliance and nary an obligation?

The stream became a rippling silver sheet under the moon, which was out just for them. All of the universe must have subjugated itself to true love. Leaves swept across the ground, giving the scene just the right artistic flourish. And was that a night bird singing, the notes of its song lifting the scene to an even higher level of idealized romance?

"Tekeli-li! Tekeli-li!"

A ring of robed men—twelve of them—stood around the circle. Hoods hid their faces, and they pressed their palms together in front of their chests. The murmured chanting came from their shadowed lips.

"Golarom Beelzebub, r'lia yog soggoth m'li mene tiki la'lia Beelzebub ..."

How did her hand feel in his?

Warm.

How did her eyes look in that light?

Deeper than the universe.

How did it feel to stand in that radiating circle of want, happiness, and riches?

He didn't know because he wasn't standing with Elsa. Emil stood with her.

He stood in the shadows, coveting. He was cold. Snot dripped from his nose. He shivered. His back and leg felt like fragile winter sticks weighted down with ice.

Himmler, the thirteenth of the coven, stood in the center of the circle, a pentagram of blood drawn beneath his bare feet. He wore priestly vestments and held a book in his hands. Its cover appeared to be made from human skin and was scratched with heathenish symbols. A pot bubbled next to him, heated by a gas flame that jetted up from the floor. Steam percolated over the pot's lip and cascaded to the stones. It wormed toward the chained men like a living thing and smelled of carrion.

He stood alone, under the barren moon, in the deserted park, beneath the skeletal trees, near the stinking stream. The wind doesn't ruffle the shadows surrounding him.

He held a brick so tight that his fingers ached, and its sharp edges dug into his palm almost deep enough to draw blood.

Did he hate?

Of course he did! What else did bitterness and frustration birth into existence?

He whispered something. Something cruel? Something threatening? What did it matter? Wasn't everything said in such a situation one or the other?

"Der Hagel bedeutend Lucifer, Hagel!" Himmler *intoned. It was the German language, but the syntax and cadence were off, like it was written by something from another dimension that knew the tongue but not the grammar.*

"Ich habe ein Anliegen an Sie, machtig Schatten, ein Hollesgabe. Der Einbruch dies hausgemacht Felge und macht Bestie Menschen stark und dreist, der Schreken aus jung und alt."

Did she grimace? Did she scream? Did her heart beat faster in her chest? Did her eyes lose their glint? Her breath stop? Her face grow ashen?

Yes, yes, and yes to all that and more—because that was all he could accomplish with his handicap of imperfection. The wind blew stronger, rippling his coat, blowing his hair back from his feverish forehead and chilling him to the bone.

He drew his arms around himself, but his only warmth was from the fires burning inside.

A wind grew in the chamber, making the torches flicker and hiss. The air turned colder. His flesh humped into goose bumps. Despite his shivering, large drops of sweat grew from his forehead, and rivulets ran down his skin.

He became even woozier and felt like vomiting. Himmler doubled in his vision as the man sprinkled ingredients into the pot. He recognized some of the plants: hemlock, nightshade, belladonna, wolfsbane, and something that he was sure was opium.

"Der Konig aus boser Geist die Heere, Ich beten du absenden der bedeutend duster Schatten da macht Menschen der Schrek! Kommen!"

The world became an eldritch graveyard under the moon, which affected the tides of madness. The entire universe conspired to drive a man beyond his endurance. A batch of dead leaves rustled across the ground, whispering insane secrets. And was that a night bird singing a song of mourning ... or of fear for what drew near?

"Kommen!"

An oppressive presence filled the room, making it hard to breath. His lungs labored and his eyes burned within the invisible acridity. Tears ran down his cheeks, and he blinked them away. When he could see again, he noticed a man in a flowing black robe had joined Himmler. His face was hidden in folds of cloth. Fresh jackal skins, dripping blood and dangling sinew, hung over his arm.

The man moved around the circle, almost floating. He went to Gunther first and spread the vile pelt on top of his body. Gunther's face twisted with revulsion and fear. He tried to struggle out from underneath the skin, but the chains were too heavy to move.

The man in black went to Verning and Hagen next, covering them with the dog skins. He spread the pelt over

Stark last. It clung to him, sticky and hot, the coagulated blood like paste.

How did her hands feel pounding at him?

Passionate.

How did her eyes look in that moment?

Respectful, oh, so respectful.

How did it feel to dive into the burning sea of sin and wallow in its depths?

Himmler dumped more ingredients into the pot, roots and what appeared to be a handful of lard but was surely something more sinister.

"*Ich betteln! Ich beten! Ich anflehen du allmachtig Lucifer, macht mir die Gunstlinge aus die wolf! Macht mir Menschenfressers! Macht mir Fraufressers! Macht mir Kindfressers!*"

"*Tekeli-li! Tekeli-li!*"

He strode toward Emil and Elsa. They didn't hear him until he stepped on a stick that cracked like a broken bone. They turned toward him, startled.

The strength of the wind in the chamber increased. It moaned like the forlorn cry of a dying whale. The chanting men quickened the pace of their stanza.

"*Golarom Beelzebub, r'lia yog soggoth m'li mene tiki la'lia Beelzebub ...*"

Himmler raised his hands. The fingers of one curled into a twisted symbol. The other held a knife. He brought the two together over the pot.

"*Tekeli-li! Tekeli-li! Tekeli-li!*"

The chanting men swayed like heads of grain in a violent storm, voices growing higher and more frantic. Their robes rippled in the wind.

Himmler's blood dripped.

The man in black reached into the boiling pot with a bare hand. He brought out a palm full of foul jelly and turned toward Gunther.

"Oh!" Elsa quipped. "You frightened us, Erick. What are you doing here?"

Emil looked so strong, sure and always good enough. "You know him?"

"He works with me at the coat factory. Emil, meet Erick."

"Pleased to meet you." Emil extended his hand and smiled, such a perfect smile.

"No!" Gunther screamed. His face was a paroxysm of terror. His white hair stood on end. His eyes were open so wide that his eyeballs threatened to tumble out of their sockets. Then the man in black smeared the boiling jelly into Gunther's face.

"Tekeli-li! Tekeli-li! Tekeli-li!"

The man in black grabbed another handful of goo. He carried the simmering clump of depraved mixings to Verning. Verning laughed, a sound of madness mixed with genuine mirth. He twitched with lunatic frenzy, and his cackles became a shrill scream as the man in black force fed him the vile concoction.

"Tekeli-li! Tekeli-li! Tekeli-li!"

The dog pelts sank into Gunther and Verning's flesh. They screamed and bayed in the smoke and firelight. Hagen's silent cry joined them as the man in black smeared the burning goop into his face.

And then it was Stark's turn. The stuff from the pot was scalding. It burned his lips, tongue and throat, raising blisters. It tasted like rotten fish. He shrieked as it hit his belly and seemed to burn a hole through his gut and spread through his veins.

The wind swelled in fury to that of a raging tornado. A legion of shadows twisted across the bricks, made by capering, unseen things.

He swung the shattered brick. Emil went down with a fractured skull. Elsa tried to scream.

Himmler screamed the final incantations with the look of a man who lost control of his car and went sailing off the edge of a cliff.

"Das Herz, der Aufbau und die Seele aufschlagen die Krafte aus Ubel! Die Schmelze die Kugel, abstumpfen das Messer, erythraean der Club, der Anschlag Schrek hin-ein Menschen, die Bestie und das Reptil so sie darf nicht die Jagdbeute der Werwolf. Mein der Ausdruck ist stark, starker als Tod oder die Dauerhaftigkeit aus die Helden!

"Shhh, darling, shhhh."

He advanced on Elsa.

Seizures gripped Stark. The swallowed molten burning coursed through him. He thrashed and trembled on the floor, the dog pelt alive and clinging to him, trying to crush him in a steel grip.

A bright bolt of pain galvanized his muscles and jackknifed him rigid straight. The skin along his spine, arms and legs split open like hungry mouths. The dog pelt forced itself into the crevasses of his flesh, worming its way inside of him, tearing its way through muscles and bones and spirit.

Elsa managed a single word.

"Tekeli-li! Tekeli-li! Tekeli-li!"

"Why?"

Tight bands of pain constricted every inch of his body. He felt the thing spreading inside of him, a million hot needles stitching through his entire being. It grew and swelled, puffing him up like a balloon.

He heard a symphony of cracking bones inside his head. The roof of his mouth split. Blood ran down his scalded throat. His skull came apart at the seams, and his skeleton tried to force its way though his skin, freeing itself from its crippled prison.

His spine twisted and humped and crunched. Cramps coursed through his body in undulating waves. Burning. Freezing. Dying. Birthing. Thick hair speared out of his pores. Sprouting teeth punched through the bottom of his chin.

"Because I love you," he whispered.

The brick falls.

Elsa falls.

And he falls upon her.

The wind rose to a final hurricane dervish that blew the torches out, plunging the chamber into darkness. Then it disappeared. All was quiet.

Except for the snarling.

Himmler led Dr. Rascher down a stone staircase and into the basement of Wewelsburg like Montresor leading Fortunato. Two guards followed. They half-carried, half-dragged a thin Jewish woman in a stained white gown. Her bare feet slapped against the stairs, and black hair obscured her features. She kept her eyes on the floor and did not resist. The bruises she carried were lessons that she learned too well.

"Did it really work?" Rascher asked in an excited tone of voice. He ran a compulsive hand through his hair until it stood up in comical spikes.

"Would I have called you away from your experiments if it hadn't?" Himmler replied. "You do important work, Sigmund. Your time is too valuable to waste."

"Thank you, Reichsführer."

Himmler nodded like a king who acknowledged the existence of a peasant. "How are the high-altitude tests going by the way?"

"The chamber can now simulate a free fall from thirteen thousand feet. The sudden change in pressure causes bubbles to form in the bloodstream. Subjects report it feels like being crushed in a wine press. Some bite off their tongues and foam at the mouth. One tried to claw his own face off before his brain hemorrhaged."

"Have the freezing and resuscitation experiments been going as smoothly?"

"Oh yes," Rascher nodded with great enthusiasm. "We've collected hundreds of pages of data in that department. For instance, a hot bath is much more effective than warm blankets in the reviving process. Sometimes hands and feet are lost to frostbite, of course, but plenty more test fodder exists in the camps."

"Have you tried animal heat?"

"Pardon?" Rascher frowned.

"Animal heat," Himmler repeated. "You put the frozen subject between naked women. That's what the Frisian Islanders did for shipwrecked sailors."

"Interesting, we'll have to try that."

"You should," Himmler agreed. "And be sure to inform me of when you do so I may be on hand to observe. I'm most curious about the possibility."

"Certainly, Reichsführer. It would be an honor to have you visit, and you must take time to view some of our other successes. We now have a device that sterilizes a person unawares. You simply install it under a counter and make the subject step up to it under the pretext of filling out forms. As they write, the device bombards their genitals with radiation. Each device could handle two hundred men per day."

"You don't say." Himmler was visibly impressed. The stairwell ended, and they emerged into a hallway with six steel doors. "Here we are, Doctor." Himmler gestured to the nearest barred window. "Take a look at what I have wrought."

"Yes indeed," Rascher licked his lips. "Yes, yes, yes." He stepped up to the window and peered inside. His mouth went wide. Trying to cross humans with German Shepherds was one of Rascher's most ambitious dreams. He attempted to gestate human ovum from dog sperm, and vice versa, many times. And now here it was; mysticism had succeeded where science had failed. He didn't know whether to laugh or cry.

"Unfortunately, we must keep them caged for now," Himmler said. "We've had some mishaps. The book says it takes time for them to learn control."

"What kind of mishaps?"

"A drop of blood spilled in preparation prevents streams of blood from being spilled in action," Himmler said cryptically. "Now ... it's feeding time. You should enjoy this, Rascher. I think you'll find it right up your alley."

One of the guards approached a door with exaggerated caution and slid open the meal slot. A low growl rumbled through the opening.

The Jewish girl stopped being docile, realizing the rules of the game had changed. What did it matter if resistance meant pain? It was apparent that not resisting now meant something worse. The guards dragged her toward the door. She struggled and grunted against them, trying to dig her heels into the stones. A furry arm shot out of the slot, and clawed fingers wrapped around her shin. She screamed. The soldiers retreated to a safe distance. The arm ripped the girl off her feet and pulled her leg through the narrow opening. Her screams grew louder. Something snarled.

Then the sound of chewing.

"God!" the girl shrieked. "God! God! God!"

"The quickest way to a man's heart is through his stomach," Himmler said.

A terrific tearing sound filled the air, followed by an inhuman howl of triumph. The girl fell away from the opening. Her leg remained. "Jesus! Jesus! Jesus!" She tried to crawl, mindless with pain and panic. The hand shot through the slot once more and hit her chest like a harpoon, claws sinking deep with greed and power.

Her screams abruptly cut off.

"She called for Jesus," Rascher commented, like he observed an amoeba through a microscope. "Now, isn't that ironic?"

Stark smelled them long before they reached his cell. Himmler stank of cologne, something like juniper mixed with gasoline and perhaps a dash of urine. The other man smelled like alcohol and soap. The two guards had the tang of sweat and steel. The food smelled sweet, an intoxicating odor of fear and submission.

Stark heard every word of their conversation; he even heard their heartbeats as they drew closer. The thought of tearing the organs from their chests and crushing them between his teeth made him shiver. The transformation tore loose then with the snap of tendon and bone. Hair, teeth, and claws sprouted. Stark didn't think of it as changing; he was still himself. He merely phased into a different form, a better form, a stronger, more cunning and hungry form …oh, so hungry. He called it the Shift.

Stark recognized the man peering through the door. He remembered how Rascher looked at him during the physical, like a superior. Now fear and awe distorted Rascher's face into something servile. Stark savored it in that moment before the feast.

Feeding brought pleasure, and time brought pain. When Stark wasn't overcome by the Shift, he lay on the floor and hugged his knees to his chest. Coherent thought came and went like the shadows of clouds passing across a prairie. Sometimes he forgot his name. Sometimes he thought he was still a boy who was sick in bed.

Stark spent much of his youth bedridden. Such were better times. He loved stories and lost each day in a book. Plus, he had no frame of reference to define his place in the world. He wasn't a cripple. He wasn't a weakling. He wasn't imperfect. He was just a boy who got sick a lot and liked to read. The seeds of hate and frustration were still there, of course. Sometimes the books were bittersweet. He knew he would never hunt a white whale, climb a mountain and discover Shangri-La, or save a damsel from a vampire. At best, he could only utter, "And God bless us, every one." Plus, he sensed the resentment of his parents. He wasn't a son. He was the thing in the back room that reminded a person life wasn't fair and made them pay for it besides. What he didn't know was his condition was a result of his father punching his mother in the belly when she was pregnant. Nor did he know his mother once held her hand around his neck until his face turned blue, and then fled the room crying. But he sensed those things the way a person senses an approaching storm, and if he sometimes stuck pins through beetles and watched them die with a vacant grin on his face, well, boys will be boys.

Now he froze in deepest space. Now he burned in perdition's flames. Noises stabbed his ears and pummeled his brain while the stench of nearby sewage pipes sickened him.

Once in awhile, a limb wouldn't shift back and throbbed like an ulcerated tooth. He picked at his skin and tore out long strips. He scratched and chewed the stone floor, grinding his teeth and nails to bleeding nubs. It didn't matter; they grew back. And all the while, he had the feeling of something digging through his body, like a worm burrowing through an apple. It ate everything inside of him and shit it back into place.

Sometimes Himmler whispered at the window while Stark gnawed on a bone, cracking it open with his teeth and sucking out the marrow.

"A man whose mind is undismayed by sorrow, who has no further longing for pleasure, nor passion, fear or wrath is called a man of steadied thought, a silent sage, thus spoke Lord Krishna in the Bhagavad-Gita. Control, you must learn control. Listen to me! Unconditional and highest freedom of will comes from obedience to our masters."

Stark tried to tell Himmler that Lord Krishna was wrong, but he couldn't remember the right words. Plus, his throat was too dry, and his tongue was swollen with sores from the constant transformation of his mouth. A man whose mind is undismayed by sorrow, who has no further longing for pleasure, nor passion, fear or wrath is not a man of steadied thought or a silent sage. He is a temple plundered of its treasures and turned into a haunted palace where demons caper.

Stark could also hear the others endure their metamorphosis. Gunther cried without cease, forlorn sobs that echoed through the stone halls; Verning cursed people who were not there, insane ravings; and Hagen screamed and screamed and screamed. The cacophony rivaled the wailing and gnashing of teeth in hell.

But how could Hagen scream? He was mute.

160

And then it occurred to Stark—he was not a cripple after the Shift.

Control, you must learn control ...

Stark focused his hate. He bore down in his mind and tried to snatch the tail of the wild thing that raged through him. Sometimes he caught it, and it would tear loose, but he kept pursuing. He chased and clutched and grabbed and tried to hold on with all his strength—until that day came when he finally mounted it and rode it. He was clumsy at first, but he learned. Eventually he could shift at will. He shifted until his back, legs, and body became strong and then stopped ... unless he wanted to go further.

And all it cost was everything.

Stark entered a makeshift examination room. It consisted of a bed, a table covered with electronic instruments, a small chest of medical tools and other assorted laboratory equipment, including beakers, flasks and a Bunsen burner.

"Take off your clothes," Rascher said with a twitchy smile. "Please."

Normally, Stark hated being nude in front of others. He didn't want them to see his skinny limbs and twisted skeletal system, but things change. He removed his shirt and pants. Muscles rippled across his form in clean taut lines.

Rascher beckoned to the bed. "Sit, please."

Stark obeyed.

Rascher put a stethoscope to his chest. "How do you feel?"

"Perfect."

STEVE RUTHENBECK

"Breath in ... out ... good boy." Rascher picked up a pair of electrodes connected to what looked like a typewriter without keys. "Lie down, please."

Stark reclined. Rascher attached the wires to his chest.

"Roll over."

Rascher attached two more electrodes to Stark's back and a final pair to his temples. Then he went to the keyless typewriter and fiddled with its knobs. Paper spewed from a slot while a set of wires scratched zigzag lines across its surface. Rascher watched them with rapt attention. "Fascinating," he muttered, marking an occasional spot on the paper with his pen. That went on for five minutes. Then Rascher pulled a set of ink blots out and held them in front of Stark's face. "What do you see?"

"A monster on a bike."

Rascher flipped to the next inkblot.

"Negro women kissing."

"This one?"

"A butterfly smashed in a book."

"Last one."

"A snarling wolf."

Rascher smiled at Stark's final interpretation. He put the inkblots away and set a steel ball in the middle of the bedside table. "Try to move it with your mind."

Stark gave the doctor a disbelieving expression.

"Please," Rascher said, "for science."

Stark shrugged and concentrated on making the ball roll off the table. Nothing happened. Rascher watched the paper unfurling from the machine. The ball continued to go nowhere. Paper continued to flow. Rascher let the experiment run another minute and then ended it.

"That's enough." He noted the results, then pulled a small rubber bag out of his medical chest and handed it to Stark. "I want you to defecate in that."

"Now?"

"Is that an option?"

"No."

"Then at your convenience. Now ...let's see you shift."

Stark closed his eyes and willed the transformation to happen. Hair grew out of his skin, starting at his feet and swirling up to his face. His bones cracked and re-shaped themselves. It didn't hurt anymore. It felt good, like stretching after getting out of bed.

He smelled Rascher grow nervous. The scent was like rotten oranges. The needles on the machine scratched at a blur. The lines became a single black bar of peaks and valleys. Finally, the needles froze, and the machine died with a clunk and a puff of smoke.

"My god," Rascher whispered and dropped his clipboard.

There were many other tests. Rascher measured how fast they could run and how much weight they could lift. He tested their eyesight and reflexes. He took samples of their hair, blood, and tissue. He made them tell him their dreams under hypnosis. Bite pres-sure, vertical leap, hearing, and smelling abilities were also measured.

One day Rascher and Himmler took them out into the woods, wearing thick overcoats in the morning chill. Stark, Gunther, Verning, and Hagen weren't both-ered by the temperature, however. They breathed deep, enjoying the smell of the trees.

Verning picked up a stick, snapped it in half between his muscular hands and held it in front of Hagen's nose. "Fetch, boy! Fetch!"

"*Verpiss dich, Arschloch*," Hagen said.

Stark laughed. Even Gunther smiled, which was a rare occurrence after what happened to them. The smile didn't last long, however.

Four Jews were brought to them. They huddled with suspicious eyes, wondering what was going to happen to them. They stared at Himmler in disbelief when he told them to run. Himmler fired his pistol into the air until they took off. The gunshots echoed through the early morning stillness. Himmler looked at his watch. Fifteen minutes later he turned to Stark, Gunther, Verning, and Hagen and said, "Sic 'em!"

Himmler's room was furnished with a gilded desk, easy chairs and a bed. An oil painting showed King Henrich defeating the Magyar horse archers. A Gobelin tapestry illustrated a fully developed virginal girl, a future mother. On the opposite wall stood the statue of a woman with a lad who approached manhood.

Himmler sat at the desk and wore silk pajamas. His hair was messy, and his eyes were bloodshot behind his glasses. He sipped foul smelling tea, the odor of which reminded Stark of rotting corpses. Himmler tried to smile when they entered, but it was more of a grimace than anything else. He had stained teeth.

"My stomach," he explained. "Some days it feels like I swallowed a hot coal, but everyone has their cross to bear, and ours is a heavy one. Sometimes I wonder how history will remember us. The first steps to utopia are always heinous, but the end result justifies the means, yes?" Even though Himmler seemed to be a man brimming with confidence, Stark saw the contradicting undercurrent on his face. When all masks are removed, everyone is still the same—searching for approval.

"Sure," Stark replied.

"No matter," Himmler waved a hand in the air. "Jam yesterday and jam tomorrow, but we must work for our bread today. Gentlemen, I am pleased to inform you that you are now official members of the SS, its most secret and elite squad."

Verning and Hagen smiled. Gunther remained stolid. Stark's chest swelled with pride, and who knew where he could go from there? All he knew was that he planned to go far, farther than anyone could imagine. He sensed it was his destiny.

Yellow eyes on a black map.

Himmler passed out four boxes. The men discovered they contained SS uniforms. Stark touched the smooth black material of the tunic and button-fly trousers. Putting them on would be like slipping into a new skin. He couldn't wait to find a mirror. The box also contained a belt, a ceremonial dagger and a cap with a silver death's head. Stark tried the hat on. A sharp pain stabbed his skull like someone drilled an ice pick through his forehead. He cried out and swatted the cap off his scalp.

"What's wrong?" Himmler's voice drifted through the haze of hurt.

"My head," Stark gasped. "Something pricked me." He dabbed at the skin of his hairline and checked his fingertips for blood. None showed.

Himmler picked the hat off the floor and studied it for a few moments. He plucked the silver death's head off its crest. "Perhaps this is the culprit. The pin may have poked through the material." He held the grinning badge out to Stark. As soon as it touched Stark's palm, he hissed in pain and dropped it.

"It's red hot!"

Himmler picked the pin up with his bare hand and showed no ill effects. He held the shiny skull before his face, scowling in deep thought. Then his forehead smoothed.

"*Silver,*" he whispered.

CHAPTER

16

SURRENDER

CAIN AND RITTER entered a cottage. Ritter took a cautious lead with his flashlight. The living room contained a sparse collection of furniture and nothing more. A doorway gave passage into a kitchen, and a stairway led to an upper story.

Ritter's flashlight illuminated a snarling face. He squawked and refrained from blowing the creature to hell with his Thompson. The growling visage didn't belong to a dogman, however; it was just a mounted fox head.

The trophy glared at Ritter with dull marble eyes. Ritter gave it the finger and cursed his jumpy nerves. He wiped sweat from his forehead and turned to Cain.

"You check upstairs. I've got down here."

Cain gave no indication that he heard.

Ritter punched him in the shoulder. "Hey, asshole, wake up."

Cain raised his head. His face was pale, almost luminous in the dark. Brown smudges underscored his bloodshot eyes. Silent tears ran down his cheeks.

"What the hell's wrong with you?"

"My arm," Cain whispered and displayed his bitten limb. "It hurts."

"Yeah? Well, buck the fuck up." Ritter left Cain and entered the kitchen. He found the silverware drawer and examined a spoon under his flashlight. He had no experience with silver spoons, but he knew plain old pug steel when he saw it. He cast the spoon aside and rummaged through the rest of the utensils. Nothing.

He searched the cupboards. Maybe the owners of the house had silver candlesticks, a teapot, something, anything. He even searched a windowsill cup for silver coins and peeked inside a pot on the stove. It appeared to be filled with some sort of stew made from tulip bulbs. That was war for you. The invading army took all the food, and the indigenous population had to live off whatever they could scrounge up. Ritter gagged at the thought of how that shit would taste—cloying as all fuck—and reentered the living room.

He searched the china cabinet for any silver dishes, ashtrays, or what-the-hell-ever. Fortune refused to smile upon him. He slapped a frustrated hand on the table. The gesture reminded him of the day his father blew his brains out and took his mother along for the ride.

Goddamn 'em all to hell! This is not how things are supposed to be!

Ritter cast the memory aside. Better things existed to think about anyway, things that could turn *supposed to be* into reality, for instance. Ritter had to get that goddamn box. Then he'd be set forever. He licked his lips. The flashlight highlighted the lump of his brow and line of his elemental jaw. He looked like a Neanderthal as he grinned.

No more struggling, scraping, and planning.

Everyday would be gravy, nothing but gravy.

The box danced in Ritter's head, twisting and turning, dazzling him with desire. Something ran down his chin and startled him out of the vision. He touched his mouth, and his fingertips came away bloody. He had chewed through his lower lip. He wiped the blood on his fatigues and went through the rest of the downstairs. He fumed because he knew the search was futile. The place wasn't exactly decorated by the type of people who would own silver trinkets. But they needed it ... *needed* it.

Maybe the next cottage. Ritter went to the foot of the stairs. "Cain, let's go!"

No response.

"What the hell you doing up there?"

Thunder rumbled, but the upstairs remained silent.

Ritter reached into his bag of lucky ears and pulled out one of the cured pieces of flesh. He nervously rubbed it between his thumb and forefinger. "Cain!"

Still no answer.

"You goddamn worthless son of a bitch!"

Climbing the stairs was like climbing Mount Everest. Cain reached the top and stood on the verge of tumbling back down. Maybe the fall would crack his head open. That would be a relief.

The pressure inside was too much. It swelled with increasing misery, coming in like the tide on a shore of jagged rocks, dashing small sea creatures to death on the sharp edges. The house spun around him. He stumbled into a wall and pressed against it like a man navigating a narrow ledge above a gaping abyss.

His arm burned with molten heat. Surely acid soaked the bandages. Cain tore at them with his fingers and teeth. The pain receded to a small degree as cool air touched the bitten skin.

The wound wasn't even bleeding. It was almost healed. The fang marks were mere dimples in the flesh. Thick black hair sprouted from them.

Cain stumbled into a bedroom and shined his light around. The bobbing circle of illumination made him sick to his stomach. He flicked it off and could still see clearly. His neck itched. He scratched it. Coarse hairs grated under his fingernails.

Cain tripped his way toward the bed. He had to lie down for a minute. A minute wouldn't hurt anything. He would just close his eyes and rest for a bit. If only he wasn't so damn hungry. His stomach growled, but the noise seemed to come from his throat.

Cain smelled the mattress filling: goose down. His parents had geese when he was a child. They cut their heads off, and blood gouted from their necks. His mouth watered. The wind beat a shutter across the street, across the town.

Cain heard them all, distant applause at the curtain call of life. He listened to something highball through his veins like a virulent infection—a slithering swish. It was the sound of blood rushing through his body.

Ba-dump ... ba-dump ... ba-dump ...

Cain's heartbeat filled his head. Weird thoughts rose up from the cesspool of his subconscious and trailed slime through his brain. His name was called from the bottom of a deep well. *Cain ... Cain ... Cain ...*

He shivered. Burning. Freezing. Like when he stood in the bell tower. He was worried about Cheryl and his newborn child then. *What if? What if? What if?* The questions came back to him. The voice whispered in between them.

170

Cain strained to hear what it said. He sensed it had an answer—*the* answer.

What if the baby was born fine, but Cheryl wasn't? What if Cheryl was fine but the baby wasn't? What if it was a Mongoloid?

Wuu sss ah ck.

What if it had cerebral palsy? What if it had TB? What it if had polio?

Woo giss aw fck.

What if Cheryl dropped it on its head? What if the baby was blind? Deaf? What if it was born with its heart on the outside of its chest?

Ooh giss a fuck?

What if it was twins? Then twice as many things could go wrong …

Who gives a fuck?

Answering a question with a question. No worries existed anymore. It was a magic phrase. *Open Sesame! Abracadabra! Presto! Chango!* Cain smiled. He liked the sound his lips made sliding across his teeth. The pain ceased. It only hurt when he fought. Life's a pleasure when nothing is true and everything is permitted.

Yes, who gives a fuck for Cheryl? She's only good for one thing, and pretty soon she'll be worthless in that department, too. She just wants to pull you under. Women are like alligators once they get their claws into you. They bury you in mud and come back to eat you at their leisure. But what do you expect from a gender who goes through life with an open wound? And who gives a fuck for the baby? A parasite. They take and nothing more. They may as well have proboscises instead of noses—something sharp to jab into your chest and suck your blood.

Cain ripped at his clothes until they were rags at his feet.

Who gives a fuck for anything?

Dump-ba! Dump-ba! Dump-ba! Dump-ba!

Ritter's flashlight failed as he climbed the stairs. The beam faded ... faded ... faded ... plunging everything into darkness.

"Shit!" Ritter shook the light. The batteries rattled inside of the metal tube. It came back on for a moment, enough to get him to the top of the stairs and show him a short hall; then it died once more. Ritter slapped it against his palm. Nothing. Its light was hidden under the proverbial basket.

"Cain!" Ritter hissed. "Where are you?"

Sweat pricked his forehead and ran down his face. What if *they* got him? What if *they* were waiting for him to bumble into them right now? Ritter imagined claws flexing in the darkness. He raised his Thompson and passed a doorway. Lightning flashed. He saw a bed with a lump under its covers.

Ritter's fear evaporated into anger.

"Cain! Get up, you fucking wimp!"

Thunder boomed.

"Cain!"

No response.

Ritter laid hold of Cain's sleeping form. "Get up, I said!"

The new and improved Cain erupted from the blankets in a blur of black fur and fangs. A clawed hand grabbed Ritter's neck. Beady red eyes gleamed in the dark, and teeth glittered around a snarl.

"Jesus," Ritter tried to say, but the paw around his throat allowed no words to escape. "You're supposed to be—"

Then the hand lifted Ritter off his feet. Sharp claws sliced into his belly, and the sounds of feeding merged with grunts of pain.

A bag of ears spilled across the floor, and a fresh one plopped among them.

CHAPTER 47

DEFEAT

"FIND ANYTHING?" Kenway asked by rote. He didn't notice Chaplain's lack of response. His attention was focused on the life he held in his hands.

Kenway clutched a framed photograph. A man and a woman on skis leaned against each other within its frame. They both laughed, arms wrapped around each other for support. Their cheeks touched, and their eyes glinted with a happy sparkle. Each time the lightning flashed, Kenway saw his face superimposed over them, reflected in the glass of the picture frame.

He reached up and rubbed his cheek, imagining how the man in the photo must feel. He stood like that with Jennifer once. They were on a dock, watching the sun set behind a lake. It felt good. Now all he felt was raspy stubble as he remembered how she looked when he tried to bring her the tulips.

Down on all fours, the other behind her, their eyes lolling like animals ...

Kenway's eyes roved over the pictures on the fireplace mantle. Here the man and the woman stood in a suit and white dress at the altar of the town church. A preacher blessed their union while Christ witnessed from his crucifix. A single candle burned beside them.

There the man and the woman posed next to the cottage. A white dog sat beside their feet and looked at the camera with alert eyes and a closed muzzle—wolf-like. Another photo showed the man grin and hold an infant wrapped in a blanket above his head. The woman rocked the baby in another frozen moment while the man stood behind them. A final photograph, larger than the rest, showed the man and the woman with a group of people. Everyone smiled—old, young, everyone.

It was all so easy for some.

Kenway replaced the photograph and noted the frame—proof that people liked to contain things. The frame gave them a way to contain even memories. It was human nature to put things and other people in boxes, to save and collect, perhaps to give themselves the illusion they controlled their life, or maybe just for comfort. They lived in boxes. They drove boxes. They bought food and necessities in boxes. They sat on boxes, dreamed on boxes, put babies to sleep in boxes, and got buried in boxes.

Sometimes they even hid things in boxes—horrible things, secret things, like putting them out of sight somehow made them forgivable. Such things always had a way of escaping, however, as Pandora learned. Darkness wants to be in the light. Everything either wants to get in or get out. Everything is either trapped or safe, but always contained.

Kenway thought of the box and heard something crash in the bedroom.

Chaplain!

The dollhouse had white walls and black shingles. Its windows were made of real glass and had forest green shutters. A little brass knocker hung in the middle of the front door and glittered with happy idealism. Miniature rooms contained comfortable looking furniture and tiny swatches of carpet. A father doll sat at a small desk and wrote something, maybe a sermon. A mother doll prepared a meal in the kitchen. A lump rested under the covers of a matchbox bed—a doll child—perhaps a daughter.

Chaplain clenched his teeth until their enamel cracked.

Kenway's voice drifted down the hall: "Find anything?"

Chaplain knew where to find plenty of silver, but what did it matter? It was all a fool's errand. The box was no prize. It was just another dollhouse, and they were its dolls.

But at least it didn't look back:

The floodgates containing Chaplain's fury burst open. A high-pressure whistle escaped from between his clenched teeth. He kicked the miniature home. Its walls collapsed like Jericho's as its roof caved in. Furniture flew from orderly spots.

The dolls covered their heads as Judgment Day befell them and their happy lives crumbled into senseless chaos. Chaplain could almost hear their tiny screams. He stomped on the house again and again, grinding it into dust under his heel.

But it wasn't enough.

Chaplain turned his rage on the room. He slammed his gun butt through the wall. He tipped over a dresser, drew his knife and slashed the bed. Feathers swirled around him, caught up in the wind of his fury. His actions were the futile reflexes of a twitching corpse, however. The room meant nothing to him. He wanted to destroy the past.

Kenway burst through the door with his gun at ready.

Chaplain spun. Slobber hissed through his bared teeth.

"What the hell's wrong with you?" Kenway demanded.

Chaplain didn't answer. He remembered the day he died. He drew his knife down his arm, but the pain did nothing to mask the memories. It just made them worse.

✠　✠　✠

CHAPLAIN SAT AT HIS DESK and looked out the window, trying to generate an idea for Sunday's sermon. An apple tree stood in the middle of the lawn. White blossoms covered its branches. Insects flitted between their petals in search of nectar. The message came to him then. He saw it all from beginning to end. He typed.

Do you know how a worm gets inside of an apple? People once thought that it burrows a hole from the outside, but that is not the case. An insect lays an egg in the apple blossom. The worm hatches inside the heart of the fruit and eats its way out. In a similar fashion, humans beings are born with a sinful nature. It's a voracious beast that lives within and desires to devour our souls. The struggle between man and his sinful nature is a great war. It's a war that has taken billions of casualties since the beginning of time. It's a war that we cannot win ... but it has been won for us.

"What big eyes you have!"

A bonnet-wearing wolf filled Chaplain's vision. He uttered a squawk of surprise and laughed.

Ruth was seven years-old and the spitting image of her mother—blond hair, blue-eyes, and rosy cheeks nicked with dimples. The wolf from *Little Red Riding Hood* was her favorite doll. Chaplain picked her up and set her in his lap. "You shouldn't sneak up on your dad like that. You'll give him gray hair."

Ruth giggled at the notion. "Come play fairy tales with me."

"Can't," Chaplain flicked the end of her nose. "I'm writing Sunday's sermon."

"Pleeeeeze!"

"Sorry, pumpkin. Work before play."

"But it's 11:45," Ruth argued, "It'll be 11:50 by the time you get rid of me. Then it'll take you two minutes to get started again, and mom'll tell you it's almost dinner time three minutes after that. Then it'll take you another two minutes to get restarted, and by then you'll have to stop and eat anyway. So why don't you just play fairy tales with me for a whole fifteen minutes? Then you can work on your sermon all afternoon."

Ruth's attempt at logical debate made Chaplain smile. Sometimes he found her so smart and beautiful it hurt.

"All right, you talked me into it."

Ruth cheered and lead him to her room. Her dollhouse had white walls, black shingles and lots of tiny furniture. She had a collection of fairy tale characters to go with it, such as Jack in the Beanstalk, Little Red Riding Hood, the Wolf, the Three Little Pigs, the Tortoise and the Hare. She also had eight lead soldiers in Civil War uniforms. They besieged the dollhouse while the animals watched from its windows.

"What are we playing?" Chaplain asked.

"The soldiers are fighting the animals."

"Why are they doing that?"

"It's just the way things are," Ruth shrugged and handed Chaplain her favorite toy. "Here, you be Wolfie."

They played the saga out the best they could in the time they had.

"Dinner!" a woman called ten minutes later.

Chaplain jumped to his feet. "Last one there has to do dishes!"

Ruth squealed, picked up her wolf doll and ran down the hall. Chaplain chased her into the dining room. Esther set the last of the food on the table. Gold hair framed her aristocratic features while a white apron molded to her contours. God's marriage equation flashed through Chaplain's head when he saw her: $1 + 1 = 1$. She was everything to him, with Ruth being the physical manifestation of that union.

Sometimes, in the dead of night when the dark had weight, Chaplain would wonder: *what would I become if I lost them?*

Esther gave her husband and daughter a good-natured scowl as they burst into the room. She favored Chaplain with the greatest portion, however. "You're teaching her bad manners, my dear. You're going to end up with a ragamuffin instead of a lady."

"Now we're in trouble." Chaplain winked at Ruth. "I told you not to run."

"Did not!" Ruth shook her head with glee. "You told me to run *super* fast!"

"Fibs," Chaplain said with all innocence and turned to Esther with a half-grin. "She must get that from your side of the family."

Esther smacked his backside with a spoon. "Watch it, buster. By the way, sweet daughter of mine, what's the eighth commandment again? Isn't it something about lying? Perhaps you better recite it for your father. He seems to be having a lapse."

"Thou shalt not bear false witness against thy neighbor!" Ruth quoted in a sing-song voice. "What does this mean? We should fear and love God that we may not deceitfully belie, betray, slander, nor defame our neighbor, but defend him, speak well of him, and put the best construction on everything."

"Very good," Chaplain nodded. "You passed the test. This whole conversation was just a ploy to see if you did your memory work."

Esther rolled her eyes.

Ruth noticed her mother's expression. "Don't worry, Mom. He's not setting a bad example. I knew he was kidding the *whole* time."

"Discernment is a fine thing," Esther agreed. "You must have gotten that from his side of the family. If we had it on mine, I would have married someone else."

"Okay, okay," Chaplain laughed. "I give up. Let the witty banter cease and the eating commence." The three of them sat down and folded their hands while Chaplain said grace. "Come, Lord Jesus, be our guest and let these gifts to us be blessed, and thank you for my rapier-witted wife and daughter of good memory."

"And thank you for my slightly slow-on-the-uptake husband," Esther added with a bemused smile. "He makes being rapier-witted so easy."

"And thank you for my goofy mom and dad," Ruth finished. "Amen."

Chaplain picked up the gravy bowl. "One lump or two?"

A knock at the door interrupted Esther's retort. "You're lucky," she waggled a finger at Chaplain and got up to see to their visitors.

Chaplain picked at his food while she was gone. Whenever they got a knock it usually meant one of two things.

Either someone was stopping by for a friendly chat, which was unlikely over the noon hour, or it was bad news—someone died, someone got hurt, someone got sick, or someone needed help, money, or advice.

He hoped it was nothing serious. Eventually, Esther lead two men into the dining room.

They wore grubby clothes. Beards covered their faces, and shaggy hair sprouted from beneath sweat-stained hats. One of them was huge, topping three hundred pounds or more. He stood at least six foot nine and had to duck coming through the doorway. His partner was just the opposite—short and skinny. He had a crooked nose that looked like it got broken in a fistfight. They both smiled, showing yellow teeth.

Chaplain felt a twinge of distaste. He wasn't fond of bums. Too many were parasites who had no interest in holding down jobs when they could mooch off others. Then he silently berated himself for such an uncharitable thought. They were God's children, too. Who knew what befell them to put them in their present situation? Maybe they were robbed or lost their jobs or were just trying to get home.

"Gentlemen," Esther said, "this is my husband, Pastor Chaplain."

The big one grinned. "Pastor Chaplain, huh? Isn't that kind of redundant?"

"I guess God just knew what line of work he wanted me in from the beginning."

"Well, it's good to know you serve a purpose. My name's Farrow." The big man jerked a thumb at his partner. "This here's my friend, Phil LeSteen."

Phil shook Chaplain's hand. His palm was slick with sweat and felt amphibious. "That's quite a grip you've got there, pastor."

"I like to help the church members with harvest." Chaplain explained. "Physical labor's good for a man. It keeps him honest."

"Ain't that the truth," Phil nodded while his tongue probed a cold sore.

Despite their appearance, neither man had the slow wits or faraway eyes of an alcoholic. Most of the vagrants who stopped by did. The church was on the main road out of town, which the hoboes took to as soon as they hopped off the train or were kicked off by the rail warden. The church was usually their first stop.

It was a tricky thing to help such men. When they asked for money, nine times out of ten it didn't go toward getting them back home or helping them pay for grandma's operation; it went toward booze. Still, Chaplain tried to give them some sort of assistance. It wasn't a perfect world. One could only reflect the love of Christ the best they could.

"Farrow and Phil are on their way to Louisiana," Esther said. "They haven't had anything to eat for two days and wondered if we could spare something."

"Certainly," Chaplain replied. "There's plenty to go around. Have a seat."

"Much obliged." Farrow sat down. The chair creaked under his weight.

Esther set out plates for the two men.

Chaplain noticed Farrow's eyes follow her backside and chest as she moved about the room. He signed inwardly and lost a little more respect for the two men.

Meanwhile, Phil turned his attention to Ruth. His nostrils flared like a rat scenting a piece of cheese. "And who might you be, darling?"

"Ruth," she said shyly.

"You like jokes, Ruth?"

"Sure."

"Why did six run away from seven?"

"I don't know."

"Seven ate nine!"

Ruth smiled.

"A hamburger walks into a bar, and the bartender says, we don't serve food here."

It took Ruth a few seconds to get it; then she laughed.

"That's it," Phil said. "A little girl with a smile as pretty as yours should laugh all the time. Laughing's good for you, just ask your mom."

"Is it, mom?"

"It sure is," Esther smiled. She returned to her seat and passed food around the table. "So, what takes you two gentlemen to Louisiana?"

"It's home," Farrow replied. "We were out west picking apples, but decided to go back and enlist. The country's going to need all the fighting men it can get before too long. That Hitler won't be satisfied until he owns the whole planet."

"I'm afraid you're right," Chaplain agreed. "It's a sad state of affairs, but the world will never lack for wars. Even Jesus said as much." Chaplain belittled himself for judging the two men earlier. And maybe Farrow did have a rogue eye, but he and his friend were at least trying to do their best for their country—a noble endeavor.

"That sure is a nice doll," Phil gestured at Ruth's Grandma Wolf while he slurped up a spoonful of corn. "Do you like animals, sugar pie?"

"Uh-huh."

"Well, let me tell you a dirty joke about an animal then. A pig fell in mud!" He wrinkled his nose and snorted in Ruth's ear. "Oink! Oink! Oink!"

Ruth laughed with delight.

"Yeah, animals are fun," Phil gave Ruth an amicable smile. "Me and Farrow used to be around them all the time. We worked in a circus, you know."

"Really?"

"Yep. It had lions, tigers, bears, elephants, horses, monkeys. It even had a snake."

"Keyword being *had*," Farrow broke in.

"What happened?" Ruth asked.

"We were performing in Peoria," Phil explained. "It was the final act of the show. After some death-defying stunts with the lions, the animal trainer—"

"Name of Mike," Farrow interrupted.

"Yeah, Mike, brought out a thirty-foot boa constrictor for the big finale."

"What's a bow conscriptor?" Ruth asked.

"Bo-ah con-strict-or," Esther corrected her. "It's a snake."

"A thirty-foot snake?" Ruth scoffed. "You sure you're not making that up?"

"I'm not exaggerating, darling. Some snakes grow even bigger than that."

"The ones around here don't," Ruth said and continued on in the scatter-shot conversation style of the young. "The devil was a snake when he made Eve eat the apple in the Garden of Eden. Maybe he was a boa constrictor then?"

"Well, I don't know anything about that," Phil replied. "All I know is what happened to Mark that day—"

"Mike," Farrow said.

"Right, Mike. Anyway, he took the snake out of its cage and wrapped it around himself until he was completely covered by the beast."

Ruth's eyes widened.

"Everything was going fine. He did the same trick lots of times. Then the boa raised its head and just stared into

184

Mike's face. Next thing you know, Mike lets out this horrible scream. The crowd cheered. They thought it was all part of the act. Then they heard bones crack as the snake crushed Mike in its coils. The boa's natural instincts returned just like that. One second it was a pet. The next second it was a killer."

"Oh my!" Esther exclaimed, "that's awful!"

"Yes, ma'am," Farrow agreed with her sentiment. "But that's how it is; animals have that bad nature to them. Sometimes it just kicks in. People are the same way. You never know when someone will go rabid on you and bite. And the worse part is," he paused with weighty emphasis, *"you can never see it coming."*

"What did they do with the snake?" Ruth asked.

"They cut its head off," Phil replied matter-of-factly. "It was the only way they could get it to let go of Mike. Hey, do you want to see a snake?"

Ruth wasn't born yesterday. "You don't have no snake with you."

"Sure do. Farrow's got one, too."

"Where?"

"In our trousers."

"Excuse me?" Chaplain broke into the conversation. He couldn't have heard that right. Saying such a thing to a child—to anyone—was just too wrong. He rose from his seat, propelled by incredibility, and Farrow shoved him back into his chair.

By then, Esther was up. "What are you—"

Farrow grabbed her in a bear hug and laughed.

A knife appeared at Chaplain's throat before he could regain his composure. It all happened so fast, from peace to peril, just like that.

"Don't move," Phil hissed.

Jesus, God, what's happening?

Ruth started crying and covered her face.

Phil spoke with infinite gentleness. "Stop crying, baby. We're just playing a game. Now, how about you get in that closet while we grown ups have a private chat?" He whispered in Chaplain's ear. "Get her in there, or you'll be sorry."

Chaplain's voice trembled. "Go in the closet, Ruth. It'll be okay."

Thou shalt not bear false witness …

"Daddy?"

"Go in the closet," Esther added her shrill voice to the mix.

Ruth nodded, sniffling back tears. She took her doll into the closet and pulled the door shut, casting them one final heartbreaking glance.

Farrow immediately jammed a chair under the closet's doorknob. Then he turned to the window, ripped down the curtains and shredded them.

Chaplain cringed. "What're you doing?"

Move! Do something!

"Don't get any bright ideas," Phil read Chaplain's mind and kept the knife pressed against his throat, "and you'll make it out of this just fine, preacher man."

"Why are you—"

"Because we can," Farrow cut Chaplain off and began tying him to the chair. The curtain strips dug deep grooves into his wrists. He hissed in pain.

Move, you fool, before it's too late!

No, don't do anything stupid.

"Comfy?" Farrow asked once Chaplain was secure.

"I don't know why you're doing this, but I'm begging you to stop."

"A preacher shouldn't be so adverse to sharing, you know."

"What do you want? Money?"

Farrow turned to Esther and smiled. "Take off your clothes."

Esther gasped, dumbfounded, and then her gaze swiveled to Chaplain. Silent, futile, communication passed between the two of them, and he saw that her love bound her tighter than the curtain strips around his wrists.

"No," Chaplain said. "God, no …"

"I said, take off your clothes!" Farrow barked.

Esther didn't move.

"Show them how it works, Phil."

Phil slashed the knife across Chaplain's chest, drawing an ugly gash along his ribs. Chaplain cried out. Esther screamed.

Muffled cries came from the closet: "Mommy? Daddy?"

"Those are the rules of the game, sweetheart," Farrow said. "You don't do what I say, and your husband pays for it. Got it?"

Esther blinked back shock.

"Do you understand?" Farrow shouted.

"Y-y-yes, but—"

"Then shut up and strip!"

The psychotic sheen of Phil and Farrow's faces matched the shine of the knife at Chaplain's throat. Esther realized she had no choice and undid her apron with trembling fingers. It dropped to the ground and pooled around her feet.

"Take your time," Farrow smiled.

Chaplain's mind jammed up with the senselessness of the situation. How did things come to this? He was just writing his sermon. He was just playing with Ruth. They were just eating dinner, having witty banter. The sun was still shining outside. The apple tree was probably waving in the breeze, its petals falling to the ground and covering the grass like a miniature snowstorm. They just tried to help a pair of drifters like they had done a dozen times before. And now ... now.

Do something!

Esther undid her skirt and revealed bloomers that went down to mid-thigh. She reached up and unbuttoned her shirt. Falling tears dotted its material. She let the garment drift to the floor like an oversized leaf. Then she stood in her underwear. She seemed to shrink in on herself like a flower dying in the desert sun.

"Oh yeah," Phil whispered. He pressed himself against Chaplain's back. Chaplain felt the man's excitement and wanted to be sick.

"Don't," Chaplain groaned, one final plea.

Phil replied with another joke: "Where's a pig who's on fire from?"

Then the butt of the knife slammed into Chaplain's skull and all went black.

Chaplain awoke. How much later, he didn't know. His head throbbed in time to the beat of his heart. Two thoughts stabbed through his brain like drill bits: Ruth! Esther! The chair lay broken beneath him. He must have tipped over after Phil cold-cocked him. The cracked backrest allowed him to wiggle his arms free. He tore at the curtain strips holding his wrists with his teeth. He smelled his own sour sweat and something else. What was it? Burning pork? He looked around wildly. No sign of Farrow or Phil. The table was still set with their shared meal.

The Last Supper ...

Come Lord Jesus, be our guest ...

Everything was silent ... except for a faint sizzling sound. Chaplain's right hand slipped free. Then he untied his legs and stood up. A wave of dizziness overcame him.

The vision of his left eye dissolved into a hazy snowstorm. He had a concussion.

Ruth! Esther!

Chaplain stumbled into the kitchen. The stench and sizzling grew stronger. He spotted their source and stopped as if he had run into a brick wall. His face went slack. His eyes bugged. An invisible spear skewered his insides.

Oh, Christ, oh, God, oh ...no ...

Esther sat on top of the stove, strangled by a hank of curtain. Her tongue protruded from her mouth like a dead slug while her buttocks rested on the lit stove burners. Flesh sizzled. Smoke rose. A word was carved into her chest: *Burningham.*

Where's a pig who's on fire from?

1 − 1 = 0

Maniacal laughter screamed inside Chaplain's head. He wanted to fall down and die and puke and scream and rip the world apart with his bare hands, but Ruth, *Ruth!* He stumbled back into the dining room, tearing open the broom closet.

Empty.

"Ruth! Where are you?"

Chaplain tripped his way to his daughter's room. The concussion made it hard to keep his balance. He fell through the doorway. The dollhouse was still in the middle of the floor. The fight with the animals left the soldiers scattered around its base. The wolf doll gazed up at Chaplain with sympathetic eyes.

What big eyes you have ...

The bed had a child-sized lump under its covers.

"Ruth?"

Let her be okay, scared, hiding under the covers, just hiding, just scared, not hurt, not ... touched ... not ...

A drop of blood stained the comforter. Chaplain's heart seized up in his chest. The pain of it nearly incapacitated him. The drop was small, no more than dime-sized. That's all there was, just one drop. One tiny drop ...

Oh God, let her be okay, please, Jesus ...

Chaplain pulled the bedspread away.

The scream was too big to fit through his throat. It got caught in his sternum and expanded, growing larger and larger until it threatened to burst his chest like an over-inflated balloon. The world swam. The jagged sound of breaking glass filled his ears. He went to his knees, turning away; he had to turn way. Vomit barreled up his throat and exploded out of his mouth in a geyser spray.

As he lay on the floor, he looked straight into the dollhouse, past the animals and soldiers, into the very heart of the structure and the treasure that it contained.

A pair of blue eyes gazed through its front window ...

Chaplain shrieked as his life shifted out of the white and into the black.

CHAPTER 18

FORGE

THE FIRE BURNED white hot and hissed like a dragon in a trap. Heat waves distorted reality and pushed the cold away. For the first time since they jumped, the men knew warmth.

None of them took time to savor the sensation, however. The Major threw another wooden balustrade into the hastily constructed brick forge. Berg and Kenway worked fireplace bellows and fanned its flames to a molten temperature.

Mac sat on a nearby pew with two flowerpots, a pliers and a lap full of bullets. He removed slugs from shell casings and pushed their noses into the potted soil.

Chaplain watched the door—token guard duty. If the beasts wanted in, they'd get in; it was that simple—unless they were too busy with Cain and Ritter. The two men hadn't returned. The odds of them doing so grew longer with each passing minute.

The Major leaned over the forge. The heat baked his face and brought tears to his eyes. "More air. We have to get this thing burning merry hell."

Kenway and Berg had their shirts off and gritted their teeth with exertion. The muscles of their arms and chests bulged as they worked the bellows. Sweat dripped from their bodies and extinguished whatever sparks landed on their skin.

The Major laid the metal grillwork of a music stand across the forge and set a frying pan on top of it. The hottest part of the flames licked its bottom.

"What if the pan melts?" Kenway asked.

"Not a chance. Silver melts before iron. Keep pumping. Tell me when the pan gets red hot." The Major went to check on Mac's progress. "What's the story?"

"It's a bitch," Mac growled and yanked another bullet apart. He set the casing aside, careful not to spill any of its powder, and pressed the slug into the dirt.

"How many do you have?"

"Twenty-seven."

The Major grabbed a handful of bullets and a second pair of pliers. "We'll do a hundred. We don't have enough silver for much more than that anyway."

"We don't have many bullets either."

"Life's a pain in the ass," the Major agreed. "Deal with it."

Firelight etched all of their faces in demonic lines and shadows as they performed their tasks and stoked the fires of madness. Visions of the box filled their heads—obsession, wishing, and fantastic desire. Finally, Kenway came out of the fugue long enough to notice that the center of the frying pan glowed a dull orange.

"It's ready!"

The Major rejoined them. He spit into the pan and watched it evaporate into instant nothingness. "It'll do." He reached into his pack and pulled out the silver lock and two keys that Mac found in one of the houses. Acid etched the lock's surface, creating a beautiful pattern of flowers and vines entwined around the word "*Amour*". The Major dropped the creation into the frying pan. "Burn, baby, burn."

Eventually, the hasp of the lock sagged and touched the bottom of the frying pan. The keys lost their definition and took on flat shapes. Liquid appeared at the base of the lock and oozed across the pan like yolk from a fried egg.

The Major wrapped a wet rag around his hand, drew his knife, and poked at the lock and keys. They took on a sludgy consistency. He smeared them across the bottom of the frying pan. The melting process increased as the surface area of the lock and keys grew wider. The Major stirred the gleaming mess with his knife until all solidity was gone.

"The trials of existence shape us, on Earth—life's forge, pray that you live as a plowshare, and don't get tempered as a sword ..."

The words of Chaplain's verse hung in the air. The fire's glow brought out the skeletal structure of his face. A ghastly smile creased his lips. The other men experienced vertigo from staring into his deep emptiness.

"Where did you learn that?" Berg asked.

"I didn't learn it. I live it."

"Fuck the poetry," the Major hissed. "Bring the bullets."

Mac slid the slug-filled flowerpot next to the Major. The Major picked up the frying pan and poured the silver into the hollow backs of the bullets. Once finished, he set the frying pan back on the forge where it gleamed with the residue of liquid silver.

The Major wiped sweat from his brow. "All right, now we let them cool."

A hollow boom echoed through the church, and a cold wind swept over the five men as they turned toward the open front doors. Rain cascaded into the cathedral with the pitter patter of rat's feet. A shadow stood in the tomb-like opening. Lightning crashed behind it, illuminating its ragged silhouette.

Berg recognized the figure. "Cain!"

The soldier staggered into the church. The other men could see that he was in rough shape as he neared the light of the fire. His face was dark and muddy. Ragged clothes hung from his bloody frame. His wide, blank eyes stared.

The Major stepped forward. "We gave up on you. What happened?"

Cain opened his mouth to answer, but all that came out was a series of unintelligible grunts. The corners of his lips curled down into a silent sob.

"Where's Ritter?"

"*What if?*" Cain whispered. "*What if? What if?*"

"He's in shock," Kenway said.

"Tough shit," the Major replied. "We don't have time for that." He questioned Cain once more. "Where's Ritter? Do you know if he's still alive?"

"Ritter?" Cain repeated, confused.

The Major frowned. Cain's face wasn't covered with mud. It was covered with beard growth. The dark hair went all the way down his neck and up his cheeks, almost to his lower eyelids. His eyebrows had even merged into a single line that slashed across his brow from temple to temple. "What the hell?"

Cain tried to speak again. "I … I'm …" Then a sly smile spread across his lips like seagull shit running down the side of a building, "*I'm hungry!*" His eyes flashed red. Fangs distended from his upper jaw. He raised clawed hands.

"Christ!" the Major shouted. "Shoot the bastard!"

194

Chaplain put a burst of bullets into Cain's guts. Cain bounced off a pew and collapsed to the ground. He lay there, dazed and panting. Blood oozed from his wounds.

The other soldiers grabbed their weapons and gathered around him.

"He got bit," Kenway said, his voice high with horror. "Remember? He got bit back at the bank. Maybe it transmits, like rabies. Infected. Maybe—"

Cain's dry chuckle interrupted Kenway's theory. "More," he gasped, "so much more." His voice sounded like gravel in a tin drum. Drool dripped from his maw, and his eyes glittered with malevolence. "Nothing but eating and not eating."

"What are we going to do with him?" Berg's voice cracked.

It didn't take the Major long to answer. "Let's see how the new bullets work."

Cain smiled around sharp fangs. "*Even a man who's pure in heart and says his prayers at night, may become a wolf when the wolfsbane blooms, and the autumn moon is bright.*" The men recognized the quote as coming from Universal Picture's, *The Wolf Man.* Cain's words trailed off into a lunatic gale of laughter, which then turned into a violent shaking fit. His body trembled like each cell was an animal fighting against its neighbor. The veins of his neck stood out in harsh relief, pumped to the point of bursting. He yowled and his flesh bubbled and popped over reshaping bones.

"Jesus," Mac half-prayed, half-swore.

"You couldn't be more wrong!" Cain growled around bleeding gums and rearranging teeth. "I wish you could know what I know. Maybe some of you will. But I can't tell you on an empty stomach!" He exploded to his feet in a blur of motion.

Chaplain pulled the trigger of his Thompson. The Major and Mac fired their .45s. Bullets chewed up the portion of floor the beast occupied an instant before. He scrambled into the darkness of the church. His laughter echoed through the building.

"Fan out!" the Major ordered. "Get the son of a bitch!"

Flashlights speared the gloom. Claws clicked on stone. Kenway spun toward the source of the noise. Nothing. He swallowed the taste of fear. Lightning flashed through stained-glass windows, illuminating martyr deaths while thunder boomed.

"Here!" Mac shouted. A burst of machinegun fire blasted through the church. "Get over here! Now!" The men converged on the spot.

"Where?" Berg shouted.

A curl of smoke drifted from Mac's gun. "Under the seats."

The men turned in nervous circles, weapons to shoulders and flashlights held beneath barrels. Kenway spotted a black shape ducking between pews. "There!"

The men opened fire. Cain sprinted, becoming beastlier with each stride. He jumped up and ran across the pews, feet stepping from backrest to backrest. He leapt onto the wall and dangled from a windowsill like a monkey. Slugs shattered the glass above him. It rained across the floor with a musical tinkle. Cain dropped back down into the shadows, out of sight. He shouted a garbled, misquoted William Blake verse.

"Man, man, burning bright, in the forests of the night, what immortal hand or eye can frame thy fearful symmetry?"

Seconds passed. The storm beat against the church. Hearts beat against chests.

"Where'd he go?" the Major whispered.

Trigger fingers itched. Eyes blinked away sweat. Teeth chewed on lower lips. Ears strained for the sound of movement. Someone sniffed.

"I think I smell him," Berg said. "He's close."

Then Berg screamed like a woman giving birth. Growling filled the air as he was dragged under the pews. His gun went off, and he put a full clip into the ceiling. Chunks of stone and wood rained down on the others.

"Son of a bitch!" Mac shouted and grabbed one of Berg's flailing arms.

"He's got me!" Berg screamed. "Jesus Christ, he's got me!"

Mac heaved. The sound of tearing cloth filled the air. Berg screamed louder. Mac dropped his rifle and grabbed hold of Berg with both hands.

"Help me!" Berg shrieked.

Kenway dove onto the floor. He shoved the barrel of his Thompson underneath the pew and caught a momentary glimpse of beady eyes and snarling teeth. Then he opened fire. The Cain-thing scrambled away like a gigantic crab.

Mac pulled Berg to his feet. Berg's pants were shredded. Blood flowed.

"Oh, God," Berg moaned. "Oh, Jesus. My legs." He pulled the tattered material apart with trembling fingers, trying to gauge the extent of the wounds.

The Major stepped forward to examine Berg's injuries, as well. Something caught his eye. He spun around with his flashlight. "Look out!"

Cain, more dog than man now, hefted a pew over his head and threw it at the group of men with vicious strength. They dove to the floor. It slammed into the altar behind them. The impact shook the crucifix hanging above it. Christ swayed and then dropped from his mounts. The base of his cross smashed into the top of the altar, and then the entire thing tipped forward like a falling tree, heading straight for Chaplain.

Chaplain watched the stone Christ swoop toward him. The sight registered no surprise, only a bitter resignation to the inevitable.

It's about time. I'm already dead anyway.

He put his hands up, closed his eyes and tumbled backwards in a reflexive motion of avoidance.

A tremendous crash. Chaplain opened his eyes. Christ's face was inches from his own. The arms of the crucifix hit the pews on either side of the aisle and stopped its downward progress. Chaplain looked up into the fire-lit visage. It contained neither anguish nor sorrow nor wrath. It held only pity and disappointment.

Why don't you just finish me, God? Please—

Rough hands grabbed Chaplain under his armpits and dragged him out from beneath Christ's implacable gaze.

"You all right?" Kenway asked.

"No," Chaplain shrugged his hand away.

A hairy form smashed into Kenway. The two of them hit the floor. Cain snarled and spit. Kenway buried his hands in the hair of the dogman's cheeks and tried to hold the twisted face at bay. The monster's snout sank with irresistible force and opened wide to rip out his throat. Hot saliva dripped in Kenway's face.

"Get him off me!"

Chaplain threw himself at Cain. The two of them rolled down the aisle. A slavering muzzle came for Chaplain's face. He raised a hand to ward it off. Teeth sank into his palm. Chaplain cried out, ripped the hand free and punched the beast in the nose. It howled in rage.

Chaplain slammed his knee into the monster's groin. It tumbled off him. Chaplain scuttled away on his hands, heels and rear and smashed into something hot. *The forge!* He grabbed the handle of the frying pan and flung it at the monster. Drops of molten silver splattered across the dogman's chest. Cain screamed as it melted into his flesh. Smoke rose from red holes. He ran in frenzied circles, insane with agony. His high-pitched yips could have shattered crystal. Finally, the beast bounded across the church and jumped through a window in one powerful leap.

Chaplain struggled to regain his breath. Kenway appeared beside him and helped him to his feet. The Major, Berg and Mac joined them.

"From now on, if anyone gets bit, shoot them immediately," the Major growled. His eyes happened upon Berg's bloody legs. He raised his pistol and pointed it at the soldier's face. "An ounce of prevention is worth a pound of cure."

"No!" Berg cried. "He didn't bite me! They're claw marks! Look!" He pulled up his pants like a pretty woman trying to hitch a ride. Ugly scratches marked his shins and calves. There didn't appear to be any teeth marks.

Kenway examined the wounds. "I think he's right."

Berg nodded with enthusiastic agreement. "Yeah, he thinks I'm right."

"You willing to bet on that?" the Major asked.

"We watch him," Kenway said. "If something happens, I'll shoot him myself. In the meantime, we're developing a shortage of manpower in case you haven't noticed."

The Major's left eye ticked. For a moment, he looked like he would press the issue; then he backed down. "So be it, but if he gets so much as a single chest hair, kill him.

He won't be so easy after that. Now, let's finish the bullets and move out. We're going hunting. We only get twenty silver slugs each. Make them count."

Unnoticed by any of them, Chaplain flexed his bitten hand. He winced in pain and wiped the blood on his pants.

CHAPTER

CIVIL WAR

THE UNIVERSE CONTAINS billions of galaxies. Gold veins the size of Mount Everest exist, as do planetary cores of solid diamond. Storms erode hills into valleys. Earthquakes turn canyons into mountains. Volcanoes bury planets in their own molten guts. Super tornadoes spew the ashes into space. Comets streak through the frozen reaches and tear the nebulas apart. Worlds collide. Rogue stars pulse. Solar systems burn.

Within the perpetual destruction, a blue jewel totters on the brink between life and death. A small change in ratio among its atmospheric gases would result in worldwide suffocation. Slowing the speed of its rotation would turn it into a ball of permafrost. Any closer to the sun and its surface would boil. Any closer to the moon and tsunamis would sweep over its continents twice a day. While such water makes life possible, the salt content of its oceans renders them poison. The sun evaporates the seawater into clouds, however, and they scatter fresh water over the earth as rain.

The cold rain fell without cease as the storm stalled over Le Coeur. The lightning cracks might have been whips spurring on the men below. They possessed souls, minds, consciences, inclinations, and complex biological structures found nowhere else in the universe, yet they chose to slither on their bellies through mud and over stone, working their way toward where Michael and the Dragon held sway over all.

The eyes of the one called Kenway looked up into the raging sky, and the mind behind them wondered if the sun would ever shine on the godforsaken hellhole they found themselves in, while the one named Berg sighted his Thompson, and the Major whispered important instruction in his ear: "The silver's going to fuck up the slug's weight. It'll tumble. Don't get cute. Aim for the chest. Got it?"

"Got it."

Everything a machine winding down to an inevitable conclusion.

Stark, Gunther, Verning, and Hagen sat around a table, picking at the remains of their meal. Verning raised a finger and frowned with slight effort. The digit's nail grew long and tapered. He dug the claw into his forearm and worked it back and forth. Blood dotted the table as he popped the bullet out of his flesh with a practiced flick of the wrist. He palmed the slug while the wound in his arm closed.

"I wonder how many times I've been shot now."

"A hundred?" Hagen guessed around chews. An observer might have thought his answer facetious, but it wasn't; it was matter-of-fact.

Verning considered the number and nodded. "Probably, still hurts like hell, though." He tossed the slug over his shoulder. "The first time I got hit was outside of Wewelsburg, when we trained on the British POWs. You remember that?"

Hagen nodded. It all seemed like such a long time ago. Stark sucked at shreds of meat stuck between his teeth. Fire glinted in his eyes over whatever burning thoughts wormed through his mind. Gunther slumped in his chair. Despite his robust physique, he looked tired and on the verge of crumbling into dust.

✠   ✠   ✠

THEY WERE EVERYWHERE and nowhere in the war, moving from place to place, task to task, mission to mission, shades among shadows.

They operated as scouts at Dunkirk when over three hundred thousand British troops retreated across the English Channel.

They carried out covert operations in Africa. They watched tanks battle in great clouds of dust while the sun burned men black and the sand lice drank their blood.

They killed dissidents within the Nazi party. Whether the men were actual traitors or merely hindrances to Himmler's political ambitions was unclear.

They fought in Russia until winter froze the German advance dead in its tracks, and men snapped off frostbitten fingers and lit fires under their vehicles to keep them running.

Then the Russians came out of the shifting snow with superior tanks and fanatic troops who drank antifreeze when they had no vodka. The Germans retreated under the onslaught. The snow turned red, and bloody icicles dangled from wounds.

They were in Berlin when the opposition started in earnest, and the Empty Cross Organization, led by Ernst and Gertrude Von Roth, wrote their famous pamphlet:

Who counts the dead? Hitler? Don't be deceived. Thousands fall in Russia each day. Grief enters the cottages of the Fatherland and no one wipes away the tears of the mothers. Hitler lies to those whose dearest treasure he robbed and drove to senseless death. If he says peace, he means war. If he uses the name of the Almighty, he means the power of evil, the fallen angel, Satan. His mouth is the stinking gate of hell, and his power is debased. Whoever doubts the existence of demonic powers has misunderstood the metaphysical background to this war. Behind the concrete and material perceptions, behind all factual, logical consideration stands the irrational, i.e., the battle against the demons, against the emissaries of the Anti-Christ.

They took the Von Roths to the torture chambers. Ernst was repeatedly asphyxiated and revived. The guards finally kicked him to death while he watched Gertrude being violated with an electric cattle prod. Then she was hung with piano wire.

As things fell apart, they were assigned special duties, such as transporting spoils of war to secure locations. Finally, just before D-Day, Himmler sent them on a clandestine journey to Italy to recover something unique—the box.

✠   ✠   ✠

"I FORGOT WHAT it's like to even be afraid of death," Verning said.

It was meant to come out as a boast, but it was oddly pathetic. Fearing death was part of being a man.

"I wonder how long we can live like this. Will we ever get old? Sick?"

No one had an answer.

Verning turned to Hagen. "When was your first time?"

"The Jewish uprising in Warsaw. I was bunker hunting with a Waffen-SS squad. This girl came out of the rubble with her hands up. She was pretty, maybe eighteen. The men took her to the commander for interrogation. She pulled a grenade out of her halter and blew up everyone around her. This boy came running out of the alley then. Maybe it was her brother. He had a pistol and was screaming and shooting. One of the slugs caught me in the shoulder. I thought a bee had stung me."

"The Jews fought hard," Gunther said. "You have to respect that."

"Bullshit," Stark snapped. "Anyone will fight hard when their back's against the wall. It won't matter in the end. They're animals."

"So are we," Gunther replied, "now. And this war is lost. Hitler's insane. You know that as well as I do. *Mein Kampf,* indeed. More like, *Mein Irrtum.*"

✠ ✠ ✠

THEY SAW HITLER peak June 21, 1940—the day France surrendered. He arrived at the Compiegne Forest in his Mercedes, his face solemn, yet brimming with a scornful joy at reversing fate. He had a spring in his step as he walked to the granite block dedicated to Germany's defeat in World War I. Its inscription read: *Here on the eleventh of November 1918 succumbed the criminal pride of the German Empire—vanquished by the free people which it tried to enslave.* Then he turned his back and walked away. The gesture was a master-piece of contempt. But things fell apart …

They visited Hitler's Bavarian retreat a few weeks prior to their last mission. The Eagle's Nest, as the location was named, stood on a mountaintop six thousand feet above Berchtesgaden.

The home was simple but luxurious. It afforded a breath-taking view of the Alps and even stood above the clouds when the weather was right. The place gave the impression of godlike megalomania, domination, and solitude.

Hitler had aged greatly from the man who gave fiery speeches and accepted France's surrender at the start of the war. He had a puffy face. His left arm, leg and hand shook. He smelled of medicine, amphetamines, and sickness, perhaps syphilis. He paced up and down the floor in a food-stained uniform. Pastry frosting caked his fingernails.

Hitler raved at his guests, which included high-level Nazi leaders. They nodded their heads in the right places as if Hitler had them on strings. His mistress, Eva Braun, was also present. She was blond, slender, and submissive. Hitler met her after his first love, Geli Raubal, killed herself. Raubal was also his niece. Rumor had it she committed suicide be-cause she couldn't stomach Hitler's bedroom fetishes.

"We will win!" Hitler exclaimed. "It's providence and destiny and fate! Oh, the weapons we will soon bring into battle. Jet fighters! Vergeltun rockets! U-boats with unprec-edented speed! They will prevent an Allied invasion and allow us to transfer our western armies to the east for the decisive battle against the exhausted Russians!"

The 'exhausted' Russians currently sped toward Berlin with gigantic armies of tanks and men.

"Churchill is only good for shoving cigars up his ass! Roosevelt is a cripple who should be put down like a horse with a broken leg! They will come begging when I unleash my V-2s!" He paused to view his captive audience. Their plastic looks weren't convincing enough. "You don't believe me? Come! I will show you!"

Hitler forced them into cars. They drove to an underground facility where slave laborers constructed secret weapons. The cave's air stank of shit. Dead bodies hung here and there with signs around their necks: *Lazy. Stealing food. Dissenter.*

The lowest chambers were lit with soul-sucking lights that turned skin green. The faces of the slaves were gaunt skulls with dull eyes. They wore dirty coveralls. Their hands put together a chaotic jumble of parts that appeared to form strange saucer-shaped aircraft. No rhyme or reason existed to anything. Not even hatred could be found on the faces of the slaves. They were just corpses waiting for the release of decomposition.

"You see!" Hitler exclaimed, throwing his arms wide and grinning with righteous assurance. "We're working miracles!"

✠ ✠ ✠

"WE'LL WIN." Stark insisted. "There's nothing to worry about."

"That's because we have nothing left," Gunther argued. "We'll finish out the war here. Nobody's coming for us. Why do you think the Americans came?" He pointed at the box. It simply sat there in resplendent opulence. "They know about that."

"So?"

"So how could they know unless they intercepted the convoy? We should just go home—or at least pretend that we can go home. I have a wife."

"And we have orders," Stark put closed to the matter. "We will stay. We will wait. We will guard. So shut up, old man."

"What do orders matter anymore? We're damned, and you talk of duty?"

"I said, shut up."

Gunther shook his head. "Christ, this is all so wrong."

Stark laughed with absolute mirth.

"What's so funny?"

"You're a fine one to be a spokesman for morality," Stark said between guffaws. "Look at what you're eating."

Gunther glanced down at the remains of his meal. The bones of Jacobson's arm were almost completely stripped of flesh. He dropped the severed limb, really seeing it for the first time. He moaned in disgust and self-loathing.

Stark had to wipe tears from his eyes before his laughter tapered off.

Eventually, Hagen spoke just to speak. "I have a wife, too." The other men looked at him with surprise. None of them knew. Gunther even managed some sympathy. Hagen turned to him with a hopeful expression. "Have you seen yours since …?"

"No." Gunther shook his head. "Maybe she thinks I'm dead."

He said it like it wasn't such a bad thing.

"Me either," Hagen went on. "She's not beautiful, my wife. A beautiful woman wouldn't have married a deaf mute, but I loved her, and she loved me. I wonder what she will say when she hears me talk. Maybe I will sing her a song, huh?"

"What will you sing?" Verning asked.

Hagen smiled, stood up and began in a surprisingly beautiful voice. The words carried through the bank. For a few seconds, they even drowned out the storm. But they were all wrong. It was the German language, but the grammar and syntax were off, just like Himmler's stanzas in the basement of Wewelsburg.

"Mein Herz, Mein Blut, Mein Seele, Deinetwillen, Bitte zuruckkommen, zuruckkommen, zuruckkommen, Dein Liebe die Losungen mein gebrochen halbieren, Es abfullen mir und absaufen das Ubel, Ich habe zuruckkommen, zuruckkommen, zuruckkommen."

The others stared into space. Hagen's words wound them up in cocoons of self-reflection. The song showed them how things were with all smoke and mirrors removed. It showed them what they were by describing what they lost, like light illuminating an object so that people could identify its shadow.

"Mein Herz, Mein Blut, Mein Seele, Mit Gewinn arbeiten, Ich kann geboren werden, Ausgenommen daß die Anlage einaschern, Ich kann geboren werden, Ausgenommen daß die Höllen die Brande, Alles unsauber, unsauber, unsauber."

Stark smirked at the fine jest of it all. To him, it was nothing to complain about. Better to reign in hell than serve in heaven. Verning didn't particularly care either. Violence made the world go around, and now he was a fine agent of it. He would take what he wanted when he wanted. Gunther wondered if hanging himself would work. Probably. They weren't invincible. The possibility was worth investigating.

"Ich habe vorangehen einher mit du, Ich zuruckziehen, zuruckziehen, zuruckziehen."

A sudden shot rang out. Hagen pitched over and crashed to the floor. He screamed and cried and gurgled. Blood and smoke poured from the wound in his throat. The other three dove for cover as more bullets whizzed overhead.

Hagen reached out to them with open hands. Gore flooded his chest. His skin turned translucent as his veins

emptied their contents onto the floor. He looked to be in excruciating pain. His feet drummed on the tiles.

At last he grew silent and still, like a windup toy slowly
stopping. His blank eyes looked surprised and perhaps a bit
relieved. The others stared at him in shock.

"*Silver*," Stark said it like a curse word.

Verning suddenly remembered fear. "What do we do?"

"We fight! They're not the only ones with guns!"

CHAPTER

BALANCE

"DID YOU HIT ONE?" The Major's voice was hoarse with eagerness. He and Berg lay at the base of the Michael-Dragon statue. The Major's vulpine eyes squinted at the bank through the rain. Vague shadows moved inside of the building.

"I think so..."

"Did it work?"

"He went down ugly."

A savage grin split the Major's face. "We're going in." He waved at Chaplain, Kenway, and Mac. They vaulted over the courtyard wall and sprinted through ankle-deep water. The Major gave them the word, "We've got the bastards now! Let's go!" Then he lunged to his feet and charged the bank. The men followed, teeth clenched, eyes alight, and trigger fingers itching as the box beckoned them onward.

A slew of machinegun bullets impacted around them and threw up geysers of rainwater. Mac cursed in pain. Lightning illuminated a dogman positioned at the corner of the bank. Its snarling teeth and yellow eyes gleamed. An ammo bag hung from its furry shoulder while an MP-40 submachine gun smoked in its hands. Its clawed fingers removed the spent magazine and dug into the bag for a fresh one.

"Break off!" the Major shouted. "Cover!"

The beast opened fire again, muscles vibrating with weapon recoil. Shell casings ejected from its gun and splashed in the puddles around its feet. The men ran zigzag routes to make themselves more difficult targets. Despite that, Chaplain grunted in surprise and pain as he went up and over the courtyard wall. Bullets bounced off the bricks and drew sparks at his heels.

"Motherfuckers!" the Major raged. "Who's hit?"

Mac used his teeth to tie a handkerchief around his forearm. Blood ran down his wrist and dripped off his fingers. "Don't mean shit," he said. "Flesh wound."

Chaplain checked his bloody shoulder. "Just a scratch," he muttered. The hand that Cain bit hurt much worse than the bullet wound. It throbbed with an ethereal heat. He wondered how long he had before he changed. He remembered the staring eyes of the crucifix and tried to muster up a drop of trust that had been absent for so long.

"They've got guns!" Berg cried in surprise. His voice was shrill with the announcement. His lips trembled, either from cold or nerves.

"No shit, Sherlock," the Major hissed. "Chaplain, Kenway, Mac, hold this position. Berg and I will work around behind them. Got it?"

A chorus of: "Yes, sir!"

"Hoo-fucking-yah," the Major grinned and pulled Berg after him.

Berg tried to remember how many bullets he shot at the bank. It all happened so fast. One target stood up, straight into his sights, like the guy was reciting a poem or something. Berg aimed for his heart. The bullet didn't fly true, but it caught the German nevertheless. Then the others jumped out of their chairs. He fired. How many times? Four? Five? The question was of grave importance. He only had twenty silver rounds.

The Major poked his head around the corner of the wall. He saw shadows, a rainy street and shadowy buildings getting rained on. No telling what else was out there ... waiting. The Major grabbed the front of Berg's shirt and growled in his face.

"You've been promoted to point. Go!"

Kenway peeked over the wall. The dogman was gone. Nothing moved except for ripples on the surfaces of the many puddles. The town was certainly flooding. Some places were under three feet of water and had a current that could suck you along if you weren't careful. What a lovely fucking place. Then bullets buzzed in from everywhere. They ricocheted off the stone wall with sharp twangs and cracks. Brick fragments peppered Kenway's face, drawing blood. He caught glimpses of two muzzle blasts—one from the right, the other from the left. The monsters had them in a crossfire.

"Displace!"

The three of them sprinted across the street.

Kenway felt a slug bite into his ass. "Son of a bitch!" he cried out and dropped to his knees.

Chaplain hauled him back to his feet. "Keep going!"

Kenway gritted his teeth and ran on, his limp gradually returning to a normal stride as adrenaline and necessity negated the pain.

Mac looked back. Two beasts pursued them, firing guns with one paw and loping along on three legs. Bullets zinged past Mac and took out chunks of a stucco wall. He returned fire, pulling the trigger three times. The beasts veered apart. One disappeared around a building. The other took cover behind a log pile and fired a long burst.

Mac tucked into a roll. Bullets whined off the cobblestones. A stray slug tugged at his jacket collar. He put his Thompson to his shoulder and pulled the trigger twice more. The dogman ducked behind the woodpile as the slugs threw splinters into its face. Mac disengaged the target and followed Kenway and Chaplain into an alley.

The wind howled through the corridor, driving raindrops like shotgun pellets. Mac put on a burst of speed to catch up to his fellow Zombie Squad members. Something hit his forehead with terrific force and knocked him off his feet. He hit the ground hard. A flash of lightning revealed a wire clothesline. Kenway and Chaplain were shorter than him and had passed harmlessly beneath it. They didn't notice Mac fall. They turned the corner at the far end of the alley and disappeared from view.

"Wait up!" Mac shouted. His voice was lost in the wind. One of the dogmen entered the corridor in pursuit. "Shit!" Mac rolled to the side. Bullets hit the ground next to him and threw sparks across his chest. He returned fire. The monster ducked behind the corner. Mac pushed himself to his feet and ran forward. The second dogman turned into the alley ahead of him. He was trapped. "No!" Mac fired by reflex, sending two bullets toward the beast. It twisted out of sight. Mac spun around just in time to see the other dogman take aim once more. "Christ!" He dove between two piles of flower boxes. Bullets riddled the wood crates, throwing up dirt and slivers. Mac stuck his Thompson out and returned fire. A bullet took a chunk of cartilage out of his ear. Another took a piece of meat out of his calf. "Chaplain! Kenway! Help!"

A hand clutched Berg's shoulder. He was so keyed up from running point that he nearly screamed. The hand turned into a pointing finger.

"That street!" the Major directed. "Move!"

Berg wiped sweat from his forehead and licked his lips. His eyes swiveled in every direction. The area contained a hundred possible ambush points. Plus, the question still nagged at him: Four or five? Did he have fifteen or sixteen rounds left?

The problem reminded him of his school years. He remembered going up to the classroom blackboard and standing before an arithmetic problem on those last hot days of summer. Sweat ran down the small of his back and pricked the skin of his forehead, like it was now. The chalk was a hard lump in his hand, like his rifle. The place smelled of moldy books, like Le Coeur. The equation was weird hieroglyphics written by an ancient race, like the design on the cover of the box. All of the other kids sat behind him, watching, judging, and laughing as he failed. He wouldn't have cared so much, but Becky Thatcher laughed, too. Becky with her blond hair and white stockings, and sometimes when he saw her from just the right angle, he felt something slip and catch in his belly like a badly used gear. Sometimes he had visions of becoming smart when he walked home after class. He dreamed of studying until he was a genius, but no amount of work he did mattered. The numbers would never add up.

Berg just wanted the box. Then it wouldn't matter anymore. He wouldn't be stupid. He'd be someone. Maybe he'd even see Becky Thatcher again, and his chances with her would be greatly improved, maybe even as high as four out of five.

Four or five?

Berg and the Major raced to the end of the street, making the final turn in their circuitous route back to the bank. They worked their way through the tables of a corner café and came face to face with a dogman. Rain dripped off its shaggy fur. It looked almost as surprised as they did. It and Berg opened fire at the same time.

Mac huddled in a fetal position. Bullets buzzed by him like angry bees. One took a chip of fore grip out of his Thompson. Others blasted brick shards out of the wall, which embedded themselves in Mac's skin. Another bullet grazed the back of his hand, leaving a trail of blood and pain. Mac pulled his pistol and fired without aiming. The bullets weren't silver, but the dogmen didn't know that.

"Chaplain! Kenway! Where the fuck are you guys?"

Thompsons firing on semi-auto answered Mac's cry. He raised his head and peered over the flower boxes. The beast at the far end of the alley retreated under a hail of bullets. One of the slugs hit the monster in the thigh. Smoke poured from the wound. Then Kenway popped into the mouth of the alley, his rifle to his shoulder.

"Come on!" he yelled and sent a volley of bullets over Mac's head. The beast at the other end of the corridor drew back under the onslaught. Mac pushed himself to his feet and half-ran, half-stumbled to join his companions.

"Why'd you leave me?" Mac shouted.

"Why'd you stop?" Kenway yelled back.

"A clothesline damn near took my head off." Mac ran a shaky hand through his hair. He had lost his helmet in the alley. "How many rounds you got left?"

"Eleven," Kenway said.

"Fourteen," Chaplain answered.

"I've got seven. We need a plan."

A storm of bullets stopped any plot before it started. The men ran down the street. Ricochets whined away at their heels. They ducked around a corner. A dogman gave chase. A sudden idea occurred to Mac—do the unexpected. He stepped back around the edge of the building. The pursuing monster skidded to a stop. Its yellow eyes went wide with surprise. "Goodbye, shithead," Mac smiled and pulled the trigger.

Nothing happened.

Mac looked down, incredulous. A misshapen silver slug was jammed the Thompson's receiver. He looked back up at the monster, the tables turned. It grinned around lupine fangs and raised its own machinegun. Mac dove for the ground. Bullets sprayed over his head. Chaplain lunged around the corner then, firing as he came.

The beast yowled in surprise and pain as a slug glanced off its ribs. It dropped to all fours and fled, spraying a final burst of bullets in Mac and Chaplain's direction. One of them took Chaplain in the hip. He fell back onto the wall.

Mac pushed himself to his feet. He worked the Thompson's bolt by hand, ejecting the bad round. It bounced across the street. He didn't bother picking it up.

Chaplain leaned against the wall, a hand pressed to his hip.

"You all right?" Kenway asked.

Chaplain grimaced, examining the extent of the wound. "Yeah," he nodded. "It went clean through. No bone."

"We have to move," Mac said. "Now."

Down the street, the monsters regrouped and worked their way toward the three soldiers, darting from trees to benches to doorways. One ducked behind a horse cart filled with potato sacks.

The cart had a chock behind one of its wheels since it was parked on the peak of a fairly steep hill. A large wooden sign reading, *Boucherie*, hung above it and swayed in the wind like a giant guillotine blade.

"I've got a plan!" Mac ejected his clip of silver bullets and inserted one filled with standard rounds. Then he unloaded the clip at the hanging sign. It blew off its mounts and landed on the beast hunkered behind the cart with a splintery crash. Mac reinserted the silver bullets and ran into the street. "Cover me!"

Berg cried out and pulled the trigger of his Thompson. He remembered to count this time. *One, two, three, four!* One of the bullets tore a gouge in the creature's arm. Blood and smoke poured out. It growled in rage and fired its own weapon. A slug hit Berg's left biceps; the other caught his left side. He slumped to the ground. The Major stuck his rifle around the corner and pulled the trigger. The beast bounded away with unnatural speed. The Major kneeled over Berg. "Get up!"

"I'm hit!"

The Major surveyed the damage. "You'll live. Come on, we wounded it!"

"It hurts."

The Major grabbed a handful of Berg's shirt and jerked him to his feet. "I said get up and after the son of a bitch! You'll feel better once you start moving!"

Berg swayed on his feet. Burning pain emanated from his wounds. His hand was red with blood. *My blood?*

The Major grabbed him by the arm and dragged him along before he could fall. Berg stumbled next to him like an obedient puppy.

"Tell me how many rounds you've got left?" the Major demanded.

The pain seemed to clarify Berg's thought process—funny that it should work that way. *Four shots! I just fired four shots! Plus ... four of five at the bank?* The Major expected an answer. That further motivated Berg to make up his mind. *Four, it had to be four, so that's eight total. Then I've got thirteen left ... no! Twelve! Or maybe ...*

"Thirteen?" Berg guessed.

"Perfect!" the Major said.

They ran toward a stone and wood barn. The Major shoved Berg through its door. "It went in there. After it!"

It was pitch black inside. Lighting flashed through a spider web of roof cracks but did nothing to illuminate the interior. The storm also made it impossible to hear any sound of movement. Berg forgot all about his wounds in his attempt to ascertain whether or not the beast was present within. The Major entered behind him.

"Flush it out."

"What? How?"

The Major didn't have time to answer. The strobe-like flashes of the monster's MP-40 illuminated the place. The movements of the Major and Berg appeared jerky and spasmodic under the stuttering light. They both hit the ground and rolled to their knees, swinging their rifles toward their adversary and returning fire.

Nine! Ten! Eleven! Thirteen! Fourteen! Berg counted as he pulled the trigger. *No, I forgot a number! I forgot twelve! Thirteen, I was on thirteen!*

The dogman leapt ten feet straight up and disappearing into the hayloft. The Major yanked a grenade off his belt and tossed it up after the beast. It blew with a sharp crack that took down the hayloft and a portion of the roof.

The Major and Berg threw themselves out of the way of the falling lumber and straw. The rain washed the dust from the air as soon as it billowed upward from the crashing debris. The two men recovered and trained their guns on the pile of rubble. Something lurched and tore itself free from the jumbled mess of blasted timber. The Major fired four quick rounds.

"Shit!" he cursed. "It's getting away! After it!" He made his way out of the barn, pushing Berg ahead him. The creature limped its way around the corner of a building. The Major's features grew manic.

"We got this son of a bitch now!"

The Major shoved Berg forward. Berg stumbled and then found his momentum. The thrill of the hunt made him forget his pain. They were winning, and it was just like running down a wounded coon back home. For a moment, he almost felt sorry for the beast, but the moment was fleeting. Berg grinned and for a second he looked almost as crazy as the Major.

Mac charged the dogman as it struggled to crawl out from beneath the heavy sign. Behind him, Chaplain and Kenway opened fire on the other creature.

"You're mine, asshole!" Mac shouted.

The beast intensified its efforts to free itself. It was the same one Mac had in his sights when his weapon didn't properly feed. He could tell because its black fur had a grayish tinge. The thing wouldn't be so lucky this time.

Mac raised his rifle and popped off three quick rounds. The combination of him running, the wobbling bullets, and the struggling dogman did not bode well for accuracy. One round struck the sign. Another clanged off the street. The third took the beast in the forearm. It howled and freed its gun hand.

Mac dove to the side, came up, and fired again. One of the bullets missed. The second struck the monster's weapon. Sparks flew, and the broken gun clattered to the street. "For the love of God, would you just die!" Mac screamed in frustration and popped off his last round.

It hit the cobblestones near the beast's nose.

No way! No *fucking* way!

The dogman freed itself of the sign. Mac threw his Thompson aside and grabbed a fifty-pound sack of potatoes off the cart. He slammed it down on the beast's head.

The blow would have broken the neck of a man, but the thing was way more than a man. It went to its knees and lashed out with a clawed hand, knocking Mac off his feet. The beast loomed over him, ready to have his guts for breakfast, and Mac was overcome with the smell of wet fur. Then he saw its foot step into a loop of cart rope. From there, his eyes swiveled to the wheel chock. He kicked it. It popped loose with surprising ease, and the wheel rolled over his foot; he screamed as it crushed his toes.

The beast looked down just in time to see the rope tighten around its ankle, and then it was yanked off its feet and dragged down the steep slope. The cart picked up speed. The monster's claws skittered along the cobblestones. Its eyes gleamed with rage.

The street curved at the bottom of the hill. The cart bounced up and over the curb and slammed through the front wall of a flower shop. Mac didn't wait around to watch anymore. He grabbed his weapon and limped/sprinted back to Chaplain and Kenway, wincing at the pain of his smashed toes. Bullets from the other beast's machinegun followed his tracks. The firing of Kenway and Chaplain caused the monster to seek cover.

"I'm out!" Mac slapped in his last clip of regular bullets.

"Me, too," Kenway said.

Chaplain popped the magazine of silver rounds from of his Thompson and checked its load. It was empty. They ran for the church.

The Major and Berg rounded the corner for the coup de grace.

The dogman fooled them.

It had only pretended to be badly hurt. Now it huddled in the branches of a tree, gun trained on the Major and Berg, just waiting for them to charge into its sights. Lightning flashed behind it. Its eyes glowed yellow. Drool dripped from its fangs.

A soft curse escaped the Major's lips. "Goddamn it all—"

Berg reacted instantaneously, pulling the trigger of his Thompson, still insanely counting the rounds. *Fourteen! Fifteen! Sixteen! Seventeen! Eighteen! Nineteen!* None of the bullets hit the creature. He was too frantic and out of control. Berg knew his end had come. It all seemed to happen in slow motion. He could actually see the muscles of the creature's forearm tighten as it pulled the trigger. It seemed he could even see the bullets streaking for him, and they all had his name carved into their tips. Then he felt a hand grab the back of his shirt and yank.

The Major! I'm saved.

But instead of jerking Berg out of the creature's line of fire, the Major used him as a human shield. Bullets slammed into Berg's chest and splashed blood. Then he was dropped, discarded like a used rag. He hit the ground on his face. His nose snapped on the cobblestones. The pain was lost in the burning agony engulfing his body. He heard the Major's fleeing footsteps. Somehow, he rolled onto his side.

The monster leapt out of the tree and walked toward him. Berg's gun was there, just inches from his fingertips. *Nineteen.* One round left. He reached for the weapon with supreme effort of will. Blood worked its way up his throat and spilled out of the corner of his mouth like thin vomit. He coughed. His lungs felt full of liquid. It hurt, god how it hurt. Tears joined the rain on his face.

The beast came for him with infinite slowness.

One last try, he thought. *One last try.* He jerked the weapon up with the last of his strength. The monster faltered with frightened astonishment. Berg pulled the trigger.

The gun clicked on an empty chamber.

He had fired five shots at the bank after all. Phantom laughter rang in his head as the monster lunged for his throat. He saw a chalkboard filled with numbers that made no sense growing blacker ... blacker ... black.

CHAPTER 24

DISSENT

STARK GLOWERED AT THE CHURCH. Blood and smoke seeped from the bullet hole in his biceps. He gritted his teeth and dug the silver out with his fingers. The acrid smell of burned flesh brought tears to his eyes. They were the first tears he shed in a long time. His chest heaved with rage. The situation had been amusing at first but no longer. Pain brought doubt, and death brought confusion. They were hurt and Hagen was dead. Stark had no feelings for the man, but he was part of the pack. He understood the agony and the ecstasy of the Shift, and if he could be killed, so could they.

Gunther and Verning remained in canine form. They licked their wounds and emitted soft whines of pain. A tendril of smoke rose from Gunther's forearm. The bullet was lodged in the bone, and he couldn't extract it.

Verning tried to heal his thigh. He pinched the wound closed with his teeth, but the enchanted flesh refused to mend. Silver made it mortal and subject to the natural healing process.

Stark's fury grew in proportion to the raging storm. He had to destroy the men in the church. If he failed, then it all meant nothing. The cause he found to rally around was just a demented farce, and he had no greater destiny. Then he was nothing more than a goddamn murdering, raping cripple, after all.

Elsa's voice rang in his head. *Why?*

Stark's features wavered between dog and man. "Come out!" he screamed at the church. "Come out and we'll make it quick! If you don't, I'm going to rip your faces off and shove them up your asses! I'm going to eat your livers and squeeze the shit from your intestines! I'm going to make you beg for me to kill you!"

Stark fell to his knees. His claws gouged the earth in rabid frustration. He wanted to destroy creation itself to get even with life. "Come out, you bastards! Come out and fight like men!"

No response came from the church. It simply stood there, impassive and hulking. Its silence mocked him. Stark resisted the urge to charge it, burst through its doors, and tear them to pieces.

That wouldn't do; they had silver, but Stark had weapons, too. His hands clenched into fists, and his claws stabbed through his palms.

"*I am Übermensch*," he whispered to no one and lead Gunther and Verning into the darkness.

The Major stoked a fire in the forge. He sat on a pew and looked into its flames, chewing on, but not tasting, a chocolate bar. The rest of the men warmed themselves, tending to their wounds and trying to stand under the weight of great weariness.

Kenway pulled down his pants and examined his backside. Blood leaked from the bullet hole in his right buttock. He powdered the wound with sulfide and injected half an ampoule of morphine. The drug did nothing to ease the pain of his bullet-cracked pelvic bone, however. He tried not to groan as cold sweat dotted his brow.

Chaplain licked his lips over and over again. Shallow pants puffed his cheeks, but very little blood flowed from his wounds. It was as if his shoulder and hip injuries had already nearly healed. The eyes of his pale face stared at the fallen crucifix. He twitched periodically, like he heard sounds beyond the auditory ranges of the others.

Mac tied a bandage around his calf and steeled himself to examine his toes. Unable to put it off any longer, he gritted his teeth and removed his boot. Blood soaked his sock. He peeled it away with careful fingers and winced at the sight.

Bruises turned his toes black, and they jutted out from his foot at crazy angles. Pus congealed around their nails like jam. He wrapped them as tightly as possible and jabbed a syringe of morphine into his thigh. It made him feel like he floated just above the surface of the pain. He pulled his boot back on with an animal squeak of misery.

"What happened to Berg?" Kenway suddenly demanded.

The Major answered without batting an eyelash. "He got shot trying to cover me."

Shirking responsibility for the death of another was no great trick for the Major. He'd been practicing since he was sixteen. His girlfriend got pregnant at that time. He arranged for an abortion six months later. The quack was a drunken lout with hairy knuckles. Unfortunately, if you buy cheap, you get cheap. The doctor scraped out a little more uterus than fetus. The Major's girlfriend bled to death on the kitchen table where the procedure was performed. The blood pooled around a tiny baby arm that was tossed aside like a cigarette butt. The doctor shrugged and said, "Don't worry, that's perfectly normal," then swigged from a bottle of wine. The Major got angry. His girlfriend had been a good lay, so he broke the wine bottle over the doctor's head and ran.

"What do we do now?" Mac asked.

"We need more silver," the Major said with utmost rationality.

"Yeah? Well, who's going to go out and look for it? You?"

"If I tell you to go, you'll go," the Major answered with a shrug. "I've got rank, and an order's an order."

Mac turned away and mumbled something under his breath.

"What did you say?" the Major asked with a raised eyebrow.

"*Come out!*" a voice screamed. The men turned toward the door of the church, grabbing their weapons. "*Come out and we'll make it quick!*"

The Major smirked. The men looked at him like the mates of the Pequod must have looked at Captain Ahab. The wind howled as the voice continued to rave.

"*If you don't, I'm going to rip your faces off and shove them up your asses! I'm going to eat your livers and squeeze the shit from your intestines! I'm going to make you beg for me to kill you! Come out, you bastards! Come out and fight like men!*"

"Bad dreams," the Major said in a high keening voice.

"Maybe it *is* a dream," Kenway latched on to the idea. The morphine he injected made it all seem perfectly plausible. "That would explain everything. Otherwise, it's just too insane, what we're after, what we're fighting, but if it's all a dream …"

"It's no dream," Chaplain said.

"Then maybe we're dead," Kenway went on. "Maybe the *Lazarus* crashed with us on board. Maybe this is hell … and they're its demons."

Chaplain shook his head. "This isn't hell."

"How do you know?" Kenway asked.

"Hell's a lot worse."

Chaplain flexed his bitten hand and winced. Strange thoughts wormed through his head, thoughts of shredding and blood. His skin itched. The world seemed to drain of color and exist in black and white sepia tones.

"You know," the Major said, "this reminds me of a story. There was this guy who wanted more, because that was all he needed to be happy, you see, but there was no practical way for him to get it, so he made a deal with the devil. Satan gave him everything he wanted, on condition, of course. The condition was that ole Splitfoot got the guy's soul if he died *inside* of a church and if he died *outside* of a church. But the guy thought of a loophole toward the end of his life. You know what he did?"

Silence greeted the question.

"He sealed himself up inside a church wall. Then he died in the crawlspace. Technically, he wasn't inside the church, but he wasn't outside of it either. Pretty clever, huh? But ultimately, it didn't mean shit; he still died. And that's the moral of the story, kids. In the end, there's no escaping anything. That's why only one thing matters: how much you have while you're alive. *Having*, gentlemen, that's happiness."

The fire crackled in the quiet that greeted the conclusion of the Major's story. The men stared into its depths, each lost in their own world. They looked like they wanted to jump into its flames—moths flocking to the oblivion of the candle.

The Major went on: "And I, for one, am not leaving this shit hole of a town until I have." He turned and faced Mac in particular. "Now get out there and find me that proverbial silver lining. I'll keep the home fires burning."

"I'm not going back out there," Mac growled.

The Major nodded in understanding and sympathy. Then he pulled his pistol and pointed it at Mac's face. "Think about it for a few seconds, will you? I'll even count them off for you. How does three sound? Will that give you enough time to decide?"

"Jesus," Kenway said. "What are you're doing?"

"I'm giving you all a choice," the Major replied. His eyes glittered and a smile split his face. "Kick in an ante up or get the fuck off the planet. One ..."

Chaplain stepped forward to defuse the situation. If the Major wanted silver, he could get him silver. But before he could speak up, he heard something—for real, this time. He cocked his head and listened. "What's that noise?"

"Inevitability," the Major whispered, hearing nothing. "Two ..."

Gradually the sound became louder, audible over the storm. It sounded like ... a horde of chirping crickets? It increased in volume and became accompanied by a loud rumbling. Realization of what it was dawned on all four men at once ... just as the massive Panzer Wolf exploded through the wall in a cloud of shattered brick.

The tank lunged at them on squeaking treads and ground everything in its path to dust.

CHAPTER

MASKS

THE CHURCH GREW in the Wolf's view slot. Stark gunned the twelve-cylinder, six hundred-fifty horsepower engine. The thirty-ton war machine blasted through the church wall like it was made of tissue paper.

And I'll huff, and I'll puff, and I'll blow your goddamn house down!

Stark spotted his enemies among the pews. Gears strained and clashed as he wrenched the front end of the Panzer in line with his adversaries.

"Fire!"

Verning sat in the turret and pulled the trigger of the tank's three-inch cannon. A hollow boom slammed through the machine and jerked its chassis with violent recoil. The spent shell ejected with a mechanical thrust of pistons. The smell of cordite permeated everything as the smoke of ignited gunpowder sucked back into the interior of the Wolf through the cannon barrel. Verning pressed his face back to the gun sight. Gunther shoved another greased round into the cannon breech.

"Up!"

"Acquired!"

"Fire!"

The Major, Kenway, Chaplain, and Mac scattered before the juggernaut. The thunderclap of its cannon shook mortar from the church walls and shattered its windows. The space the soldiers occupied erupted into an explosion of broken floor. Chunks of stone winged across the rectory and punched holes through the pulpit.

The Wolf dug into a spinning turn. Pews were sucked under its treads and shattered into splinters.

The Major found himself speared by the light beams of the tank. He heard the hydraulic wheeze of its cannon acquiring a target—him.

"Shit!" He dove to the ground.

The tank fired a heartbeat later. The shell detonated at the base of the communion rail. The oak banister blew into a thousand pieces. Slivers of wood embedded themselves in the ceiling. Chunks of stone slammed into organ pipes, and discordant music rang out over the destruction.

Stark's teeth lengthened. Black hair sprouted from his forehead. He spotted a ghostly figure in the murk ahead and gave chase. The back end of the Panzer swung around in a rattling skid that swept away several rows of pews and smashed them through the wall.

The Wolf was quick and mobile for a tank. It had the same engine as a Panzer Tiger yet weighed only two-thirds

STEVE RUTHENBECK

as much. An MG-34 machinegun mounted on a bubble turret near the driver supplemented its main cannon. Its combination of speed, maneuverability and weapons made it a formidable adversary. Under Stark's direction, it tore through the church like a bull through a china shop.

Kenway lost his bearings in the gloom. The sound of the tank filled the world. Its headlights cut sword beams of illumination through the dust. They slashed across him, stopped, and came back. He turned and fled. The tank pursued like a lion after a mouse.

Kenway darted between the pillars supporting the balcony. The tank's cannon boomed. The round passed over Kenway's head and tore a ragged hole through the wall. Debris rained around his sprinting form. The tank smashed through the pillars behind him. The balcony tipped forward and tore free. It toppled to the floor with an apocalyptic crash, flattening pews and breaking over the Wolf like water over a rock.

Mac struggled through the choking haze. He pulled the neck of his shirt over his mouth and squinted his eyes down to slits. He ran into the wall and fumbled his way along it, trying to find an exit. The Wolf powered through a sharp turn behind him.

"Nine 'o' clock!" Verning screamed into his headset.

Stark manhandled the Wolf onto the designated course and spotted the figure moving along the wall. He steered with one hand, leaned over and grabbed the MG-34 in the bubble turret beside him. He pulled the trigger and simultaneously hit the gas. He was unaware he was screaming. His eyes gleamed bright yellow.

Mac saw the line of red hot tracers blasting from the Wolf's MG-34. They stitched a trail down the wall behind him and ricocheted along crazy tangents into the interior of the church. Mac threw himself to the floor. The rounds seared through the air above his head. The Panzer lurched into a half turn and came into line behind him. Its left side plowed through the church wall and tore down its length.

"Jesus!" Mac half-swore, half-prayed and pushed himself to his feet. He ran three steps while looking back over his shoulder at oncoming doom. His wounded toes smashed into a hunk of brick. Intense pain bolted up his leg and sank sharp teeth into his groin. He screamed in abject agony and tumbled to the floor.

The Wolf bore down on him through a cloud of dust. The wall collapsed behind it. The church roof groaned and sagged. Thick beams tore loose from ceiling arches and crashed to the floor. The front of the tank grew larger and larger. Mac watched its treads grind bricks into dust.

Stark leaned forward in anticipation. His black pupils reflected Mac's struggling form. He blinked and saw Mr. Leberwitz. Then Emil. Then Elsa. Then everyone … an orgasmic expression filled his face, and a wide smile framed his drooling tongue.

The floor vibrated. The Wolf loomed and blotted out all of existence. Mac's bladder let go, and he realized he would die soaked in his own piss. He screamed in denial. The sound of it was lost in the noise of the Panzer's engine. Mac smelled its hot exhaust and saw the individual rivets of its armor. He closed his eyes.

And then rough hands grabbed him and jerked. Rain beat against his face. He discovered he was outside, yanked through the hole where the Wolf first plowed into the church.

The Panzer tried to stop, but its mass and momentum prevented the maneuver. It dug into a power skid instead and took out the rest of the church wall.

The Major hauled Mac to his feet. They ran. The west side of the church collapsed at their heels like a massive mudslide. They stopped and looked back at the destruction. Half of the cathedral appeared to have been leveled by a fleet of B-17s. The Wolf lurched and moved under the rubble like a dinosaur trying to escape a tar pit.

"We've got to go!" Mac screamed.

Lightning illuminating the Major's incredulous expression. "Go? What do you mean, go? We've got them right where we want them, you fucking pantywaist!"

"You're crazy!"

"*They're in a tank!*" the Major shouted, like it was all so painfully obvious. "They're trapped! Once we get them out in the open we can finish them!"

"How?"

"With these!" The Major pulled a pair of grenades off his bandoleer. "They're not silver, but blowing them to pieces should be just as effective!"

Mac seemed to watch from afar as he accepted a grenade from the Major. Wasn't this the same man who just threatened him with a gun? And now he was going to go after a monster-driven tank on orders from that man?

Madness!

But what if the Major was right? Then the box was theirs. The box, the box, the beautiful box.

It was worth it.

The Wolf erupted from the remains of the church like a dragon bursting from an underground burrow. Its lights threw cones of illumination through the rain. They came around on a running figure: Kenway. The tank's cannon fired. A smoking crater appeared at Kenway's heels as he sprinted through the rain. He stumbled but kept his balance. The Wolf barreled after him with an angry growl of horsepower.

"Over here!" the Major shouted.

Somehow, Kenway heard them over the din of the storm and the MG-34 machinegun fire tearing up the cobblestones behind him. He arrowed in their direction. The Major and Mac met him halfway, and they sprinted into the heart of the Le Coeur with the Wolf in hot pursuit.

Stark's rage fueled the Shift. He went feral in the confines of the buried tank. Black fur covered his body and a fang-filled snout telescoped from his face. He bent the Panzer's steering wheel in a brutal grip and slammed its gearshift into low.

"*Move!*" he snarled.

The Wolf struggled under the weight of the fallen church.

"*Move!*"

Its tracks dug at the debris, struggling for purchase.

"*Move!*"

It crawled forward inch by inch, its motor bogging down under the strain.

"*Move!*"

The tank slipped and caught and slipped again.

"Come on, you tub of shit, *move!*"

The steering wheel trembled under Stark's hands like a dying animal. Just when it appeared the machine had reached the limits of its power, the rubble shifted and the tank made infinitesimal progress, seemingly propelled by the will of Stark himself.

"Yes!"

The Panzer strained and groaned and tore at the trap holding it.

"Move! Move! Move!"

Forward, forward, up, up from the black and into the dark and wet and storm, and finally, the Wolf burst free in an embryonic explosion of rubble. Stark's eyes burned like yellow flame as he scanned the street ahead of him. Now, which way did they fucking go?

"Target?"

"Negative," Verning snarled.

"Negative," Gunther repeated, then, "Target! Three 'o' clock!"

Stark wrestled the Wolf into a right turn. A lone figure ran through the rain. Stark gunned the engine and pursued with a howl of rage. Verning fired the cannon. Stark fired the MG-34. Somehow, they both missed.

"Du hast glück, du Schuft!"

The figure ran through the barrage and joined two others. The three of them ducked in among the cottages. Stark soon lost them.

He slammed the heels of his paws against the steering wheel in venomous frustration. Goddamn the dark! Goddamn the storm! Goddamn everything! He guided the Wolf through the streets, making random turns that approximated a search. Finally, he flushed out his quarry.

"Du bist mein, mann," he snarled and gave chase.

The Major sprinted across the cobblestones. He looked over his shoulder and smiled. The Wolf took the bait and followed. Now, if only Kenway and Mac could be as successful in their task—not that he planned to stick around to find out.

He would lose the Panzer once they attacked. Three of the furry assholes remained by his count. One drove the tank, another manned the cannon and the third probably had reload duty. That meant no one guarded the bank. All he had to do was walk in and take the box. He could load it onto the Krupp truck and be gone before the smoke cleared.

Fuck everyone else. A man has to look out for himself.

Kenway and Mac emerged from their hiding place and sprinted after the Panzer. Its exhaust burned their lungs and eyes. Mac's foot throbbed and pained him with each step. Kenway's bullet wound broke open and bled a great deal.

Neither of them stopped, however. There comes a point where a man can't stop any longer. Whether that point amounts to stupidity, bravery, stubbornness, or insanity is irrelevant. The end result is the same. All that matters is killing the beast and taking the prize.

Kenway caught up to the tank and leapt onto its hitch. He grabbed a loop of towrope and climbed aboard the Panzer's engine compartment. The motor vibrated beneath him like a living thing as the Wolf picked up speed.

The gap between Mac and the tank increased. Kenway stretched an arm back to his comrade. "Jump!"

Mac leapt and snatched Kenway's hand. His foot slipped off the hitch. His chest thudded into the back of the tank, and his feet dragged in the street.

Kenway heaved with all of his strength. Mac snagged the back of Kenway's neck and pulled himself aboard. They crawled to the base of the turret. Mac placed his hands on the hatch. Kenway jerked a grenade off his bandoleer. They had a brief moment of eye contact, then Mac yanked the hatch open.

Hellish red light spilled out. One of the dogmen had his faced pressed against the gun sight. The other held a shell ready for reloading. It looked up, startled. Kenway cocked his arm to throw the grenade.

The canine gunner picked that moment to fire the cannon at the fleeing Major. The recoil made the Panzer lurch like a bucking bronco. Mac lost his grip on the hatch. It slammed shut. The grenade tumbled out of Kenway's grasp. It rolled over the front of the turret and exploded at its base.

"Grenades!" Gunther screamed. "They're on top of us!"

Stark cursed. The man ahead of them was just a diversion. He snarled and ripped the Panzer's wheel back and forth, trying to shake the attackers off their hull.

The Wolf tore down the street at better than thirty miles per hour. Kenway and Mac held on to hooks meant to hold spare track sections. Their lower bodies rolled with the motion of the tank. Sometimes a leg went over the edge and came dangerously close to getting sucked into its treads. The radio antenna whipped back and forth and lashed Kenway's cheek. The turret swung around with a giant servomechanism whir.

Kenway realized the gunner intended to wipe them off the tank with the cannon barrel.

"Get over it!" he shouted.

He scrabbled across the revolving turret. The barrel swung around to a nine 'o' clock position. Mac tried to follow, bloodying his knuckles on the Wolf's rough Zimmerit anti-magnetic mine paste.

The Panzer jigged to the right. Mac lost his balance and slipped over its side. His caught the cannon barrel and hung there like a hammock, feet wedged against the edge of the tank and body dangling over its treads.

They rolled beneath him in a blur of metal teeth that threw up fans of rainwater. The hiss of it sounded like the machine licked its lips, anxious to eat him. His hands slipped on the smooth wet metal of the cannon barrel.

Kenway threw himself across the top of the turret and tried to grab Mac's belt. His mouth smashed into the edge of the hatch, and his front teeth shattered in a glassy explosion of pain. He swallowed the shards and a mouthful of blood.

"Give me the Walther!" Verning shouted. Gunther snatched the pistol off its wall mount and gave it to his companion. Verning cocked it and pushed the hatch open. He poked his snout out and found himself face to face with one of the Americans.

"Jesus!" Kenway cried in fear and revulsion, inches away from the burning yellow eyes of a dogman. He slammed a reflexive elbow into the beast's surprised face. The monster tumbled back inside of the Wolf.

Verning toppled out of his seat and banged his head on the steel edge of the cannon breech. His elbow hit the turret controls.
"Verning? Gunther? What happened?" Stark shouted.

Kenway stretched. His fingertips just grazed Mac's waist. The cannon suddenly reversed its spin and pulled Mac out of his reach. Mac's feet slid off the tank. Its treads seemed to speed up in anticipation of tearing him to pieces.

The street blurred before Stark. He didn't care about his direction. He only cared about the troops on top of them. Russia gave him firsthand experience with what happened to tankers when grenades went off in their machines.
Stark kept the engine floored and cut a zigzag course through Le Coeur. His forearms bulged with effort from guiding the Wolf at such a high rate of speed through such violent maneuvers. Its transmission system had to be taxed

to its limits. Any more pressure and the Panzer would shit out its drive train in a trail of twisted parts.

Something crashed in the turret. "Verning? Gunther? What happened?"

Then the cannon barrel swung back over Stark's view port. He stared in disbelief at the soldier hanging from it, his arms and legs wrapped around the tube of steel like it was a fireman's pole. Stark cranked the wheel and hit a brake pedal, swinging the Wolf around and pointing it straight at a cottage. He smiled with grim intensity.

He'd scrape the sons of bitches off their hull.

Mac tilted his head back and saw the upside down view of an approaching home.

"Fuck me!"

He shimmied down the cannon barrel and rejoined Kenway as the Wolf plowed through the French cottage. Wood and plaster exploded around them in a storm of destruction. Crunches and doomsday squeals filled the air.

The speed of the tank and their position behind its turret afforded them protection from the majority of debris. Nevertheless, something snagged Kenway's collar and ripped out the back of his shirt. A random piece of lumber cut a slash down the length of Mac's arm.

Then the Wolf burst through the other side of the cottage. It smashed an outhouse into toothpicks and blew a woodpile into the air like someone stuffed a stick of dynamite beneath it.

The Panzer continued across the street and blasted through another home made of brick and stucco. Shattered mortar rained over Kenway and Mac. Their screams were lost in the noise of the Wolf plowing through a living room.

Its barrel sliced into the ceiling like a knife. Steel treads flattened furniture and then crushed a refrigerator like a tin can. The machine's right fender clipped an oven and sent it flying through the wall.

A light fixture whizzed by just inches above Kenway's head. Something scrapped across the back of his hands and peeled away skin like a cheese grater. One of his boots was torn off. A stray piece of table sheered through his pants and shaved the hair off his leg.

The neck of Mac's jacket billowed up and acted like a funnel that sucked in grit, dust and what he would later discover to be a fork. A loop of electrical wire hooked around his little finger and yanked it back until it dislocated with a snapping pop. Then the Wolf was through the home and into the streets once more.

Verning popped through the hatch with the Walther P-38 in his paw. He was surprised to see one of the Americans still clung to the turret. The man missed a boot and half of his pant leg. The rain washed through the filth covering his face and made him look like a painted Indian. Verning aimed his pistol between the soldier's wide eyes. Before he could pull the trigger, he was grabbed from behind.

Mac put the beast in a headlock and knocked its gun hand to the side. The shot went wild. Kenway pounced and grabbed the furry arm holding the weapon.

The growls of man and beast were indistinguishable. The flesh of the dogman felt hideously alive and vital under Mac's grip, like a hot water bottle filled with boiling piss. He felt the hairy skin ripple as it continued through the transformation process. Claws ripped at his arm while Kenway struggled to snatch the pistol from the monster's iron fingers.

Verning raged under the men's attack. His position and the swaying of the tank prevented him from gaining any leverage. His savage twisting and flailing activated both the turret controls and the Panzer's defensive smoke screen.

"Gunther!" he growled. "Get up here, goddamn it!"

Gunther wormed out of his seat and moved to a forward hatch.

A cloud of white smoke billowed into Mac's face. It burned his eyes and seared his lungs. He retained his hold on the monster, however, and then the turret swung away beneath him. A tight band of pressure bit into his belly. He looked down to discover a strap of his harness snagged under the turret's lip. As the turret moved, it pulled him along with inexorable force. He lost his grip on the dogman's neck.

Kenway gagged on the smoke, and a furry fist clubbed him upside the head. He tumbled backwards and landed on the engine compartment. The dogman raised its pistol. Smoke engulfed the beast in a noxious cloud.

Kenway rolled to the side. Bullets glanced off the hull of the tank around him. Its treads grumbled inches from his face. His hand happened upon a shovel strapped to the track skirting.

Mac struggled with the buckle of his harness. The strap dug into his guts until it felt like it would cut him in half. *Jesus!* The turret pulled him around, and the side of the tank drew closer. Soon he'd be dragged into its treads and ground into hamburger. *Christ!*

The hatch at his feet popped open. A dogman stuck its head out. Mac kicked the steel lid, and it slammed into the beast's face. The monster absorbed the blow with a snarl of rage. Its hands reached for Mac's legs.

242

"Motherfuck!"

Mac kicked the hatch again and again. The steel lid rebounded off the monster's nose and made it angrier. Mac got his fingers under the harness buckle and ripped at it with all of his strength.

Kenway hefted the shovel and lunged into the cloud of smoke enveloping the turret. He swung the tool with everything that he had. The handle vibrated, and a loud clang sounded as the shovel hit the dogman on top of its skull. Kenway raised the spade to clobber it again. This time he turned the head of the tool on edge.

Stark heard the snarls of pain and anger in his headset. Somehow, through it all, the Americans held on and still fought.

Enough!

Stark slammed a boot full of left brake and twisted the wheel. The Wolf dug into a monstrous skid and tore down the street sideways. Its heavy treads threw up sparks and ragged chunks of broken cobblestone.

The left track clanked to full stop. The right track ran at a blur and whipped the huge machine into a violent spin. The Wolf's skidding treads threw an amazing sheet of water thirty feet high into the nearby cemetery.

Smoke continued to billow from its dispensers and formed a contrail that followed the tank's progress, ending in a thick spiral as the machine came to a stop and rocked on its heavy-duty shock absorbers.

Centrifugal force threw Kenway and Mac off the Wolf's hull. They flew through the air and landed on the grassy bank of Le Coeur's cemetery, plowing deep grooves into the wet weeds.

They were fortunate to hit dirt instead of stone. Still, the impact wasn't without cost. Kenway hit his shoulder hard enough to dislocate it. He screamed through gritted teeth. Mac landed with a bone-jarring crunch that caused him to bit off a chunk of his tongue. Other than that, he was still mobile. He scrambled to his feet, grabbed Kenway and half-carried him, half-guided him through the graves.

"Come on, asshole! Run!"

CHAPTER

13

FACES

CHAPLAIN STAGGERED OUT of the church and watched the tank roar off in pursuit of the others. The French countryside was right there, but he didn't run. It was too late to run anyway.

He couldn't escape the infection that coursed through his veins. Symptoms overcame him. His vision sharpened. Smells grew stronger. His skin itched like a thousand invisible ants marched across it. Red thoughts wormed through the sludge at the bottom of his mind and made him feel like a rotten apple.

The Major was right; there was no escaping anything.

But there was another reason he didn't run.

He just … couldn't.

He lapsed after the deaths of Ruth and Esther to be sure. He drank. He got in fights. He felt up whatever bar whore was drunk enough to give him a free handful while

245

lice crawled from between her thighs like rats fleeing a sinking ship. He burned. He froze. Hate radiated off him like black sunshine. Whatever fresh air drifted into his stinking dives was strangled by stale smoke and despair. The song of the wretched masses serenaded him—the music of vomited booze and blood. At some point, the nameless cunt in his lap would try to drag him back to her place with whiskey-breath promises. He would tell her to go to hell and wander off with just her curses for company. When it came to selling off the last few bits of himself, he just … couldn't.

And when morning found him in his moldy cockroach-infested apartment with the sounds of an arguing Mexican family drifting down the hall like piss rolling downhill, he would stick a gun in his mouth and question God. The metal gave a taste to the anguish Farrow and Phil unleashed in his life. His brain screamed, *Shoot! Blow the memories out of your goddamn skull, you miserable fuck!* But he just … couldn't.

Then the war came. It was the perfect outlet for all of the hate and rage. Every enemy soldier was Farrow and Phil. How many could he kill before the anger and grief ran its course? Might as well ask how many angels can dance on the head of a pin?

And when it came to deserting the others and just leaving them to the dogmen while the box sat in the background like some dark idol, he just—couldn't.

Chaplain stumbled around to the front of the church. The Kubelwagen was still on its steps. The escape from the bank seemed like forever ago, but it was still the same night; it felt like it had always been the same night. Concepts like day and the sun seemed like nothing more than myths. Chaplain grabbed the Kubel's spare can of gasoline. He hefted it onto his shoulder and followed the path of the Wolf.

A giddy smile slit the Major's lips. He lifted the lid of the box the way a groom lifts the dress of his bride on their wedding night. *Beautiful.* He put his hands inside of it, groping the fantasy. Visions of plenty ran through his head. His body trembled with excitement, anxious to possess the means to follow any road he chose.

He could go places that others only dreamed about. He could ascend to heights where wishes took on tangible form. Satiation. Wealth. Godlike power at his fingertips. He burned. He froze. Greed radiated off him like heat from a fire. The price was right for selling out. Everyone yearns to say to hell with everything, but few have the means to follow through. The box gave the Major the means. He could have his own empire, a palace even—marble columns, perfumed air, and servants bringing food and drink. He'd fuck a woman with silk hair, peach tits, and myrrh pussy every night, and not standard fucking either, but the kind that put them in hospitals.

And when morning found him in the lap of luxury, without a care in the world, he would consume the sweetness with a silver spoon, lick the Christless thing clean and think: *You have everything that you could ever want, you magnificent fuck!*

And all he had to do was get out of Le Coeur and out of the war because the box was *Having* and *Could* all rolled into one—the Big One.

The open box was a mouth that smiled upon the Major with great favor—right before it chewed and swallowed. The Major shook his head and pulled himself out of his daze. How long had he stood there daydreaming? He checked his watch. Cracks covered its face. Broken hands pointed out six minutes, six seconds after six.

No matter. My time has come.

The Major closed the box and picked it up. He wanted to fall under its weight but bore it with maniacal energy. He staggered past Hagen's dead body without so much as a second glance. He exited the bank and moved across the courtyard.

The Panzer's engine fired up with a predatory roar. The Wolf sprang from the shadows in which it hid and came on like hell's fury itself.

"God no," the Major muttered. "You can't! Not now! It's mine! *Mine!*"

They waited over fifteen minutes for the Major to exit the bank. The box had him so mesmerized that they drove into the courtyard and parked without him even being aware of their presence.

If the box wanted you to look, you looked. Finally, it released the American. Stark waited for him to move out into the open. Then he started the Wolf and tore forward. The man ran. Stark pursued.

The Wolf clipped the Michael-Dragon statue as it rumbled past the sculpture. The Michael figure broke from its mounts and toppled to the ground like a disposed monarch made of stone. Rainwater flowed around its wings.

Stark reached for the MG-34. He fired a burst that raked across the Major's legs. The fleeing man crumbled to the cobblestones. The box slid out of his hands.

"No!"

The Major clutched his knee. The joint was blown apart. He crawled toward the box; the tank came for him—the irresistible force and the immovable object.

"No! No! No!"

The Major drew his .45. Its bullets glanced off the Wolf's armor without effect. Desperate, the Major threw the empty pistol at the Panzer. The gun was crushed under grumbling treads. The Major dragged himself toward the box.

The noise of the tank swelled. Excruciating pain overtook the Major's feet. He couldn't crawl anymore. A great weight rolled up his legs. He screamed the scream of the damned and reached for the box. Flesh squelched. Bones splintered. Something burst from his side like a ruptured water pipe. The tank rolled up his back, compressing him like a tube of toothpaste. Veins exploded. Heart valves tore. Blood leaked from his eyes. His innards squeezed up his esophagus and cut off his screams. The tank rumbled over his spine and snapped it. Guts spilled from the Major's mouth and dashed themselves on the stones in Judas fashion. His arms flopped, beating the ground in a spastic rhythm like a child with a temper tantrum. Images flashed through his head. He saw the fantasy life of the box. He saw the beaten face of Franz laughing at him, and then his skull was crushed like an eggshell.

Chaplain entered the courtyard as the Major fired his pistol at the Wolf. He ran forward but was too late. The Major's high-pitched scream wavered through the air. The man was beyond salvation, but Chaplain could still stop the Panzer.

He leapt over the fallen Michael statue, which appeared to crawl along the ground, still trying to raise its sword in final defiance against the Dragon. Chaplain climbed onto the Panzer's rear end and lifted the heavy hatch of its engine compartment. Cooling fans blew hot air into his face. He opened the can of gasoline from the Kubel and stuffed his last grenade into it. Then he dropped the container into the Wolf's engine compartment and ran.

The grenade blew. Flames erupted from the Panzer's backend. Fire found its way into fuel lines and fed back into the vehicle's gas tank.

The grenade's detonation nearly burst their eardrums. Verning and Gunther screamed as flames entered the tank's interior. Stark looked back and saw fire engulf the cannon rounds. The three of them scrambled for the machine's hatches.

The Wolf exploded into a huge fireball that lit up the courtyard like it was day. Seventy rounds of cannon shells, three thousand rounds of ammunition, and pieces of Panzer rocketed into the sky like a deadly fireworks show.

CHAPTER

MIRROR

GUNTHER ERWACHE!

The thought waved through Gunther's head like one of the first Nazi flags, which contained a swastika and the slogan, "Deutschland Erwache!"

✠   ✠   ✠

GERMANY AWAKE! the cry went up from backroom meeting halls. *Shake off the stupor of control and regain your rightful place in history. In a Nazi-governed Germany, every farmer will have his soil, every factory worker his craft, every man his purpose, every woman her husband, every child their dream!*

Hitler attended his first Nazi meeting in September 1919. Maybe he believed, even then, he was destined to be Germany's savior and the world's ruler. Why else would

Providence rescue him from the trenches of World War I? Why did the phantom voice tell him to take cover seconds before an incoming artillery shell killed everyone around him, if not to spare him for great things?

The meeting was held in a Munich pub. Hitler listened to the speakers, took a pamphlet and left. He awoke early the next morning and watched mice nibble on the bread crumbs he scattered the night before.

I had known so much poverty in my life, he later wrote, *that I was well able to imagine the hunger and hence the pleasure of the creatures.*

Bored, Hitler inspected the pamphlet. He discovered he agreed with many of the Nazi ideas. He had similar views on the shortcomings of democracy; the inherent evils of labor unions, communism, and capitalism; the power of the worker; and especially on the matter of racial cancers, such as the Jews and Slavs. Inspired, Hitler joined the group and built them up from a backroom gang of nobodies to the ruling party of the nation by the 1930s.

No one took the Nazis seriously at first. They seemed to be nothing more than a gang of rabble rousers, failed artists, bohemian losers, and sexual perverts.

The climate of Germany was ripe for revolution, however. Its frustrated citizens were ready to latch onto any brass ring that dangled down from above, and Hitler didn't just peddle hope; he supplied results.

People had jobs. The economy boomed. The military grew strong. Foreign policy was a grand romp of victories where Hitler made asses out of the Allies, who were too divided and blind to grasp the truth of what was building up beyond the Rhine. And the infection spread.

By 1934, 95 percent of registered voters went to the polls. 90 percent—thirty-eight million—supported Hitler.

Even at the Dachau concentration camp, 96 percent of the inmates voted for the government that put them there.

Gunther was one of the supporters. He served in the Great War and despaired over what happened to his country and way of life in the aftermath. He lost his house and had to live with a cousin. He did odd jobs to survive, such as shoveling shit for potatoes or scraping slime from the underside of piers for the princely sum of a used winter coat.

One night, while lying in bed, his wife, Gisela, asked in a very quiet voice if she should prostitute herself to earn them needed money. Gunther pretended he was asleep and didn't answer. If the best a man could do was pimp for his wife, then he was no kind of man at all. He lay there for the rest of the night with his hands clenched at his sides and tears of frustration rolling down his cheeks. And nothing got better as the weeks became months and the months became years and the years became a decade.

But then Hitler came. All hopelessness was wiped away, and people believed in promises again. They stopped making ends meet and started making plans. The factories churned out products. The trains ran on time. Foreign money poured in. People had bank accounts and stocked pantries. The country even developed a tourist season.

And who cared about the cost?

The majority of Germans didn't seem to mind that they lost personal freedom. They didn't care that much of their culture was destroyed and replaced by a mindless barbarism. Hitler was liquidating the past along with all its failures, frustrations, and disappointment. That and being able to sleep at night without rumbling bellies and having interest rates was worth a few small—*very small*—sacrifices.

At least that was how Gunther explained things to Gisela whenever they discussed the subject. She was always leery of Hitler. She could never bring herself to trust the man.

When Gunther asked why, she said, "It's his moustache. Only a man with a distorted view of reality would think that moustache looks good."

Other times, her points had more validity.

She mentioned the night Berlin students burned thousands of books labeled subversive to German thought. Authors included Jack London, Upton Sinclair, Helen Keller, Margaret Sanger, H.G. Wells, Freud, and Proust. The Nazis then deemed which literature was appropriate for the masses. They also decided which movies were acceptable and radio programs, newspaper articles, plays, songs, magazines, games … The Nazis even went so far as to label all modern art degenerate. Works by Van Gogh, Picasso, Guaguin, Matisse, and others were removed from German museums. The Nazis declared that works of art which could not be understood but needed a swollen set of instructions to prove their right to exist and find their way to neurotics who were receptive to such stupid and insolent nonsense would not be tolerated.

Other things disturbed Gisela, as well. Paperwork ran rampant. Each transaction splintered off into forty different forms. Every citizen needed a workbook that listed their skills and experience or else they couldn't get jobs. The school system was revamped. Lessons had to correspond to Nazi ideology. Girls joined the Young Maidens to learn household skills. Boys joined the Hitler Youth to learn how to fight. Gestapo gangs whisked people away in the dead of night and called it "protective custody." The Sondergericht, or Special Court, sentenced people to concentration camps for any vague reason. Himmler's Security Service, the Sicherheitsdienst, employed people to spy on their fellow citizens and report any anti-government comments or activities. Your son, father, wife, best friend, boss or secretary might be an informer. You just never knew.

And always, everywhere they went, were the signs: "Jews Strictly Forbidden In This Town," "Jews Enter This Place At Your Own Risk" and at a sharp bend in the road near Ludwigshafen, "Dive Carefully! Sharp curve! Jews 75 Miles An Hour."

Gunther told Gisela she was overreacting.

She told him to open his eyes.

But Gunther kept them closed. And if he ever got the urge to peek, he would ask himself a single question to make the impulse go away: *Would you rather the Nazis be in charge or would you rather see Gisela fucking for bread?*

Yet, some doubts did squeeze through. As a man who was raised in the church, Gunther grew nervous with the Nazi meddling in that area. The Party guaranteed liberty for all religious denominations ... as long as they were not a danger to the moral feelings of the German race. The regime wanted a positive Christianity.

By "positive Christianity" they meant one that incorporated Nazi ideas into its doctrines. Unfortunately, what the Nazis stood for and what the Bible taught rarely matched up. In that case, the Bible had to change.

The Old Testament, with its tales of "Jewish cattle merchants and pimps," had to go. The New Testament teachings of Jesus were revised to meet the requirements of the Nazi Party. Resolutions were drawn up that demanded "One People, One Reich, One Faith" and required all pastors to take an oath of allegiance to Hitler and institute the changes to their beliefs. Those who refused were arrested and sent to concentration camps or taken behind buildings and shot.

The Nazi persecution of Christians did not arouse the majority of Germans. A people who had so lightly given up their political, cultural, and economic freedoms were not going to die or risk imprisonment to preserve freedom of worship. Few even cared that the Nazis intended to destroy Christianity and replace it with a Nazi paganism.

The Bible would no longer be published in a Nazi world. *Mein Kampf* would replace it on church altars and in people's bookshelves. Furthermore, the cross would be supplanted with the only unconquerable symbol—the swastika.

Such things did bother Gunther, however. He learned his Bible lessons well as a boy, and if there was one axiom in the universe he believed, it was this:

Don't fuck with God. Sooner or later you'll get burned.

✠　✠　✠

GUNTHER TWITCHED on the cobblestones. His mind teetered between consciousness and unconsciousness. He smelled singed hair. The stench triggered a memory-dream of the day he awoke to the reality of the Nazi regime—the day he visited Bernich.

✠　✠　✠

THE BERNICH CONCENTRATION CAMP was located just outside of Munich. Gunther, Stark, Verning, Hagen, and Himmler arrived via a black Rolls Royce. A guard who looked like he was carved from granite and has his eyes painted on waved them through the gate. Gunther noticed two chimneys poking above the guard towers and barracks. Thick smoke poured from their tips, and ash descended over the camp like a gentle snow.

A mousy clerk met them in front of the commandant's office. He reminded Gunther of the Renfield character from the *Dracula* movie. The man was all bug eyes and a barely-contained grin. Gunther half expected him to snatch one of the flies buzzing through the air and eat it while he giggled with insane glee.

"I'm here to see Herr Lisser," Himmler said. "He is to give us a tour."

"This way please."

Instead of taking them into the office, the clerk led them around back of the building. "Lisser is doing some field work this morning."

The Jewish woman was skeletal from malnutrition. A scarf with twelve stars covered her gray hair. Tears ran down her face. Her body quaked. The tremors increased as the weight of the boy on her shoulders tired her. His hands were tied behind his back, and his features bore a resemblance to the woman that went beyond the pale complexion, sores and scrawniness—a resemblance of blood. The rope around his neck made the wooden support beam of the guard tower creak.

Ludwig Lisser strutted around the woman. He didn't shake from the cold or from weakness. His black leather SS field jacket barely stirred in the stiff wind. His officer hat topped blond hair and strong features. He tapped his baton against the woman's legs.

"Are you getting tired, *Mutter*?"

The woman whimpered.

Two soldiers in Wermacht overcoats watched the drama unfold as they restrained a pair of Dobermans. The dogs spotted Gunther, Stark, Hagen, and Verning come around the corner and whined in the back of their throats.

Lisser ceased his interrogation and approached Himmler.

Himmler raised a hand. "Do your duty. We can wait."

Lisser gave the Reichsfuehrer a curt nod and returned to the woman.

"Please," she begged him. "My son did nothing."

"Nothing? He was found with hoarded food. This is *verboten*, is it not?"

One of the woman's knees buckled. The boy on her shoulders shifted. He cried out with fear. "Don't cry, Abraham. It'll be okay. It'll—"

Lisser slammed his baton into the woman's gut. "*Answer my question!*"

"I hoarded the food!" she wailed and somehow remained standing. "My boy did nothing! I merely gave it to him. He was so hungry. We don't get enough food."

"Not enough food?" Lisser asked, honestly puzzled. "I'm confused. If you don't get enough food, then how could you have extra to hoard for your boy?"

"Please," the woman cried. "Have mercy."

"Am I not being merciful? You should both be shot. Yet, here you are, both alive"—Lisser smiled, his lips moving like worms on a hook—"up to this point."

"It won't happen again," the woman insisted. Her shaking muscles now resembled an epileptic fit. The boy on her shoulders tottered back and forth. He could no longer contain his weeping. It made his balance even more precarious.

"Of course it won't," Lisser agreed. "And now you're only reaping what you have sown. If you hadn't given the boy extra food he wouldn't be so heavy!"

Stark laughed. The dogs pricked their ears at the sound.

Gunther looked at the sky. He thought he saw a stern face in the clouds, the face of God passing judgement on them all, and then the woman's legs gave way and she fell into the mud and the boy kicked the air as she struggled to her feet, screaming and calling his name over and over, trying to grab him and hold him up, but his kicking legs pushed her hands away and one lashing foot broke her nose. She cried for help, and blood poured down her face as she struggled.

The boy gradually grew still, and she sank to her knees and wailed his name while his blank eyes stared at nothing.

Every child their dream!

Lisser grabbed the woman by her hair and yanked her head back. "Silence!"

She cried harder. He slammed his baton into her stomach, doubling her over, then into her back until her cries became broken wheezes. He noticed the red dots on his jacket and hissed with disgust.

"Goddamn Jews," he spat and took out his handkerchief. "They get blood all over everything." He dabbed at the red stains and only succeeded in smearing them in further. "Son of a bitch!" He threw the handkerchief down and turned to the two soldiers with the guard dogs. "Set them loose."

Gunther turned away. He couldn't watch.

Open your eyes.

He looked out past the barbwire fence and into the forest. Lovely fir trees covered with snow, like when he was a boy and his father hitched the horses up to the sleigh and they would go to church on Sunday morning and visit the bakery for cream pies and there were no bombs and tanks and no Shift and mothers being forced to kill their sons in the mud.

Behind him, the woman shrieked. The Dobermans snarled. Flesh tore.

"*You'll pay!*" she screamed over the ravaging dogs, cursing them with her dying breath. "*All of you!*"

Gunther's heart jumped in his chest.

"*Do you hear me? God will strike you down! Somehow he will strike you down! All—*"

She gurgled and fell silent.

Lisser strode up to them like nothing unusual just happened. "Herr Himmler!" he beamed and shook the Reich-fuehrer's hand. "I'm so glad you could make it. I'm sorry for the delay, but work has a way of intruding on pleasure."

"No need to apologize," Himmler said. He gestured to Gunther and company. "These are my adjutants, Stark, Gunther, Verning, and Hagen."

"It's a pleasure to meet you all," Lisser said. "Now, on to the inspection." He led them away from the scene as the two guards wrestled the dogs off the woman's carcass. Gunther was amazed by Lisser's easy transition from murderer to tour guide. He was also horrified by how easily he, Himmler, and the others went along with it.

"We're still in the process of getting things up and running, but I'm sure you'll be pleased with the progress, Herr Himmler. We're expecting a train to arrive any minute now. Until then, you may view one of the barracks. We have ninety-five of them, four for clergymen, two for medical experiments, and the rest are for prisoners."

They entered a rectangular hut, and Lisser continued without missing a beat. "The occupants of these quarters are out clearing derelict buildings and draining a marsh. They make such wonderfully cheap labor. They cost even less to feed than horses."

Himmler put a hand to his face and pinched his nose shut.

"Ah, yes," Lisser acknowledged the odor. "It's a little ripe, isn't it? But one gets used to the smell. It's like the monkey house at the zoo. You go in and can hardly stand the stench, but after a few minutes, you don't notice it anymore. Now then, each barrack is divided into five rooms. Each room sleeps fifty-four people."

Lisser led them through stacks of cramped bunks. Some of them had straw instead of mattresses. They passed through a doorway and the smell became worse.

260

"And here we have a bathroom." Lisser went on. "There is one on each side of the building. Each contains a sink and six toilets. The toilets once had doors and partitions, but the prisoners used them for firewood. If they want no privacy, that's their business. I guess you can't expect modesty from beasts."

Said toilets were crusted with excrement and buzzing with flies. A look of whimsical humor crossed Lisser's features. "The twelve toilets are insufficient for two hundred-seventy inmates, of course, but it's good for a laugh each day. They have ten minutes between reveille and roll call to use the facilities. Since many of them have dysentery, you should see the mad scramble for the bathrooms in the morning. It's indescribable really. Shit happens, I believe the Americans say."

The sound of a distant train whistle came to their ears.

"Ah!" Lisser exclaimed. "Good! Now you'll *really* see something."

They gladly exited the bathroom, and Lisser escorted them to the north side of the camp. A loading ramp stood next to the train tracks. Soldiers surrounded it while a forlorn group of *Sonderkommandos*—Jewish prisoners elected to help in the process—waited in the wings. Gunther's sharp ears picked up some of the soldiers' comments.

"Fresh meat!"

"Some gypsies from Austria, I heard."

"That's good! Gypsies give off less soot!"

"I hope there's some pretty ones!"

"Who cares? Shade in the summer, heat in the winter. That's all I need!"

The train clacked out of the woods and bellowed smoke. Red swastika flags waved from the front of its engine. Steel wheels squeaked and slowed their revolutions. Cars clunked as their momentum ceased. A boxcar drew even with the loading platform, and the train stopped with a hiss of steam and a screech of brakes.

Haunted eyes stared through the boxcar's slats. Soldiers opened the coach's door, and prisoners spilled out like so much cordwood. They hit the platform, lice-infested things wrapped in rags and despair. Some were sick with jaundice and had yellow skin. Others coughed, the loud wet hacks of pneumonia.

"On your feet you filthy pigs!" the soldiers shouted and forced the gypsies down the ramp with dog whips and leather batons. "*Raus schnell! Alles Raus schnell!*"

"The guards perform this violent routine to stun the senses of the prisoners and to create the impression of urgency," Lisser commented on the proceedings. "That way the captives have no time to think. It's all very psychological."

"Good," Himmler approved. "Very good."

The train occupants were cajoled and beaten into lines of one hundred while the *Sonderkommandos* collected what little luggage they carried. Then the lines moved past a doctor in a white coat. He directed some to the left and some to the right.

"He's winnowing the wheat from the chaff," Lisser explained. "The young and fit go into the labor gangs after they're tattooed and shaved. The too young, too old, weak, or sick go to the showers. Come! Onto the processing rooms!"

Lisser led them away from the station and toward a row of nearby buildings. The structures had neat lawns bordered by well-tended flowerbeds.

"You're going to enjoy this, Herr Himmler. At the end of the day, you'll feel so much satisfaction at a job well done. I know I do."

The gypsies entered the processing rooms moments later. The men were separated from the women and children while a Viennese waltz emanated from hidden speakers. The women and children went first. They moved deeper into the building, all nervous and wide-eyed, like youngsters on their first day of school.

Male orderlies addressed them like chipper scout masters. They told them to undress and remember the exact spot where they left their clothes so they could retrieve them after they went through the shower and delousing rooms.

"This is all a part of the process," Lisser said. "It creates an aura of normalcy and routine. See, the benches even have numbers on to help the prisoners remember their spots. You smell the soap? You hear the water drip? Very comforting, yes?"

"Yes," Himmler agreed. "Very realistic."

The orderlies then led the women and children down a hall with a large sign: *To The Bathroom*. Each prisoner was handed a towel on the way.

"The chamber can process two thousand at a time," Lisser said, "but the number we have will be sufficient for this demonstration. This way, gentleman."

Lisser led them into an antechamber with circular windows that looked in on a large shower room. The enormous lavatory was immaculate. The pipes and faucets gleamed. The tile floors shone. Naked women and children filed in like obedient puppies.

Once all of the prisoners were inside, the door closed with a hollow boom. The women and children looked around nervously, hugging themselves and waiting for the water to fall. Would it be cold? None of them noticed the lack of floor drains. Some of them did see the observation windows, however. A little girl held her mother's hand and blinked shyly at Gunther from behind her matriarch's hip.

Gunther's mouth went dry. It all seemed so surreal. Surely what he thought was going to happen simply couldn't happen. It was all just a dream. He was asleep in Gisela's arms somewhere. Everything from Wewelsburg on was a nightmare.

Open your eyes.

"*Nah gib ihnen Zeit schon zu fressen!*" a voice cried from somewhere up above.

Tiny blue crystals rained through ceiling shafts and bounced across the floor with musical tinkles. The women and children voiced sounds of wonder.

"It's called Zyklon B," Lisser said. "A industrial derivative of cyanide that's used as a disinfectant. In a sense, I suppose that's what it's being used for even now."

The crystals evaporated into a gas that diffused through the room. The women and children screamed and coughed. Those nearest the shafts collapsed as they breathed in the most potent concentration of the chemical. The rest fought for air, clawing each other to pieces. They climbed on top of one another, not caring if they buried family and friends in their need for oxygen. A pyramid of writhing bodies formed.

"We will even find claw marks in the cement ceiling after their game of Mountain King is finished," Lisser said. "The weak, old, and children will be at the bottom, covered with blood, vomit and excrement. Sometimes they're crushed to a pulp."

It took thirty minutes for all signs of struggle to cease. The *Sonderkommandos* entered in rubber suits and gas masks, dragging fire hoses. They pulled the tangled mass of bodies apart with baling hooks and washed away the filth. Then they knocked out gold teeth and checked assholes and vaginas for hidden valuables.

The mother and daughter still held hands. The daughter looked at Gunther but no longer blinked. The cleanup crew had to break their fingers to pry them apart.

Gunther was dazed, like a man awakened in the middle of the night by a loud alarm. One moment he stood at the observation window; the next he stood outside.

The smell! Oh God, the smell!

He looked down into a pit filled with dead bodies. Thousands of them packed the hole from side to side, naked, purple, bloated and stiff with rigor mortis. A plague of flies hung in the air like a dark cloud. Their many wings created a foul breeze.

"Sometimes the ovens can't keep up," Lisser said. "We're working on that. I have this letter, Herr Himmler. What are your thoughts?" He handed a sheet of paper to the Reichsführer, who read it and passed it on to Gunther.

TO THE ADMINISTRATIVE OFFICE OF BERNICH:

Subject: Crematoria for the camp.

We acknowledge receipt of your order for two triple furnaces, including two electric elevators for raising the corpses and one emergency elevator. A practical installation for stoking coal was also ordered and one for transporting ashes.

Each furnace will have an oven measuring only 25 by 18 inches, as coffins will not be used. For transporting the corpses from the storage points to the furnaces we suggest using light carts on wheels or a conveyor belt with metal forks. We have enclosed diagrams of these drawn to scale.

Following our verbal discussion regarding the delivery of equipment of simple construction for the burning of bodies, we are submitting plans for our perfected cremation ovens which operate on coal and have hitherto given full satisfaction.

We suggest two more crematoria furnaces for the camp in the near future, and we advise you to make further inquiries to make sure that a total of six ovens will be sufficient for your requirements.

We guarantee the effectiveness of the cremation ovens as well as their durability, the use of the best materials and our faultless workmanship.

Awaiting your further word, we will be at your service

Heil Hitler!
B. I. Lorgi, F.L.A.I.

Gunther blinked with stupid shock and handed the letter to Stark. He stared down into the enormous mass of bodies, numbed. A cord of drool distended from his lower lip. The corpses heaved, like they were alive and trying to escape the pit of corrupted flesh. He rubbed his eyes. He couldn't believe what he saw. As Gunther watched, several bodies rolled off the top of the pile and flopped down to its base.

"Jesus Christ! They're still alive!"

"No, no, no," Lisser laughed. "Due to the swelling effect of decomposition, the upper bodies are pushed out of the pit by the bloating corpses beneath them. It does look like the whole pile of them is breathing, though, doesn't it? But I assure you, gentlemen, they are not. We do the job right at Bernich."

Gunther swallowed hard. Sweat dotted his brow. He turned away from the pit and faced the camp. A patrolling guard with a Doberman passed nearby. The dog stared at Gunther with yellow eyes and a canine grin, recognizing one of its own.

Jesus …

Everywhere he looked—madness. He turned to the sky. Slate gray clouds boiled across it. He saw the face of God in them again. The chimneys spewed ash straight into his eye, so he couldn't help but notice their great wickedness. The Lord did not let evil go unpunished. How long would he withhold his righteous anger from them? Gunther's eyes slid back to the guard dog, and he remembered the pain, shadows and chanting in the deepest chamber of Wewelsburg.

You'll pay! All of you!

Gunther awoke. But by then it was too late.

He was too far into the nightmare.

✠ ✠ ✠

FLAMES LICKED the blackened hull of the Panzer. Rain hissed down the sides of the steaming metal. Gunther hurt. The arm with the silver slug in was agony, and he was also burned.

They were vulnerable to fire. Fire killed everything. He saw Verning lying on the ground and licking the cobblestones, eating the remains of the soldier that Stark crushed under the Panzer's tracks.

Gunther rolled onto his stomach and crawled over to join him. He picked up strips of flesh, chewed, swallowed, and hated himself.

CHAPTER 25

OUTBREAK

THE WIND HOWLED like a wounded animal. Stark echoed its cry. The smell of his own burned flesh and the destruction of the Wolf maddened him.

For all the strength that the Shift bestowed, they weren't invincible. The thought frightened him. That made him madder still. Fear was something the cripple felt; not him, not now.

The box mocked his denial of the truth. It gleamed in the rain and reminded him of futility. The world would not shed a tear in his absence. The sun would still shine. The tides would still come in. Billions of people would never know his name.

Meanwhile, the box would find its way into the possession of someone else. That's what it did. That's all it did. Because people had to have it. That's why the Americans were so tenacious. They should have scattered. They should have curled up into balls of disbelief at what they faced, but they just kept coming. They had to have the prize.

Stark limped across the courtyard. Blisters covered his arm and one side of his face. A clear fluid seeped from the burn-cracked skin of his chest. The Shift dealt with the damage but needed food to fully heal him. Stark headed for the smear of soldier pate and passed the remains of the Michael-Dragon statue.

Michael lay face down on the cobblestones, his sword stretched out in front of him. The Dragon remained on the pedestal, snarling at the sky, finally the victor it seemed.

It was an omen, Stark decided. He would end up the victor as well, in Le Coeur and beyond. Granted, his battle wasn't for heaven, but it was for satisfaction. In the end, weren't the two one and the same?

Lightning flashed. Stark realized one of the dragon's humps was a naked man. Rain ran down the man's skin, which was as white as the alabaster stone of the statue. Burn marks streaked his chest and face, like someone threw molten steel on him. He smiled as he sat astride the beast. His maniacal expression unsettled Stark.

"Who are you?" Stark asked.

"Who are you?" the man answered.

Verning and Gunther appeared at Stark's side.

"I recognize him," Verning whispered. "He's one of the Americans. I almost took his arm off in the bank. He tasted like pussy."

"So finish the job," Stark commanded.

Verning snarled and leapt onto the base of the statue. The naked man paid him no attention. He tilted his head back and let the rain hit him in the face as he spoke.

"Do you ever wonder how many raindrops are tears? People cry. Their tears hit the ground. They evaporate under the sun, rise into the air, condense and fall again. This whole storm could be all of the tears ever shed in the world." The man turned back to Stark with the same peculiar smile. "It's a solemn thought, is it not?"

Verning lunged. The naked man dodged the attack and lashed out with a strike of his own. Verning squawked in surprise, lost his balance and tumbled to the cobblestones with a grunt of rage and pain. Blood leaked from a slash in his shoulder.

The naked man leapt from the Dragon statue to the burned-out Wolf—a jump of over twenty feet. Stark and Gunther watched with astonished expressions.

"At least it's a solemn thought until you take it one step further," the naked man continued. "More people piss on the world than cry on it, and piss is just as compatible with the hydrological cycle as tears—so is blood. Think about it."

"What are you?" Stark asked.

"What are you?" the man answered.

Verning pressed a hand to his shoulder wound. The injury refused to heal. His face twisted with pain. "What did he hit me with, silver?"

In response, the naked man raised his hand. Sharp claws protruded from his fingers. Hair grew and twisted around his arm like jungle vines growing over an ancient temple. His eyes glowed with a red light.

"You asked who and what I am," he said. "I used to be a Cain, but all those things have passed away. Only one thing matters now: what do *I* want?"

"What do you want?" Stark asked.

"To thank you," Cain said. "I used to worry about things." He grinned, showing huge fangs. "Now I just *worry* things."

Sinews and bones snapped. Joints rearranged themselves. Sleek muscles knitted together. Black fur covered his form like a creeping shadow. Finally, a dogman stood on the

Panzer. It threw its head back and howled, a wavering cry that rose into the night and seemed to grow in strength the higher it went.

The beast met Stark's eyes, winked, and then bounded away. The three of them watched it lope across the courtyard and jump over the wall. Their heightened eyesight allowed them to see the creature run through the field of haystacks bordering Le Coeur and finally take to the open road. From there, it headed out into the world.

Realization numbed Stark. "We can pass the Shift on to others," he whispered.

CHAPTER 26

CONTAINMENT

CHAPLAIN STAGGERED THROUGH the flooded streets. Cramps knifed his muscles, belly, and heart. His forehead felt so hot he expected steam to rise from his skin.

The faces of Esther and Ruth appeared in the shifting curtains of rain. He held on to a light pole and clenched his eyes shut. Their faces disappeared, but the memories remained. He forced them into a box deep inside and locked the lid.

Pain stabbed through his mouth as his teeth rearranged themselves and slashed his tongue. The movement was sickening, like feeling an incest-sired baby kicking inside of its mother's body. The blood tasted sweet and awoke thoughts as beautiful and terrible as statues built from human bones.

The demolished church stood across the street. Its steeple lay on the ground, and the vestigial of a roof overshadowed its remaining walls. Exposed rafters made the overhang look like the ribcage of some giant long since dead.

"Can't make it," Chaplain gasped and took a step like a doddering old man. "Can't make it." Another step. "Can't make it." Another. Another. Another.

He negated his way across the street and into the church. Kenway sat on one of the remaining pews. He gritted his teeth while his arm jutted out at a peculiar angle.

Mac handed him a hymnal cover. "Bite on this."

Kenway's jaw clamped down so hard that the veins of his neck stood out.

Mac grabbed his crooked arm. "Ready?"

Kenway nodded. Mac gave the limb a terrific wrench. Kenway's shoulder popped back into its socket with a crunch. A mewl of pain wheezed through his clenched teeth. He sagged in the pew, and Chaplain approached his spent form.

"Where were you?" Mac asked.

"Busy," Chaplain replied.

"You seen the Major?"

"He's dead."

Kenway and Mac wilted. Neither of them could have come up with any kind words to say about the Major, but he was their leader. He was their rudder and voice of authority, giving them direction and no alternatives. Purpose can be found in submission. Without guidance, there is chaos.

Chaplain smelled their fear, and it made him want to swoon. It smelled like pepper. The spice of it would flavor the meat.

Come Lord Jesus be our guest ...

Kenway sagged like an old man. "We have to get out of here."

"There is no getting out," Chaplain said and swayed on his feet.

The Panzer had knocked the fallen crucifix against the altar. It stood upright once more. The dim light made it impossible to read Christ's expression, but Chaplain knew what it contained. He climbed into the pulpit and looked out over his pitiful congregation. It was a far cry from how things used to be. Living is a reflex without suffering, and a fingernail trying to claw through cement when reality intrudes. Or is let in …

Farrow and Phil are on their way to Louisiana …
The words he wrote that day came back to him.

"Do you know how a worm gets inside of an apple? People once thought that it burrows a hole from the outside, but that is not the case. An insect lays an egg in the apple blossom. The worm hatches inside the heart of the fruit and eats its way out. In a similar fashion, human beings are born with a sinful nature. It's a voracious beast that lives within and desires to devour our souls. The struggle between man and his sinful nature is a great war. It's a war that has taken billions of casualties since the beginning of time. It's a war we cannot win … but it has been won for us."

Overhead, clouds boiled across the sky and took on the silver light of approaching dawn. Anger, bitterness, hate, and the infection burned through Chaplain like the fiery tornado that took Elijah to heaven. His fingers tightened on the edge of the pulpit until his nails scratched down to white wood. Thunder crashed.

"Exodus thirty-two tells us God presented the Ten Commandments to Moses on Mount Sinai. Singing came from the Israelite camp below. Moses went to investigate and found the people worshiping a golden calf. Moses challenged the Israelites with a choice: *'Whoever's on the Lord's side come to me.'* Only the sons of Levi joined him. The rest of the Israelites brought a terrible punishment upon themselves. Moses, speaking for God, told the men of Levi to put on

274

their swords and kill their neighbors. They obeyed. Three thousand people perished that day. To the rest of the Israelites, Moses said, 'I will speak to God and see if I can make atonement.' He asked the Lord to forgive them. If not, he asked to be blotted out of the Book of Life in their place."

Chaplain lost his concentration and stared at the throats of Kenway and Mac—so smooth, so supple. How would they feel between his teeth? Fine white hairs sprouted from the back of his hand. He clenched it into a fist and put it behind him.

"The event of the golden calf happened three months after God led Israel out of Egypt. They arrived at Mount Sinai several million strong, and the Lord announced his presence with a raging thunderstorm. The sky blazed with lightning. The earth shook with thunder. The display of power was incredible, and the message was clear: God is all-powerful, and no one should take him or his commandments lightly."

Pain pulsed in Chaplain's head. His brain felt like it was overheating, expanding, and cracking his skull. Then it occurred to him it was probably doing just that. But no, not yet. It wasn't the right time. He had to last just a little longer. *One more moment, one more moment, one more moment*—the mantra of those at their limit.

"Despite God's mercy and presence in their lives, the Israelites decided to cast him aside and create a new god. Gold was collected, and the golden calf was forged. A drunken orgy ensued. They danced around their false god, while the true God was on Mount Sinai and instructing Moses, 'Thou shalt have no other gods before me.'"

We're *fucked*, Mac realized in the moment. Why else would he stand in a demolished church in the middle of a storm and listen to a crazy man while monsters prowled about outside? He wanted to laugh. They came for a box, and now he wouldn't even get to be buried in one. The golden opportunity ended up a mirage.

"To hell with this horror show," he said. "I'm leaving."

"Where you going?" Chaplain asked.

The question froze Mac in mid-step. Chaplain smiled ruefully. It was always the same. People assumed their path went somewhere until someone asked them about their destination. Then they were suddenly confronted with the horrible truth—they were just wandering along, following whims to destruction. He continued.

"Idolatry occurs whenever someone puts something above God in their hearts. It can be money, pleasure, success, or even the self. A person's sinful nature wants them to worship a god that corresponds to their wants—not a God who wants what's best for them. It wants them to be slaves to earthly satisfaction rather than heavenly salvation. It wants to turn their lives into vain struggles for things of perceived worth. But no amount of possessions or money is going to buy a sinner a pardon from hell's flame come Judgment Day. Only one treasure is that precious—the blood of Jesus Christ."

Kenway rubbed his throbbing shoulder. Everything hurt, from balls to soul. The box might have made dreams come true, but it didn't guarantee living to see them.

"When Moses descended Mount Sinai, he discovered the Israelites had totally given into their sinful nature and were nothing more than beasts. As a result, many died by the sword. The Lord is slow to anger, but his justice is sure. Thankfully, so is his love. Moses came before God and said, '*Yet now, you will forgive their sin, but if not, blot me, I pray, out of the Book of Life.*' Moses did not ask God to overlook the sins of the Israelites; he asked God to punish him in their place. Unfortunately, no sinner can make atonement for his own sins, let alone the sins of others. That's why God sent Jesus."

Chaplain ran a shaky hand across his forehead and chewed on his thumbnail. Christ, he just wanted to go home. But home was gone. He couldn't even remember the Esther and Ruth of those days any longer. All he remembered was Esther's dead face as she burned on the stove and Ruth's eyes peeking out from the dollhouse. How was a person supposed to live with those images? Blood ran down his arm. He no longer chewed on his thumbnail; he nipped at his own flesh and enjoyed the taste. Self destruction— the last attempt of a person to achieve control of their life and failing.

From somewhere came a distant howl. It grew in volume and wavered through the night, building to a terrible crescendo that dwindled to a haunting echo. The sound raised the hairs on the back of Kenway and Mac's necks. Chaplain felt the howl call to him. He wanted to cease resisting and join it but forced his hand away from his lips instead.

"Jesus was God's own Son and had no sinful nature. He never deviated from the Ten Commandments. He rendered the obedience that you and I could never produce and offered the atonement that no one, not even Moses, could offer. He laid down his perfect life on the cross. God made him who knew no sin to be sin for us, that we might become righteous by faith in his atoning work. Christ's death defeated our sinful nature and won the great war for us. Through his blood sacrifice, we inherited heaven. There, we will rein with our Heavenly Father for all eternity in glorified victory."

Chaplain stumbled out of the pulpit. He couldn't stand it anymore. Those days were dead and rancid. It was a repulsive form of emotional necrophilia to revisit them. But he wasn't finished yet. He moved behind the altar and opened the cupboard that held the wine he drank after the assault on the bank. It also held the cup used for communion—the

277

silver cup used for communion. It burned his hands as he grabbed it.

"But we're not in heaven yet. For now, we're stuck on Earth, and the devil, the world, and our sinful flesh work to destroy our faith in salvation. You're going to lose. You're going to fail. You're going to watch important people desert you or destroy you. You're going to hurt. And sometimes you're going to fucking hurt. You're going to cry and scream and suffer like you can't believe. You're going to beg and plead and pray for help until it feels like you're tearing your own heart out with your fingernails. And just when you think you can't go on for one more second, you will have to go on for years and years and years, and you will doubt God even exists because he doesn't seem to answer no matter how loudly you scream from the burning forge."

Chaplain tossed the communion cup to Kenway as the agony of holding it became unbearable.

O my Father, if it is possible, let this cup pass from me; nevertheless, not as I will, but as you will.

"If you want me to tell you why, I'm only going to disappoint you. I'm not omniscient. I can only tell you what God says: he can make even the bad things work out for the greater good." Chaplain rubbed his bitten hand. "And now I don't have much time or faith left. I can tell you this, though: if you're not with him, you're against him. We're all slaves to something whether we like it or not. The only question is, are you a slave to the white or a slave to the black? With the devil, no matter how it looks, no matter what you have, you're nothing but a dog. With God, you can be a steward instead of a stooge, a tool instead of a trophy."

Chaplain went to the forge. Enough wood remained for one more fire.

"What are you doing?" Kenway asked. "Our guns are gone."

"We still have our knives."

"What are we going to do with those?"

"We're going to kill them," Chaplain said. He built the fire up to a molten temperature. Sweat and tears beaded on his face. "Maybe I do have one answer after all," he said. "Maybe I know why we ended up here." Ruth and Esther's faces appeared in the flames. "We're here because we can take it. We have nothing left to lose. We're here because God doesn't always wield tools. Sometimes he wields swords."

CHAPTER

DEATH

"WE'RE LEAVING."

Stark gazed out at the western horizon. Clouds rolled over the rim of the valley, growing brighter—the coming of a new dawn. He remembered his dream of the world map, the devouring darkness and the yellow eyes.

"What about your precious orders?" Gunther asked.

"This is bigger than any order."

Gunther realized the end result of what Stark imagined: a planet covered with ashes and wrapped in barbwire. Guard towers in place of steeples. Searchlights for illumination. Efficiency without direction. Control without balance. Philosophy without sanity. Society-supported murder. And in the middle of it all, a figure in a black castle, overlooking a swastika army that was more beast than man.

"Wrong, what you're thinking is as small-minded as it gets."

Stark's expression darkened. "You don't know a god-damn thing about it, Gunther. You only think that you've had to struggle in life, but let me tell you something that's worse than struggling—being nothing, giving everything you have and always being a nobody for it. Well, I'm not a nobody no more. I have the power to create an invincible army. Imagine thousands of soldiers just like us." A new possibility dawned on Stark like a thunderbolt. "My god, we could even give the Shift to Hitler himself!"

"You're mad."

Stark laughed. "Why not unconscionable? Demonic? Evil? Who gives a shit? I'll take any one of those labels over cripple." He faced Verning. "Orphan, too."

"*Sieg heil!*" Verning agreed. He and Stark formed the final manifestation of the *Übermensch*—a solid wall of un-reason. Their limits had ceased to exist, and a terrible will not swayed by sense remained. They stood as lifeless as the Dragon statue snarling at the sky. Such a state had more in common with the storm than humanity.

"No more," Gunther said and turned to walk away.

"Where you going?" Stark asked.

"Home."

"Home," Stark scoffed. "Pray tell me, where's that? Do you think that your wife will welcome a freak back into her bed with open arms? I might not know shit about love, but I know it's never unconditional with people. It needs to eat, and once it begins to starve, it will kill. We have no home. We're outside of everything now. We only have each other. What do you think will happen to us when the war is over? We'll have no sanction, no purpose. Killers are heroes in war and outlaws in peace, and we're worse than killers. We're monsters. We'll be hunted and despised ... unless there's more of us than them. Majority rules, Gunther, not morality.

We can be the masters of the Earth. We can perfect our own race of supermen that will rule the world!"

Gunther said what he should have said long ago. "I want no part of it."

Stark sighed and strode up to Gunther, standing chest-to-chest with the man. Gunther stayed his ground with a flex of nerve. A musky odor of fear emanated from his pores. Stark sniffed, savoring it. He looked Gunther square in the eye and spoke with utmost sincerity. "I don't think your heart is in the right place, Gunther."

"At least I still have one."

"Not anymore."

A razor-clawed hand punched into Gunther's chest. Flesh tore. Ribs cracked. Blood spouted. And then Stark held Gunther's still-beating heart in his fist. He let the apple-shaped mess fall to the ground and stomped on it with his foot, grinding it into the cobblestones. "There, that's the right place for it, I think."

High atonal music filled Gunther's ears. The world swayed, and then his knees buckled. The ground was soft. It felt like a tremendous weight rolled off his shoulders and he was about to float away.

He smiled at Stark. "Thank you."

Stark spit in Gunther's face. The man's serene expression angered him. He hated to see people that way. Everyone should be miserable. He dismissed the corpse and turned to Verning. "And what about you? Do you want to go home?"

Verning grinned. "I am home." He hadn't felt so right since Lidice.

Lidice was a village in Czechoslovakia until a high-ranking Nazi official was assassinated in Prague. German Security Police used Lidice to teach the Czechs that resistance was futile. Stark, Gunther, Verning, and Hagen witnessed the lesson.

The Germans shot all the Lidice men and carted the women and children off to concentration camps. Then they dynamited the village. The town ceased to exist and was wiped off the maps. It was all very satisfying, Verning remembered. It was progress that could be seen and measured. He especially took pleasure in standing before the crying children and telling them what they had to look forward to as orphans.

Verning asked one girl if she wanted something to remember her father by.

The girl, a slim doe-eyed waif of no more than six, nodded.

Verning told her to hold out her hand and close her eyes.

She did, and he placed her father's scalp on her palm.

Verning still remembered the girl's scream. It always brought a smile to his face, the way a man might remember a dance with a pretty girl.

And now they were going to do that to the whole world.

Verning giggled. Stark wondered what was so funny and if he was the butt of the joke. Then he realized no one would ever laugh at him again.

"Right," Stark smiled along with Verning. "Let's go."

"What about the box?"

"We *are* the box."

CHAPTER

MARCH

NO BANNERS HUNG along their path. The streets were cold and empty, leading nowhere but to an end. It was a path that many walked before them, and many would walk after them. They were nothing extraordinary. It was just their time this time. They found little comfort in that fact, however. Few deaths are worth the wait.

They encountered a half-eaten whore slouched against a wall. Decay gave her cloudy eyes and a gleeful smile. Her expression was one of sly beckoning. *Stop, stay awhile, and I will show you the way.*

But that was a trap. There was no stopping—ever. They ignored her con game and walked on, machines in motion that tried to know neither joy nor sorrow. It was the last walk after a lifetime of wandering—a search drawn through the years for dreams drawn in water, nearing its conclusion.

The sky brightened to the color of blood. Kenway looked back. Fog closed in on their path, obscuring it into gray nothingness. There was only forward now. Nothing else existed. They sloshed between decrepit buildings.

Dead plants drooped in pots, growing like scant hair out of leprosy-infected skin. One brown flower tried to struggle above its mates. They wrapped their thorns around it and dragged it back down with brutish intent. Petals from the battle littered the cobblestones. It was an ugly scene in an ugly place, and only destruction would cure it.

They passed a dead horse that lay on the ground, its pale belly ripped out and its guts strewn across the street like party favors from a ruptured piñata. The knobs of its spine were visible under its gray skin. Its cloudy eyes looked surprised to come to such an end. The animal was grotesque with woe, and they hated to look at him. He must have been wicked to deserve such pain. They took note of their own breathing in that moment and grieved for the too late recognized miracle.

They shut their eyes and turned inward as a cold moaning wind buffeted them, men needing comfort before a fight. They tried to find earlier, happier thoughts—a taste of old times to convince them their existence wasn't all for naught.

Mac saw a grinning Mr. Webster.

Chaplain saw a murdered wife and daughter.

Kenway saw a crowd of people with their backs turned.

Better the present than pasts like that. They refocused on their dark path. The wind drowned out a screeching bat, and then the sound of running water swelled into a liquid roar. They turned a corner and found a washout flowing across the street. The black water carried a mess of tangled sticks and snatched greedy handfuls of cobblestones as it rushed along, twisting like a serpent and unheeding of their plight.

They forded it without pause, going in up to their necks, hanging on to each other for support and anchoring themselves the best they could. The water sucked at them and tried to drag them down. They swallowed, gasped, and coughed.

A large branch slammed into Kenway. He became entangled in its limbs. The current drove him under. Sticks clawed at him like skeleton hands. He breathed in a mouthful of water and choked as he sank deeper. Sticks. *Styx*. Good Christ, what a stupid way to die.

His foot found the bottom and kicked off it. He snapped sticks away from his shoulders, and his hand plunged into something soft. He broke the surface and found himself face to face with a corpse, his fist buried in its bloated guts. A horrible smell of corruption enveloped him. He screamed, and the corpse rode him back under the waves. He pushed and beat against it to no avail. Then something grabbed his hair and pulled. He gasped for breath as Chaplain and Mac dragged him from the water.

They emerged from the frothing Charybdis like struggling toads and left footprints in the silt deposited by the sluice's earlier heights—the last impression they would ever make, perhaps, and nothing that would endure for long.

They continued on, skirting a huge crack that split the street where a sewer tunnel collapsed. The crevasse looked like a distorted mouth that screamed at some unimaginable horror. A wet crow watched their progress from a light pole. Its harsh caws followed them like laughter.

At last they came to the courtyard—full circle. They looked around, surprised they were there once more, like it was all a trick—a bad dream perhaps—but dogs return to their own vomit.

There ended the quest, if it could be called anything so sane. It had more akin to a fall or an obsession or madness. They stepped through the gate and entered the den of broken statues, a burned Wolf, a shattered bank, and the enemy.

And what lay in the center of the arena but the box itself? It gleamed in the diffuse morning sunlight that burned through a cleft in urine-colored clouds. On either side of it stood their adversaries, Stark and Verning, dressed in black SS uniforms, as if they wanted to pretend they were men one last time.

A bell tolled from somewhere, increasing in volume, telling of lost opportunities and years, how such could have been better and such could have been worse, but now all was swept away and lost in finality.

A faint rainbow appeared overhead.

Dauntless jaws. Grim forms. The two groups faced each other like surreal gunfighters preparing for a showdown. No one witnessed the confrontation but the shadows, and after it was all over, no one would ever know it happened.

CHAPTER

MAN

STARK NOTED their silver-coated knives. The silver blades gleamed with keen sharpness—the brightest things in sight. The knuckles of the three soldiers cracked as they tightened their grips on the weapons. Stark smelled their fear and resolve. It smelled like steel. "Let me guess, you've come for the box."

Chaplain stepped forward. "We've come for you."

Stark wasn't surprised by the answer. It was the way of things. He put his foot on the so-called prize, "Don't you want to know what it is first?"

"Do you even know?"

"No," Stark admitted. "I don't think anyone does, not anymore. We have to define it by the shadow that it casts. It doesn't tell you what it is, but it will show you where it's been." He opened the box, and its contents glimmered. Chaplain, Kenway, and Mac stared into its depths, mesmerized. Images flickered, merged, and plotted a course. All of them watched and understood, even though none of them had any context for it.

✠ ✠ ✠

A GREAT PEOPLE appeared in the world. They stabbed the sky with proud towers and built strange wonders—things that flew and traveled under the sea, rings that spoke, and boxes that held the uncontainable. They worshipped their achievements and mated death with pleasure. Life was naked multitudes bathed in blood, writhing as a single beast among marble pillars—screams, moans, laughter, and vile depravity.

The world groaned, cracked, and tilted. Volcanoes covered the continents with brimstone avalanches. Ice storms froze life into statuettes. Mountains erupted from sloping plains, and mudslides churned civilization into a quagmire. Finally, a torrential rain fell from the heavens. The oceans rose and swept everything away.

The box waited for civilization to rebuild itself. Gone were the amazing wonders of wisdom. Vanished were the tools and incredible devices—all lost in the destruction of the great cities. Man scratched out an existence instead of warping reality to his will. Uglier. Stupider. Less intuitive. Nevertheless, he was still twisted at his core.

A race arose out of the desert and constructed great monuments to their vanity—the Pyramids. They expanded their empire on the backs of Jewish slaves. While digging the foundation of a temple honoring the sun god, Amon-Ra, the slaves discovered the box in the shifting sand. The Pharaohs took it and placed it among their treasures.

The slaves rebelled. Plagues befell the land—locusts, frogs, darkness, and death. The Egyptians blamed the God of the Israelites and released them. The Jews carried the box through the wasteland and lost it to the Canaanites, who possessed it for six seasons. Then the Philistines captured it and placed it at Dagon's feet. He watched over it with fish eyes until the Ammonites attacked and stole it for themselves.

King David arose to lead the Jews. He defeated the Ammonites and took the box as spoils of war. Frightened by it, he consigned it to a storeroom and took it out only once—when he murdered a man and stole his wife. In a fit of remorse, he returned the box to its prison. There it sat, called and promised. Eventually, it escaped after the death of King Solomon, and the kingdom split into two nations: Israel and Judah.

King Ahab loved the box so much that he killed a man and converted his vineyard into a garden honoring his precious object. He then marched against Syria, and a stray arrow hit a seam in his armor. He died in his chariot, and his blood was rinsed out of the war wagon in the shadow of the box. Dogs came and licked it up.

Ahazaiah took control of the kingdom. While pondering the mystery of the box, he went for a walk on the palace roof, fell through the ceiling and killed himself. The box passed on to Jehoram, son of Ahab. Jehoram realized how he might solidify his power as he stared into it. He then took a sword and killed his brothers.

Soon, Mesha and the Moabites attacked Jehoram, stealing the box in the process. Angered, Jehoram and his army surrounded Mesha. The besieged leader clutched the box to his chest and thought of a way to save himself; he offered his son as a burnt sacrifice to his foe. Jehoram retook the box and passed it on to his wife, Athalaiah.

Athalaiah claimed Judah's throne, and the box made her grow paranoid. She saw usurpers on all sides and decided that there was only one way to protect herself. She cut off the heads of her grandchildren one by one. Ironically, the horrible deed provoked the threat that she feared the most. An assassin entered her chamber and slit her throat while she slept. The box dripped with her blood and was well satisfied.

Ahaz inherited it next. He danced in the temples of the fertility gods, surrounded himself with male and female prostitutes, and gave thanks with human sacrifices. The box watched smoke from the burning bodies drift toward the approaching Assyrian armies.

Sennacherib and his army defeated Ahaz and conquered Judah. Sennacherib then decided to attack Israel as the box sang to him. He sent a letter to King Hezekiah—*I am coming. You are doomed. Not even your God can save you.*

Sennacherib awoke the next morning and found a graveyard instead of a camp. One hundred eighty-five thousand of his men had been killed in the night—no signs of a struggle, no tracks, just piles and piles of corpses among the dying fires that had screams frozen on their faces. Terrified, Sennacherib fled and left the box behind. He went back to Assyria and was killed by his sons. Scouts of Hezekiah's army found the box and brought it to their king. It awoke unease in his heart, and he walled it up in a forgotten chamber. There it remained until Manasseh discovered a record of it in the sacred scrolls.

Manasseh practiced Moloch worship. He heated a metal statue of the god red hot and placed living infants in its arms. Manasseh sacrificed his own children and forced his people to do the same. Nabopolassar of the Babylonian Empire then marched against Israel and led Manasseh out of the city with a hook through his nose.

Nabopolassar needed Manasseh to help him fight his brother, Ashurbanipal. Manasseh refused. He then repented of the evil things he had done and begged God for forgiveness. Amazingly, Nabopolassar set him free. Manasseh returned to Jerusalem, tore down the Moloch statues and became a just king for the rest of his rule.

Since the box had no use for such a man, it went with Nabopolassar. The armies of Ashurbanipal crushed his revolt. Ashurbanipal put the rebel leaders in his royal kennels and forced them to live out the rest of their days as dogs. The box remained in Assyria until the nation succumbed to internal strife and conflict.

A nomadic tribe plucked the box from the ruins. The sun burned their faces black, and they spread camel dung on their necks to keep away the worst of its heat.

They found joy in rape and sadism, often staking victims on anthills or pulling them apart with hooks. Israel's military eventually wiped them out. The box went back to Jerusalem and into the possession of King Zedekiah. Like many of his predecessors, Zedekiah did evil with great enthusiasm, murdering many and growing fat off their blood.

Nebuccadnezzar then marched out of Babylon. Zedekiah fled with as much loot as he could carry, including the box. He was captured and taken to Nebuccadnezzar, who killed Zedekiah's sons and put out the man's eyes so he would carry the grisly image to his grave.

Nebuccadnezzar returned to Babylon with the Israelite nation in tow. The box remained in his warehouses until his son, Balshazzar, took over the throne.

In honor of himself, Balshazzar threw a party for a thousand friends. The box was present when they offered a toast to the Babylonian gods with sacred goblets from the Jerusalem temple. As they lifted the golden cups with drunken laughter, God's hand appeared and wrote on the wall: *mene, mene, tekel, parsin*—God has numbered your kingdom and finished it. You have been weighed in the balance and found wanting. Your kingdom is divided and given to the Medes and Persians.

So it came to pass that Cyrus led the Persian army against the Babylonians and defeated them, taking the box in the process. Cyrus was a shrewd ruler who cared little about things such as the box. He even allowed conquered races to return to their homelands. Jews then traveled back to Palestine and rebuilt their country.

Cambyses succeeded Cyrus and kept the box with him at all times. One day he learned people thought him insane, so he ordered an official to bring his son into the courtyard. Cambyses informed his audience he would shoot the boy. If the arrow pierced the child's heart, it was proof of his sanity. He fired, cut the boy open and was pleased to discover the missile did indeed find its target. To celebrate, Cambyses forced the boy's father to congratulate him on his fine archery skills.

Years later, Cambyses started laughing and couldn't stop. The woman he was with fled the room. When servants entered the king's chambers, they found Cambyses had slit his wrists. The box rested in his bloody hands.

The box then passed into the possession of a man named Haman, who was a favorite of King Xerxes. Haman was so high up in the Persian government that everyone had to bow in his presence. One day he encountered a man named Mordecai who refused to kneel due to his Jewish beliefs. The incident infuriated Haman. He went home and stroked the box as his anger swelled to epic proportions. He came to the conclusion he wouldn't just punish Mordecai; he would punish all the Jews.

Haman went to Xerxes and informed the king that the Jews were rebellious subjects who needed to be destroyed. He convinced Xerxes to sign a decree that made it legal to murder all of the Jews on a forthcoming date. He even built a seventy-five foot gallows outside of his home for the express purpose of executing Mordecai.

The action proved to be a grave error on Haman's part. Unknown to everyone, Queen Esther happened to be a Jew—and Mordecai's cousin.

When Haman realized his mistake, he went to Esther and begged for mercy. Xerxes walked in and found him touching the queen. By law, no man touched the queen but the king. Haman was arrested and hung on the gallows that he built for Mordecai. He saw the box through his bedroom window as he dangled at the end of the rope.

The box remained with the Persian Empire until Alexander the Great came out of Macedonia and conquered the known world. He kept it in his tent, and on nights when he was drunk and couldn't sleep, he stared at it and came to the conclusion he was a god. He decreed that people should worship him.

Shortly after, he contracted a fever and died. He left his empire "to the strongest." The ambiguous decree led to much conflict between his four generals for the next half-century.

The box ended up in the possession of Antiochus Epiphanes, who ruled Syria. He gained his power by making a deal with the Jews. Once he attained his goal, he broke his agreement and overcame the Israelites. He then built an altar to Zeus in the Jerusalem temple and forced the Jews to sacrifice a pig on it. He even made them smear the broth over the interior of the building. He chuckled about the blasphemy one night as his feet rested on the box. To him, it proved his mastery over the country.

It also proved to be the catalyst of a resistance movement. Judas Maccabeaus raised an army and drove Antiochus Epiphanes out of Jerusalem and acquired the box in the process. The Maccabeans then fought amongst themselves in the power vacuum. The box was lost in the shuffle and ended up in the hands of Herod the Great.

It was at that time that Cleopatra's face launched a thousand ships against the Roman Empire. Herod sided with Egypt, but shifted his allegiance as the battle turned. Caesar then appointed him ruler of Judah. As much as Herod was a friend of Rome, he was hated by his own people and struggled to maintain his power.

One problem in particular undermined his position. Prophecy stated the Christ child would soon be born in Bethlehem. Herod sent three wise men to investigate. When they failed to return, he paced night after night in the presence of the box and decided on the best course of action. He ordered all children under two years of age, born in Bethlehem and its surrounding districts to be killed, just in case.

Herod the Great's own life ended when his kidneys failed, and he developed a case of maggot-infested gangrene in his genitals. He suffered great pain and endured a terrible desire to scratch himself until he finally expired years later.

Herod Antipas inherited the box after his father's death. He soon divorced his first wife and married Herodias. John the Baptist publicly denounced the marriage and was forever marked by the queen.

Her chance for revenge came when her daughter, Salome, danced for Herod. He was so pleased with her performance that he promised to give her anything she wanted. Herodias told Salome to ask for the head of John the Baptist. Herod gave her what she wanted. He had no choice; a promise is a promise. Herodias placed John's head on the box, stood back, and admired the view with a faint smile.

Later in life, Herod Antipas received a special guest—Jesus Christ. Herod long desired to see the man whom his father tried to kill by murdering the Bethlehem innocents. He had heard much about Jesus and wanted to see a miracle.

Christ, a plain-looking Jew in a dirty, bloody robe, did not respond to his prodding.

Finally, in an attempt to break the man's silence, Herod showed him the box and asked him what he thought it could be and where it might have come from.

"The kingdom of heaven is like a treasure hidden in a field," Jesus said. *"Which a man found and hid, and for joy over it he goes and sells all that he has and buys the field. I am the treasure."* He pointed at the box. *"That is not. Such is your folly."*

Herod grew angry at the insolence. He called in his soldiers, and they treated Christ with contempt. They put a purple robe on his shoulders, mocked him, and beat him. Their strident shadows fell across the box as they laughed. After Jesus was taken away, Herod stood back and did nothing to prevent his illegal execution.

Herod was with a prostitute when Christ was killed on the cross. The land plunged into darkness at the moment of his death. As Herod laid in a candle's glow with the terrified whore, who thought the end of the world had come, the box gleamed at the edge of the light. Herod stared at it and shivered. He hated it from that moment on. He later went to Rome and gave it to Caesar as a gift, glad to be rid of it.

The box remained in Rome until the empire grew too big to support itself. Territories rebelled and barbarians attacked. The box ended up with the Muslim Seljuks who expanded into the Middle East. Their conquests alarmed Western Christians who were brainwashed by the lies of a corrupt Papacy. The Popes saw the Muslim movements as a chance to expand their political and religious power.

And so started the Crusades when Pope Urban II preached a sermon to a crowd of people in a French field not far from Le Coeur. Urban II outlined a plan for Christian armies to march into the Holy Land to destroy the infidels, reclaim the cities, and bring back religious artifacts. Five major armies were assembled. The Christian forces met the main Seljuk army at Dorylaeum and scored one of their first victories.

The box was captured in the battle and sent back to the Vatican. There it was a party to as much murder, corruption, and evil as ever before. Then a monk named Martin Luther called for religious reform in 1517. The simple act caused repercussions that changed the face of the world. The box ended up in the catacombs of a small Venice church. There it remained until four Nazi soldiers named Stark, Gunther, Verning, and Hagen brought it up from the depths once more. It would be a prize for Hitler, something to admire once the rest of the world belonged to him.

The box featured familiar faces next: Cain, then Jacobson, Ritter, Hagen, Berg, the Major, Gunther, Mac, Verning, Stark, Chaplain, and finally Kenway.

✠ ✠ ✠

STARK TOED THE BOX SHUT as the picture show faded. "Now," he said. "We all know what comes next." He eyes glowed, and his fingernails distended into razor-sharp claws. His voice took on a gruff tone as fangs puffed out his cheeks and hair sprouted from his forehead. "So let's get this over with. I've got a world to kill."

CHAPTER 30

SUPERMAN

THEY CHARGED. Blades and claws slashed. Blood and smoke poured from wounds. Shouts and growls merged into a single sound of fury—a dog kennel insane asylum. One couldn't tell if the cries came from man or beast. They transcended both.

Stark's talons ripped through Kenway's shirt. Strips of cloth and drops of blood flew through the air like paper streamers and sparkling confetti.

Kenway didn't notice the injury. All pain was lost in violent motion. Adrenaline surged through his muscles. He slashed his blade across Stark's shoulder.

Chaplain aimed to put his silver knife into Verning's guts. Verning dodged and lunged for Mac. Tearing, shredding, savaging—killing desire beat in Verning's veins, pumped by a heart in the throes of the Shift.

Mac tried to duck the human hand changing into a monster's paw. A claw tore open his scalp as cleanly as a surgeon's knife. Blood ran into his eyes and obscured his vision to a red blur.

"I can't see!"

Verning closed.

Harsh breaths flapped Kenway's lips.

Slobber drooled from Stark's mouth. His eyes glowed bright yellow. Black hair thickened over his exposed skin. His uniform ripped and split as his muscles expanded and reshaped themselves. He watched Kenway's silver blade. The hand holding it swayed and dipped like a cobra preparing to strike.

The knife slashed.

Stark swatted the attack aside and reached in to disembowel his opponent.

Kenway jumped back. Stark's claws raked inch-deep cuts across his lower belly and nicked his abdominal muscles. He retaliated and caught Stark under the chin with a front kick. Stark stumbled backwards, rolled heels over head and recovered. He snarled and circled Kenway on dog's feet.

Mac cleared the blood from his eyes just in time to see a fang-filled snout close in on his face like a buzz-saw black hole. He jerked his head back. Sharp teeth clipped his nose off with a vicious snap. Blood poured from the hole in his face. He screamed and slashed his blade across Verning's forearm.

Verning howled and clasped a paw over the wound. Smoke and blood flowed between his fingers. Snarling, he spit the severed nose back into Mac's face.

Mac went berserk on pain and fury. *"Motherfucker!"*
Verning bashed him aside with a powerful arm.

Chaplain darted in and buried his blade in Verning's shoulder. The molten pain drove the dogman into a frenzy. Verning emanated an overpowering odor of musk as he went feral. Chaplain breathed the scent in. It mingled with the smell of blood and formed a savory aroma. Something inside of him approached the breaking point.

Meanwhile, Mac recovered and probed for a killing blow. Blood still poured from his nose and made his face a red skull with burning eyes.

Ropes of saliva flew from Verning's muzzle as he whipped his canine head back and forth. Ribbons of flesh dangled from his talons. Blood clung to strands of his fur like drops of dew on blades of grass.

He swallowed somebody's finger.

Stark surged forward in a barrage of claws and snapping teeth.

Kenway backpedaled under the onslaught and slammed into the Panzer.

A smile curled Stark's snout.

Kenway realized the monster drove him into the burned-out tank in order to corner him. Now the beast drew back a huge paw to put him out of his misery.

Kenway ducked.

Talons struck sparks off the Wolf's armor. Three of Stark's claws snapped off at the quick. He howled in pain and clutched the hand to his chest. His face contorted in concentration, and three new claws sprouted from his fingertips.

Kenway tried to escape by crawling under the Wolf.

Stark snatched his foot and pulled.

"No!" Kenway screamed. He dug the fingernails into the cobblestone cracks, trying to hold on. The monster was too strong. His nails peeled back like coins pried out of tar. The pain was excruciating, like a carrot peeler flayed the nerves of his hand.

Then the beast loomed over him, all snarling teeth and evil intent. Kenway slammed a boot into the monster's face. The dogman straightened up with a howl of rage. Kenway scrabbled to his feet and ducked around the corner of the tank. He spun around. Nothing there.

Stark leapt off the Panzer's turret.

The dogman hit Kenway like a ton of bricks. The two of them rolled across the ground. Claws, teeth and a silver knife flashed. Stark's talons gored Kenway's ribs. Kenway sank his teeth into the beast's arm and tore out a hunk of furry flesh.

Chaplain panted with excitement. He didn't even realize he lost a finger. Desire lit his eyes. Fangs filled his mouth. His nails lengthened around the knife in his hand, which grew hot and painful to hold. The sounds and smells of the fight made his stomach growl. He foamed at the mouth and slashed Verning's abdomen.

Verning howled in pain and lashed Chaplain's face with a fistful of claws. Blood trails streaked through the air at the ends of his talons. He recognized that Chaplain was on the verge of the Shift, but no understanding existed between them.

Chaplain fell to his knees, dazed. His head felt stuffed with cotton. Four deep cuts gouged his face. One of them took his right eye. It dangled against his cheek, hanging from the end of its optic nerve. Somehow, it could still see. The two different views scrambled Chaplain's brain as it tried to make sense of two images: the ground swaying like a ship's deck at sea and a monster coming to kill him.

Mac jumped onto the dogman's back and buried his knife in the side of its neck. Smoke and blood poured into his face. A sizzling bacon sound filled the air. The monster yipped in pain. Mac held on for dear life as claws shredded his skin.

"Kill the bastard!"

Mac's words came to Chaplain as if from a great distance, gradually growing in volume: "*Kill ... him ... god ... damn ... it! Kill ... him! Kill Him! KILL HIM!*"

Chaplain struggled to his feet. His double vision made it impossible to stand.

If thine right eye offend thee, pluck it out.

Chaplain ripped the dangling eyeball away. It tore out of its socket with a bone-deep sting that bolted through his body like a spear, but that didn't matter. He lunged for Verning, stabbing the beast in the torso—six, seven, eight times. He screamed as hot blood splattered his face and his arm moved like a sewing machine needle. A wet meat-chopping sound hit his ears.

Verning reacted with the full strength of fear and panic. He twisted away from Chaplain's attack and bent forward, throwing Mac over his head.

Mac slammed into the ground. His collarbone broke with a sickening snap.

Verning spun around and caught Chaplain across the jaw with a steel fist.

Chaplain flew through the air and hit the ground hard. His head rapped on the cobblestones with enough force to make him see stars.

Mac struggled to push himself up. A great weight landed on his back. His chin bounced off the hard ground and rattled his teeth together.

Verning smelled his own blood and felt himself weaken, but he couldn't stop. His rage gave him strength, and he buried his snout in Mac's lower back.

Mac shrieked as the dogman's gnawing teeth closed around his spine. He could hear the fangs rake against the vertebrae inside his own head. Electricity shot through his limbs. He spasmed and jerked like a puppet on tangled strings.

Verning twisted his head and snapped Mac's spinal cord.

Mac's legs lost all feeling. Then he was up in the air, flopping like a rag doll as the monster lifted him above its head. Still its teeth tore into him. Mac saw his stomach bulge and burst open as the dogman's snout ripped through his belly.

Blood showered Verning's chest and pitter pattered on the ground. It drove him insane with hunger. Even the pain of his wounds was lost in the savagery.

"Jesus Christ!" Mac screamed.

Chaplain sat up, mortified by the sight. It looked like Mac was a sweater, and the dogman was trying to pull him on over its head.

Mac grabbed hold of the furry face poking out of his abdomen. He sank a thumb into one of the beast's eyeballs. The monster shrieked, a coil of intestine dangling from its snout. It snatched Mac's wrist in its teeth and snapped his forearm as cleanly as a broken stick. Fading, Mac reached up to his vest and grabbed his last grenade. He tore it off and jammed it into the monster's bloody maw.

Verning gagged on the taste of metal.

Mac met the dogman's eyes. "Fuck everyone," he snarled.

Despite the fact it was his last second on Earth and the man was his enemy, Verning wholeheartedly agreed.

The grenade blew, taking Verning's head off and blowing Mac in two. The upper and lower halves of his body landed with twin splats. A red geyser sprayed from Verning's neck. His body stood in place a moment longer and then toppled over.

A warm mist of blood rained over Chaplain. Without realizing it, he licked it off his face with a tongue that was three times its normal length. His remaining eye glowed with wanton lust. He crawled toward Mac's remains with slobbering jaws. He leaned over the meat and opened his mouth wide. Then he saw his reflection in a puddle of water—gore-streaked, inhuman and about to willingly partake in all things forbidden. He recoiled and clutched his head, trying to hold it together.

"No, no, no, no! Not yet! Not fucking yet!"

Kenway got shredded. His clothes grew sodden with blood. He stabbed blindly. The blade sank into hairy flesh, and a loud howl burst his eardrum.

Stark rolled away, the knife protruding from his chest. The silver burned like acid. He ripped the blade out and flung it away.

"I'm going to eat your balls for that, pig!"

Kenway's remaining strength drained away. He couldn't catch his breath. He bled from a hundred different wounds. Where were the others? He looked left. Nothing. He looked right. Nobody. Always alone. And then he spotted a smear of blood, skin, bones, and clothing. The Major! A grenade lay among the remains. He crawled for the weapon.

Stark stalked Kenway with deliberate cruelty. No way he was going to make the man's death quick and easy. He kicked the soldier in his side.

Kenway grunted as the blow caved in four of his ribs. The foot struck him again and again. Heat highballed up his throat and he coughed out a crimson mist. The foot stomped on his right hand and ground it into the cobblestones. Another kick took him in the cheek. A gout of blood flew from his mouth as his jaw broke.

The world flashed white and black between the impacts. A strong hand closed around his neck and lifted him off the ground.

The dogman held Kenway up to its face. Kenway smelled its fetid breath. The beast buried its claws in Kenway's guts and scissored them back and forth. Kenway felt his insides get sliced and diced. The sensation was horrible, like passing razor blades.

The monster stared deep into his eyes, wanting to savor that beautiful pinched look of agony. Kenway mustered up what strength he had left and spit in the dogman's face. The beast snarled and flung him away.

He sailed through the air, weightless, and then gravity slammed him back to earth. His teeth rattled. Bones cracked. Intense pain stabbed him between the shoulder blades. He let out a huge scream and looked down to see a stone sword sticking out of his chest. He was impaled on the weapon of the broken Michael statue. The dogman advanced on him while he struggled like a bug on a pin.

Kenway's lower lip quivered. He saw the box gleaming on the ground, patiently waiting for someone else to come along, and sooner or later they would, but he would be gone—just another link in the lost-cause chain. He bit his tongue to keep from begging, and then a blur shot into view and slammed into the beast.

The impact knocked Chaplain and Stark to the ground. They rolled to their knees and stared at each other, bleeding and breathing heavily.

Chaplain smelled blood and tasted it on his tongue. The copper flavor drew the Shift to the surface and it eclipsed his essential self. His skin tingled. His being throbbed in time to the beat of his heart as the Shift shattered the shackles of his form. Chaplain began to tremble with violent seizures and cramps. He looked up and saw phantom faces in the clouds. They towered above him for as far as he could see.

Ruth? Esther?

Then they blurred through the tears that filled his remaining eye until they became one face, rising above him with untold power. He was ashamed for what he was and knew he deserved to be damned and hated, but he wasn't. He was blessed.

Stark's bulbous muscles quivered as he watched Chaplain transform. His teeth gnashed, and his yellow eyes seethed with animosity. Something gathered in the air like an electrical charge—a feeling like doom. Doom for the world. It was his time now. He was going to win. He just had to finish the matter at hand and then he would be free to go about his business. He howled a challenge. It echoed through Le Coeur, a primitive guttural roar that would have made a person clap their hands to their ears and squeeze their eyes shut in terror. A warbling scream joined it.

Chaplain threw back his head and shrieked. His veins stood out. Joints and bones cracked and expanded. Sinews snapped. His skull sloped back, and his nose and chin elongated into a canine snout. Teeth grew long, pointed and sharp. His fingernails stretched into claws, and his toenails ripped through his boots and extended into tapered talons. Lithe muscles ballooned on his form. Thick silver-white fur sprouted from his skin in a luxuriant mane. He crouched on all fours, and his ragged clothes

306

fell to his feet. His remaining eye gleamed blue and pure as he and Stark faced each other—one black, one white. A low growl issued from Chaplain's throat.

Stark charged, yellow eyes burning. He swung a clawed hand in a roundhouse punch. Chaplain side-stepped. He lashed out with claws of his own, lips curled back in a ferocious snarl, teeth flashing. His talons ripped through Stark's shoulder in a blur of flesh and hair. Blood and smoke spurted from the wound.

Stark looked at the ragged gash with surprise. His yellow eyes flashed murderous rage. He roared, and his muscles threatened to explode with raw power.

Chaplain crouched back on his haunches like a bunched clock spring. His remaining blue eye was filled with uncomplicated bloodlust.

Stark charged again, growling deep in his throat. His arm lashed back as he leapt. Chaplain met him in midair. They struck and tore at one another, twin blurs of savagery, before slamming back to earth. They rolled onto their feet and circled each other, gauging strength. Blood and smoke oozed from numerous teeth and claw marks.

They attacked at the same time. Chest to chest. Talons raking. Teeth slashing. Shredding each other with abject fury. Vicious barks ripped the air. No method existed. The battle was violence given form, mindless and wholly dedicated.

They separated. One of Chaplain's ears hung in shreds. Blood ran from a tear in Stark's muzzle. This time the respite was less than a second.

They clashed again. Fangs grabbed mouthfuls of flesh and ripped. Blood showered the ground. They flipped onto their sides and tore at one another. Stark's teeth sawed off one of Chaplain's hind legs then laid him open from haunch to neck. Chaplain bore into Stark's soft underbelly.

A high-pitched howl shattered the morning like glass. The two combatants broke apart. Chaplain stood on three legs. Blood poured from his severed leg's stump. Ribs poked through his slashed hide.

Stark whimpered. Loops of his intestines dangled on the ground. One of his feet got entangled in them. He tripped and went flat on his chest. He dragged himself along the cobblestones, going nowhere and leaving a trail of blood on the way.

Chaplain staggered after him in painful pursuit. His tongue lolled out of his mouth, and the light began to drain from his good eye.

Stark pulled himself forward inch by inch. He saw the box ahead. He was heading right for it, of course … At last his strength gave way, and he collapsed. The stones sucked at him. He felt heavy, like he was sinking. He managed to roll over. The white wolf stained red loomed above him. Stark hugged himself with misshapen arms.

"Hurts," he growled. "It always hurts … Elsa …"

Chaplain pounced.

Kenway knew he wasn't much longer for the world. He felt cold. He couldn't even remember what it was like to be warm. His lips were numb, and he couldn't feel his legs. He looked at the bloody sword sticking out of his chest. The dragon statue stood over him and seemed to laugh. His eyes grew heavy and fell shut.

He dreamed he was back in the woods, watching the wolves. One of them came up to him. He looked into its blue eye and smiled. He belonged there.

Take me with you.

But the wolf was hurt. Blood stained its white fur. Its breathing turned ragged and weak. Kenway heard its heartbeat slowing ... slowing ... slowing ...

It spoke: "Do you want to live?"

"Yes," Kenway whispered.

"It's going to cost you."

"I know."

CHAPTER 34

TRUTH

KENWAY KNELT BEFORE the box. Healing scars covered his body, and stubble darkened his cheeks. He felt woozy. He hadn't eaten—*much*—in the past three days. Dead leaves blew across the courtyard, rattling like bones. He didn't notice. Nor did he notice the crows pecking at the dead bodies lying around him—the husks Chaplain, Mac, Verning, and Stark left behind. The box consumed his complete attention.

Everything that he could ever want and nothing that he would ever need.

"My god, it's really real."

It startled Kenway to hear a voice that wasn't in his head. He twitched out of his stupor. The tendons of his neck creaked as he looked behind him. The Colonel stood there in full battle dress, ribbons and medals gleaming. Two soldiers flanked him. They looked the same—muscular bodies covered with green uniforms and topped with expressionless faces—Soldier Model #61874; just wind up and release.

The Colonel's gaze detached itself from the box long enough to acknowledge the Panzer and the bodies. "What happened here? Where's the rest of the squad?"

"Gone." Kenway whispered. The thing inside of him awoke and uncoiled as the Colonel approached. He could smell the man's desire, threat, and depravity. He clutched the object he held even tighter. "Stay away," he warned.

"Now, son," the Colonel drew his pistol, "I don't know what you've been through, but let me help you—" the Colonel broke off when he saw that Kenway held a grenade. "What do you think you're doing, private?"

Kenway shrugged and dropped the grenade in the box. "It's worth a try."

"No!" the Colonel shouted. "You goddamn fool!" He dove for the ground. The two soldiers followed. Kenway curled into a ball and covered his head.

The grenade blew, and the explosion gave way to startling silence.

The Colonel lurched to his feet and shoved the barrel of his gun against Kenway's skull. "You're going to pay for that, you stupid son of a bitch! That was mine!"

Kenway's cheek ticked. "I think … I think you had better leave."

"Why you uppity little fuck!" the Colonel screamed. "You're no one to tell me shit!" He stopped. Something in Kenway's eyes unsettled him … a peculiar tint.

"Colonel!" one of the soldiers cried. "Look …"

The box still sat there, unharmed by the grenade blast.

The Colonel favored Kenway with a lunatic smile. "You see! *You see!*"

"Nothing works," Kenway shook his head. "I even tried burning it."

The Colonel reached out to touch the polished wood.
"Beautiful ..."

"You should have left when you had the chance," Kenway growled.

Screams echoed through the courtyard as a gray shape cut through the Colonel and his men, and the crows scattered with frightened caws.

CHAPTER

ASCENT

KENWAY STOOD ON Le Coeur's bridge and held the box over the Seine River. His face stared up at him from the depths of the container's rich laminations, pale and distorted. It tried to whisper something to him. The voice sounded so right. The voice sounded so practical and oh so logical.

The voice was his own.

Kenway dropped the box before it could convince him otherwise. The box seemed to stick to his fingers for a split second. Then, it tumbled from his grasp and splashed into the water. Kenway expected it to sink, but it didn't. He watched it float down the river until the current swept it around a bend. The fact it was out of sight didn't make him feel any better, however.

He turned. The corpse with the word *Hölle* carved into its chest still stood there—the only witness. It grinned at him with black teeth and empty eye sockets.

Goodbye, it seemed to say. *It's been fun. Mayhap we'll meet again ...*

Kenway pushed the corpse over and walked away.

Kenway passed through the valley and ascended its slope. He sniffed. Cain's scent was faint but unmistakable, going on ahead of him. He turned a grim face to the sky, and the warm sun shone on his countenance. He watched as a flight group of B-17 bombers hummed through the clouds like an army of angels. Kenway followed them, heading east, toward Berlin. There was a war to be fought.

And his shadow dogged him every step of the way.

The box floated past the town of Montgaris. A group of cattle watched it go by with stupid bovine eyes. The bulls went sterile, and the cows gave bitter milk for the rest of their days. The current dragged the box beyond Paris. A soldier on a picnic with his girlfriend caught a glimpse of it. He ran to the water's edge, slipped on a rock and brained himself against a sharp stone. The box followed the Seine all the way to the English Channel. There it passed a freighter carrying wounded soldiers back home. The forward watchman picked that moment to clean his binoculars and failed to see the approaching mine. The box left the flames and cries for help in its wake and entered the Atlantic Ocean. It floated over a sunken submarine. The pressure of the deep had crushed the U-boat into a tangled mass. Fish picked at the dead sailors, and the hands of the corpses waved to the box like sinners beseeching an unhearing god. From there, the box was sucked into the North Atlantic Drift and ended up bobbing along the shore of Africa. It passed the coastal village of Katanga, and every household in the village was awaken by screaming children. Two dolphins stopped their annual migration to investigate the box in the South Equatorial Current. One of them nosed it and died of a brain embolism. The other voiced mournful cries as its sank into the depths. The box then rounded the tip of South America. As it did, a jungle tribe sacrificed a virgin to their god in the hopes it would bless their dying crops. The box rode out a gigantic storm in the middle of the Pacific, cresting waves nearly a hundred feet high. During the height of the typhoon, the box changed direction and moved against the current. It came upon a lifeboat drifting in the calm after the storm. The rubber craft contained two pilots from a reconnaissance plane that went down the night before. They saw the box as a speck on the horizon. It shadowed them until a seventy-five-foot devilfish rose from the deep and dragged the men under the waves with hooked tentacles and then shredded them with its beak. Eventually the box came to the coast of Japan. There it lingered until two mushroom clouds cracked the horizon. Then it turned and headed east—toward Hollywood.

AUTHOR'S NOTE

Writing "Dogs of War" was a fairly research intensive effort. I know enough about World War II to feel fairly confident in my answers when the subject comes up in trivia games, but I found that I couldn't bluff my way through certain parts of this novel.

I had no choice but to hit the books, and I found the following sources useful:

The Rise and Fall of the Third Reich by William L. Shirer
Himmler by Peter Padfield
The World War II Series from Time-Life Books
The Occult History of the Third Reich Video Series a Lamancha/Castle Co-Production

World War II buffs may notice that I took a few technical liberties here and there. No Panzer Wolf existed. I also played fast and loose with the properties of ammunition at one point. These things were done for thematic reasons. Forgive me.

I'd also like to acknowledge two writers for their influence: Grant Morrison for his work on "Batman: Arkham Asylum" and Richard Matheson for his novel, "Hunted Past Reason." These works guided my way through a tricky chapter in Dogs of War.

And that's all I have to say on the matter. I've noticed that author's notes sometimes end up saying too much and influence the reader's interpretation. I have no interest in doing that here. In closing, "I have written what I have written."

Let that suffice.
Steve Ruthenbeck
Okabena, Minnesota
April 2005

BatWing Press Titles

Deadlands - Life is not easy in the *Deadlands*, a nightmarish, post-holocaustic world where monstrous mutants prey on a handful of human survivors.

By Scott A. Johnson.
$16.95 Trade Paperback ISBN 1-891799-30-4

An American Haunting rips away the boundaries between real-life and fiction in its truth-based, spine-tingling exploration of evil.

By Scott A. Johnson
$24.95 Hardcover ISBN 1-891799-11-8

Dogs of War When a band of American paratroopers drop behind enemy lines in Nazi-occupied France, they encounter an enemy more terrifying than Hitler's Wehrmacht — an order of werewolves whose mission is to guard a remote village's unholy secrets.

By Steve Ruthenbeck
$16.95 Trade Paperback ISBN 1-891799-26-6